Isaac Asimov, world maestro of science fiction, was born in Russia near Smolensk in 1920 and brought to the United States by his parents three years later. He grew up in Brooklyn where he went to grammar school and at the age of eight he gained his citizen papers. A remarkable memory helped him to finish high school before he was sixteen. He then went on to Columbia University and resolved to become a chemist rather than follow the medical career his father had in mind for him. He graduated in chemistry and after a short spell in the Army he gained his doctorate in 1949 and qualified as an instructor in biochemistry at Boston University School of Medicine where he became Associate Professor in 1955, doing research in nucleic acid. Increasingly, however, the pressures of chemical research conflicted with his aspirations in the literary field, and in 1958 he retired to full-time authorship while retaining his connection with the University.

Asimov's fantastic career as a science fiction writer began in 1939 with the appearance of a short story *Marooned Off Vesta* in *Amazing Stories*. Thereafter he became a regular contributor to the leading SF magazines of the day including: *Astounding, Astonishing Stories, Super Science Stories* and *Galaxy*. He has won the Hugo Award three times and the Nebula Award once. With over one hundred and fifty books to his credit and several hundred articles, Asimov's output is prolific by any standards. Apart from his many world-famous science fiction works, Asimov has also written highly successful detective mystery stories, a four-volume *History of North America*, a two-volume *Guide to the Bible*, a biographical dictionary, encyclopaedias, textbooks as well as a long and impressive list of books on many aspects of science.

Also by Isaac Asimov

Foundation
Foundation and Empire
Second Foundation

Earth Is Room Enough
The Stars Like Dust
The Martian Way
The Currents of Space
The End of Eternity
The Naked Sun
The Caves of Steel
Asimov's Mysteries
The Gods Themselves
Nightfall One
Nightfall Two
Buy Jupiter
The Bicentennial Man

I, Robot
The Rest of the Robots

The Early Asimov: Volume I
The Early Asimov: Volume III

Nebula Award Stories 8 (ed)
The Stars in their Courses (non-fiction)
Tales of the Black Widowers (detection stories)

Isaac Asimov

The Early Asimov

or, Eleven Years of Trying

VOLUME 2

PANTHER
GRANADA PUBLISHING
London Toronto Sydney New York

Published by Granada Publishing Limited
in Panther Books 1974
Reprinted 1974, 1977, 1979

ISBN 0 586 03936 8

The Early Asimov first published in Great
Britain (in one volume) by Victor Gollancz
Ltd 1973
Copyright © 1972 by Isaac Asimov

Granada Publishing Limited
Frogmore, St Albans, Herts AL2 2NF
and
3 Upper James Street, London W1R 4BP
1221 Avenue of the Americas, New York, NY 10020, USA
117 York Street, Sydney, NSW 2000, Australia
100 Skyway Avenue, Toronto, Ontario, Canada M9W 3A6
110 Northpark Centre, 2193 Johannesburg, South Africa
CML Centre, Queen & Wyndham, Auckland 1, New Zealand

Made and printed in Great Britain by
Richard Clay (The Chaucer Press) Ltd
Bungay, Suffolk
Set in Linotype Times

Granada Publishing ®

To the memory of John Wood Campbell, Jr. (1910–1971) for reasons that this book will make amply obvious

Contents

Introduction

The summer of 1939 was full of doubts and uncertainty for me.

In June I had graduated from Columbia and obtained my bachelor of science degree. So far, so good. However, my second round of attempts to enter medical school had failed, as the first had. To be sure, I hadn't really been anxious to go to medical school and I had tried only halfheartedly, but it still left me at loose ends.

What did I do now? I did not wish to look for some nondescript job, even if these were to be found, so I had to continue with my schooling. I had been majoring in chemistry, so, failing medical school, the natural next step was to go for my degree of doctor of philosophy in that field.

The first question was whether I would be able to swing this financially. (It would have been the first question, even more so, if I had gotten into medical school.) College itself had been touch and go all four years, and my small writing income of about $200 during my senior year had been a considerable help.

Naturally, I would have to continue writing and, just as naturally, my depression made it very difficult to write. I managed one story during that summer; it was called 'Life Before Birth.'

'Live Before Birth' was my first attempt at anything other than science fiction. It was in the allied field of fantasy (as imaginative as science fiction, but without the restriction of requiring scientific plausibility).

The reason for my attempting fantasy was that at the beginning of 1939, Street & Smith began the publication of a new magazine, *Unknown*, of which Campbell was editor.

Unknown caught my fancy at once. It featured stories of what are now called 'adult fantasy,' and the writing seemed to my nineteen-year-old self to be even more advanced and literate than that in *Astounding*. Of course I wanted desperately to place a story in this new and wonderful magazine.

'Life Before Birth' was an attempt in this direction, but aside from the mere fact that it was a fantasy, I remember nothing more about it. It was submitted to Campbell on July 11 and was back in my hands on the nineteenth. It never placed anywhere and no longer exists.

August was even worse. All Europe rang with the hideous possibility of war, and on September 1, World War II began with the German invasion of Poland. I could do nothing during the crisis but listen to the radio. It was not till September 11 that I could settle down long enough to start another story, 'The Brothers.'

'The Brothers' was science fiction, and all I remember is that it was about two brothers, a good one and an evil one, and a scientific invention that one or the other was constructing. On October 5 I submitted it to Campbell, and on October 11 it was rejected. It, too, never placed and no longer exists.

So the summer had passed fruitlessly and now I had to face another problem. Columbia University was not in the least anxious to take me on as a graduate student. They felt I was going to use the position as a mere way of marking time till I could try once more to get into medical school.

I swore that this was not so, but my position was vulnerable because as a premedical student I had not been required to take a course in physical chemistry and had therefore not done so. Physical chemistry was, however, required for graduate work in chemistry.

I persisted, and finally the admissions board made the following suggestion: I would have to take a full year's selection of graduate courses, and, *at the same time*, I would have to take physical chemistry and get at least a B in that. If I failed to get the B, I was out on my ear and my tuition money would, of course, not be refunded.

One of the members of the board told me, some years later, that I was offered this in the belief that I would not accept a set of terms so loaded against me. However, since I had never had trouble with passing courses, it never occurred to me that a set of requirements that merely asked that I achieve certain grades, was loaded against me.

I agreed, and when at the end of the first semester there were only three A's in physical chemistry out of a class of sixty, and I was one of them, the probation was lifted.

By December I had gotten deeply enough into my course work to be quite certain I would fulfill all grade requirements.

10

The only uncertainty remaining was financial. I had to get back to writing.

On December 21 I began 'Homo Sol' and completed it on January 1, 1940, the day before my twentieth birthday. I submitted it on January 4, and on that day, in Campbell's office, I met Theodore Sturgeon and L. Ron Hubbard, two established members of Campbell's stable of writers. (Hubbard has since then become world famous, in a fashion, as the originator of the cults of Dianetics and Scientology.)

There is no sign in my diary of any discouragement, but after a year and a half of assiduous efforts, I had failed to sell Campbell more than one story out of the eighteen I had by then written. He had rejected eight stories before buying 'Trends,' and he had rejected seven stories since. (Two stories, which I sold elsewhere, he never saw and had no chance to reject. Had he seen them he would certainly have rejected them.)

One factor in the lack of discouragement was Campbell's unfailing interest. As long as he didn't get tired reading my stories and advising me about them so kindly, why should I get tired writing them? Then, too, my occasional sales to magazines other than *Astounding* (there had been six by then) and, especially, the opening up of a new and sympathetic market in the form of Pohl's magazines, helped keep my spirits up.

For 'Homo Sol,' my nineteenth story, there was no outright rejection. Again, Campbell asked for revisions. I had to revise it twice, but it was not to be another 'Black Friar of the Flame.' The second revision was satisfactory, and on April 17, 1940, I received my second check from Campbell (and, by that time, my seventh check, all told). What's more, it was for seventy-two dollars, the story being 7,200 words long, and was the largest check I had ever received for a story up to that time.

Oddly enough, the clearest thing I remember about that check is an incident that took place that evening in my father's candy store, where I still worked every day and where I was to continue working for two more years. A customer took offense at my neglecting to say 'Thank you' after his purchase – a crime I frequently committed because, very often, I was working without conscious attention but was concentrating deeply on the plot permutations that were sounding hollowly within

11

the cavern of my skull.

The customer decided to scold me for my obvious inattention and apparent lack of industry. 'My son,' he said, 'made fifty dollars through hard work last week. What do you do to earn a living?'

'I write,' I said, 'and I got this for a story today,' and I held up the check for him to see.

It was a very satisfactory moment.

9: Homo Sol

The seven thousand and fifty-fourth session of the Galactic Congress sat in solemn conclave in the vast semicircular hall on Eon, second planet of Arcturus.

Slowly, the president delegate rose to his feet. His broad Arcturian countenance flushed slightly with excitement as he surveyed the surrounding delegates. His sense of the dramatic caused him to pause a moment or so before making the official announcement – for, after all, the entrance of a new planetary system into the great Galactic family is not a thing likely to happen twice in any one man's lifetime.

A dead silence prevailed during that pause. The two hundred and eighty-eight delegates – one from each of the two hundred and eighty-eight oxygen-atmosphere, water-chemistry worlds of the System – waited patiently for him to speak.

Beings of every manlike type and shape were there. Some were tall and polelike, some broad and burly, some short and stumpy. There were those with long, wiry hair, those with scanty gray fuzz covering head and face, others with thick, blond curls piled high and still others entirely bald. Some possessed long, hair-covered trumpets of ears, others had tympanum membranes flush with their temples. There were those present with large gazellelike eyes of a deep-purple luminosity, others with tiny optics of a beady black. There was a delegate with green skin, one with an eight-inch proboscis and one with a vestigial tail. Internally, variation was almost infinite.

But all were alike in two things.

They were all Humanoid. They all possessed intelligence.

The president delegate's voice boomed out then: 'Delegates! The system of Sol has discovered the secret of interstellar travel and by that act becomes eligible for entrance into the Galactic Federation.'

A storm of approving shouts arose from those present and the Arcturian raised a hand for silence.

'I have here,' he continued, 'the official report from Alpha

Astounding Science Fiction, September 1940
Copyright © 1940 by Street & Smith Publications, Inc.
Copyright renewed © 1967 by Isaac Asimov

Centauri, on whose fifth planet the Humanoids of Sol have landed. The report is entirely satisfactory and so the ban upon travel into and communication with the Solarian System is lifted. Sol is free, and open to the ships of the Federation. Even now, there is in preparation an expedition to Sol, under the leadership of Joselin Arn of Alpha Centauri, to tender that System the formal invitation into the Federation.'

He paused, and from two hundred and eighty-eight throats came the stentorian shout: 'Hail, Homo Sol! Hail, Homo Sol! *Hail!*'

It was the traditional welcome of the Federation for all new worlds.

Tan Porus raised himself to his full height of five feet two – he was tall for a Rigellian – and his sharp, green eyes snapped with annoyance.

'There it is, Lo-fan. For six months that damned freak squid from Beta Draconis IV has stumped me.'

Lo-fan stroked his forehead gently with one long finger, and one hairy ear twitched several times. He had traveled eighty-five light years to be here on Arcturus II with the greatest psychologist of the Ferderation – and, more specifically, to see this strange mollusk whose reactions had stumped the great Rigellian.

He was seeing it now: a puffy, dull-purple mass of soft flesh that writhed its tentacular form in placid unconcern through the huge tank of water that held it. With unruffled serenity, it fed on the green fronds of an underwater fern.

'Seems ordinary enough,' said Lo-fan.

'Ha!' snorted Tan Porus. 'Watch this.'

He drew the curtain and plunged the room into darkness. Only a dim blue light shone upon the tank, and in the murk the Draconian squid could barely be discerned.

'Here goes the stimulus,' grunted Porus. The screen above his head burst into soft green light, focused directly upon the tank. It persisted a moment and gave way to a dull red and then almost at once to a brilliant yellow. For half a minute it shot raggedly through the spectrum and then, with a final glare of glowing white, a clear bell-like tone sounded.

And as the echoes of the note died away, a shudder passed over the squid's body. It relaxed and sank slowly to the bottom

14

of the tank.

Porus pulled aside the curtain. 'It's *sound* asleep,' he growled. 'Hasn't failed yet. Every specimen we've ever had drops as if shot the moment that note sounds.'

'Asleep, eh? That's strange. Have you got the figures on the stimulus?'

'Certainly! Right here. The exact wave lengths of the lights required are listed, plus the length of duration of each light unit, plus the exact pitch of the sounded note at the end.'

The other surveyed the figures dubiously. His forehead wrinkled and his ears rose in surprise. From an inner pocket, he drew forth a slide rule.

'What type nervous system has the animal?'

'Two-B. Plain, simple, ordinary Two-B. I've had the anatomists, physiologists and ecologists check that until they were blue in the face. Two-B is all they get. Damn fools!'

Lo-fan said nothing, but pushed the center bar of the rule back and forth carefully. He stopped and peered closely, shrugged his shoulders and reached for one of the huge volumes on the shelf above his head. He leafed through the pages and picked out numbers from among the close print. Again the slide rule.

Finally he stopped. 'It doesn't make sense,' he said helplessly.

'I know that! I've tried six times in six different ways to explain that reaction – and I failed each time. Even if I rig up a system that will explain its going to sleep, I can't get it to explain the specificity of the stimulus.'

'It's highly specific?' questioned Lo-fan, his voice reaching the higher registers.

'That's the worst part of it,' shouted Tan Porus. He leaned forward and tapped the other on the knee. 'If you shift the wave length of any of the light units by fifty angstroms either way – any *one* of them – it doesn't sleep. Shift the length of duration of a light unit two seconds either way – it doesn't sleep. Shift the pitch of the tone at the end an eighth of an octave either way – it doesn't sleep. *But* get the right combination, and it goes straight into a coma.'

Lo-fan's ears were two hairy trumpets, stiffly erect. 'Galaxy!' he whispered. 'How did you ever stumble on the combination?'

15

'I didn't. It happened at Beta Draconis. Some hick college was putting its freshmen through a lab period on light-sound reactions of molluscoids – been doing it for years. Some student runs through his light-sound combinations and his blasted specimen goes to sleep. Naturally, he's scared out of his wits and brings it to the instructor. The instructor tries it again on another squid – it goes to sleep. They shift the combination – nothing happens. They go back to the original – it goes to sleep. After they fooled around with it long enough to know they couldn't make head or tail of it, they sent it to Arcturus and wished it on me. It's six months since *I* had a real night's sleep.'

A musical note sounded and Porus turned impatiently.

'What is it?'

'Messenger from the president delegate of Congress, sir,' came in metallic tones from the telecaster on his desk.

'Send him up.'

The messenger stayed only long enough to hand Porus an impressively sealed envelope and to say in hearty tone: 'Great news, sir. The system of Sol has qualified for entrance.'

'So what?' snorted Porus beneath his breath as the other left. 'We all knew it was coming.'

He ripped off the outer sheath of cello-fiber from the envelope and removed the sheaf of papers from within. He glanced through them and grimaced.

'Oh, *Rigel*!'

'What's wrong?' asked Lo-fan.

'Those politicians keep bothering me with the most inconsequential things. You'd think there wasn't another psychologist on Eron. Look! We've been expecting the Solarian System to solve the principle of the hyperatomo any century now. They've finally done it and an expedition of theirs landed on Alpha Centauri. At once, there's a politician's holiday! We must send an expedition of our own to ask them to join the Federation. And, of course, we must have a psychologist along to ask them in a nice way so as to be sure of getting the right reaction, because, to be sure, there isn't a man in the army that ever gets proper training in psychology.'

Lo-fan nodded seriously. 'I know, I know. We have the same trouble out our way. They don't need psychology until

16

they get into trouble and then they come running.'

'Well, it's a cinch *I'm* not going to Sol. This sleeping squid is too important to neglect. It's a routine job, anyway – this business of raking in new worlds; a Type A reaction that any sophomore can handle.'

'Whom will you send?'

'I don't know. I've got several good juniors under me that can do this sort of thing with their eyes closed. I'll send one of them. And meanwhile, I'll be seeing you at the faculty meeting tomorrow, won't I?'

'You will – and hearing me, too. I'm making a speech on the finger-touch stimulus.'

'Good! I've done work on it, so I'll be interested in hearing what you have to say. Till tomorrow, then.'

Left alone, Porus turned once more to the official report on the Solarian System which the messenger had handed him. He leafed through it leisurely, without particular interest, and finally put it down with a sigh.

'Lor Haridin could do it,' he muttered to himself. 'He's a good kid – deserves a break.'

He lifted his tiny bulk out of the chair and, with the report under his arm, left his office and trotted down the long corridor outside. As he stopped before a door at the far end, the automatic flash blazed up and a voice within called out to him to enter.

The Rigellian opened the door and poked his head inside. 'Busy, Haridin?'

Lor Haridin looked up and sprang to his feet at once. 'Great space, boss, no! I haven't had anything to do since I finished work on anger reactions. You've got something for me, maybe?'

'I have – if you think you're up to it. You've heard of the Solarian System, haven't you?'

'Sure! The visors are full of it. They've got interstellar travel, haven't they?'

'That's right. An expedition is leaving Alpha Centauri for Sol in a month. They'll need a psychologist to do the fine work, and I was thinking of sending you.'

The young scientist reddened with delight to the very top of his hairless dome. 'Do you mean it, boss?'

'Why not? That is – if you think you can do it.'

'Of course I can.' Haridin drew himself up in offended hauteur. 'Type A reaction! I can't miss.'

'You'll have to learn their language, you know, and administer the stimulus in the Solarian tongue. It's not always an easy job.'

Haridin shrugged. 'I still can't miss. In a case like this, translation need only be seventy-five percent effective to get ninety-nine and six tenths percent of the desired result. That was one of the problems I had to solve on my qualifying exam. So you can't trip me up that way.'

Porus laughed. 'All right, Haridin, I know you can do it. Clean up everything here at the university and sign up for indefinite leave. And if you can, Haridin, write some sort of paper on these Solarians. If it's any good, you might get senior status on the basis of it.'

The junior psychologist frowned. 'But, boss, that's old stuff. Humanoid reactions are as well known as ... as — You *can't* write anything on them.'

'There's always something if you look hard enough, Haridin. Nothing is well known; remember that. If you'll look at Sheet 25 of the report, for instance, you'll find an item concerning the care with which the Solarians armed themselves on leaving their ship.'

The other turned to the proper page. 'That's reasonable,' said he. 'An entirely normal reaction.'

'Certainly. But they insisted on retaining their weapons throughout their stay, even when they were greeted and welcomed by fellow Humanoids. *That's* quite a perceptible deviation from the normal. Investigate it – it might be worth while.'

'As you say, boss. Thanks a lot for the chance you're giving me. And say – how's the squid coming along?'

Porus wrinkled his nose. 'My sixth try folded up and died yesterday. It's disgusting.' And with that, he was gone.

Tan Porus of Rigel trembled with rage as he folded the handful of papers he held in two and tore them across. He plugged in the telecaster with a jerk.

'Get me Santins of the math department immediately,' he snapped.

His green eyes shot fire at the placid figure that appeared on the visor almost at once. He shook his fist at the image.

'What on Eron's the idea of that analysis you sent me just now, you Betelgeusian slime worm?'

The image's eyebrows shot up in mild surprise. 'Don't blame me, Porus. They were your equations, not mine. Where did you get them?'

'Never mind where I got them. That's the business of the psychology department.'

'All right! And solving them is the business of the mathematics department. That's the seventh set of the damnedest sort of screwy equations I've ever seen. It was the worst yet. You made at least seventeen assumptions which you had no right to make. It took us two weeks to straighten you out, and finally we boiled it down —'

Porus jumped as if stung. 'I know what you boiled it down to. I just tore up the sheets. You take eighteen independent variables in twenty equations, representing two months of work, and solve them out at the bottom of the last, last page with that gem of oracular wisdom – "a" equals "a". All that work – and all I get is an identity.'

'It's still not my fault, Porus. You argued in circles, and in mathematics that means an identity and there's nothing you can do about it.' His lips twitched in a slow smile. 'What are you kicking about, anyway? "A" does equal "a," doesn't it?'

'Shut *up*!' The telecaster went dead, and the psychologist closed his lips tightly and boiled inwardly. The light signal above the telecaster flashed to life again.

'What do you want now?'

It was the calm, impersonal voice of the receptionist below that answered him. 'A messenger from the government, sir.'

'Damn the government! Tell them I'm dead.'

'It's important, sir. Lor Haridin has returned from Sol and wants to see you.'

Porus frowned. 'Sol? What Sol? Oh, I remember. Send him up, but tell him to make it snappy.'

'Come in, Haridin,' he said a little later, voice calmer, as the young Arcturian, a bit thinner, a bit more weary than he had been six months earlier when he left the Arcturian System, entered.

'Well, young man? Did you write the paper?'

The Arcturian gazed intently upon his fingernails. 'No, sir!'

'Why not?' Porus' green eyes peered narrowly at the other. 'Don't tell me you've had trouble.'

'Quite a bit, boss.' The words came with an effort. 'The psychological board itself has sent for you after hearing my report. The fact of the matter is that that the Solarian System has ... has refused to join the Federation.'

Tan Porus shot out of his chair like a jack-in-the-box and landed, purely by chance, on his feet.

'What!!'

Haridin nodded miserably and cleared his throat.

'Now, by the Great Dark Nebula,' swore the Rigellian, distractedly, 'if this isn't one sweet day! First, they tell me that "a" equals "a," and then you come in and tell me you muffed a Type A reaction – *muffed it completely*!'

The junior psychologist fired up. 'I didn't muff it. There's something wrong with the Solarians themselves. They're not normal. When I landed they went wild over us. There was a fantastic celebration – entirely unrestrained. Nothing was too good for us. I delivered the invitation before their parliament in their own language – a simple one which they call Esperanto. I'll stake my life that my translation was ninety-five percent effective.'

'Well? And then?'

'I can't understand the rest, boss. First, there was a neutral reaction and I was a little surprised, and then' – he shuddered in retrospect – 'in seven days – only seven days, boss – the entire planet had reversed itself completely. I couldn't follow their psychology, not by a hundred miles. I've brought home copies of their newspapers of the time in which they objected to joining with "alien monstrosities" and refused to be "ruled by inhumans of worlds parsecs away." I ask you, does that make sense?

'And that's only the beginning. It was light years worse than that. Why, good Galaxy, I went all the way into Type G reactions, trying to figure them out, and couldn't. In the end, we *had* to leave. We were in actual *physical* danger from those ... those Earthmen, as they call themselves.'

Tan Porus chewed his lip a while. 'Interesting! Have you your report with you?'

'No. The psychological board has it. They've been going over it with a microscope all day.'

'And what do they say?'

The young Arcturian winced. 'They don't say it openly, but they leave a strong impression of thinking the report an inaccurate one.'

'Well, I'll decide about that after I've read it. Meanwhile, come with me to Parliamentary Hall and you can answer a few questions on the way.'

Joselin Arn of Alpha Centauri rubbed stubbled jaws with his huge, six-fingered hand and peered from under beetling brows at the semicircle of diversified faces that stared down upon him. The psychological board was composed of psychologists of a score of worlds, and their united gaze was not the easiest thing in the world to withstand.

'We have been informed,' began Frian Obel, head of the board and native of Vega, home of the green-skinned men, 'that those sections of the report dealing with Sol's military state are *your* work.'

Joselin Arn inclined his head in silent agreement.

'And you are prepared to confirm what you have stated here, in spite of its inherent improbability? You are no psychologist, you know.'

'No! But I'm a soldier!' The Centaurian's jaws set stubbornly as his bass voice rumbled through the hall. 'I don't know equations and I don't know graphs – but I *do* know spaceships. I've seen theirs and I've seen ours, and theirs are better. I've seen their first interstellar ship. Give them a hundred years and they'll have a better hyperatomos than we have. I've seen their weapons. They've got almost everything we have, at a stage in their history millennia before us. What they haven't got – they'll get, and soon. What they have got, they'll improve.

'I've seen their munitions plants. Ours are more advanced, but theirs are more efficient. I've seen their soldiers – and I'd rather fight with them than against them.

'I've said all that in the report. I say it again now.'

His brusque sentences came to an end and Frian Obel waited for the murmur from the men about him to cease.

'And the rest of their science; medicine, chemistry, physics? What of them?'

'I'm not the best judge of those. You have the report there of

21

those who know, however, and to the best of my knowledge I confirm them.'

'And so these Solarians are true Humanoids?'

'By the circling worlds of Centauri, yes!'

The old scientist drew himself back in his chair with a peevish gesture and cast a rapid, frowning glance up and down the length of the table.

'Colleagues,' he said, 'we make little progress by rehashing this mess of impossibilities. We have a race of Humanoids of a superlatively technological turn; possessing at the same time an intrinsically unscientific belief in supernatural forces, an incredibly childish predilection toward individuality, singly and in groups, and, worst of all, lack of sufficient vision to embrace a galaxy-wide culture.'

He glared down upon the lowering Centaurian before him. 'Such a race must exist if we are to believe the report – and fundamental axioms of psychology must crumble. But I, for one, refuse to believe any such – to be vulgar about it – comet gas. This is plainly a case of mismanagement to be investigated by the proper authorities. I hope you all agree with me when I say that this report be consigned to the scrap heap and that a second expedition led by an expert in his line, not by an inexperienced junior psychologist or a soldier —'

The drone of the scientist's voice was buried suddenly in the crash of an iron fist against the table. Joselin Arn, his huge bulk writhing in anger, lost his temper and gave vent to martial wrath.

'Now, by the writhing spawn of Templis, by the worms that crawl and the gnats that fly, by the cesspools and the plague spots and by the hooded death itself, *I won't allow this*. Are you to sit there with your theories and your long-range wisdom and deny what I have seen with my eyes? Are my eyes' – and they flashed fire as he spoke – 'to deny themselves because of a few wriggling marks your palsied hands trace on paper?

'To the core of Centauri with these armchair wise men, say I – and the psychologists first of all. Blast these men who bury themselves in their books and their laboratories and are blind to what goes on in the living world outside. Psychology, is it? Rotten, putrid —'

A tap on his belt caused him to whirl, eyes staring, fists clenched. For a moment, he looked about vainly. Then, turning his gaze downward, he found himself looking into the enigmatic green eyes of a pygmy of a man, whose piercing stare seemed to drench his anger with ice water.

'I know you, Joselin Arn,' said Tan Porus slowly, picking his words carefully. 'You're a brave man and a good soldier, but you don't like psychologists, I see. That is wrong of you, for it is on psychology that the political success of the Federation rests. Take it away and our Union crumbles, our great Federation melts away, the Galactic System is shattered.' His voice descended into a soft, liquid croon. 'You have sworn an oath to defend the System against all its enemies, Joselin Arn – and you yourself have now become its greatest. You strike at its foundations. You dig at its roots. You poison it at its source. You are dishonored. You are disgraced. You are a traitor.'

The Centaurian soldier shook his head helplessly. As Porus spoke, deep and bitter remorse filled him. Recollection of his words of a moment ago lay heavy on his conscience. When the psychologist finished, Arn bent his head and wept. Tears ran down those lined, war-scarred cheeks, to which for forty years now they had been a stranger.

Porus spoke again, and this time his voice boomed like a thunder-clap: 'Away with your mewling whine, you coward. Danger is at hand. *Man the guns!*'

Joselin Arn snapped to attention; the sorrow that had filled him a bare second before was gone as if it had never existed.

The room rocked with laughter and the soldier grasped the situation. It had been Porus' way of punishing him. With his complete knowledge of the devious ins and outs of the Humanoid mind, he had only to push the proper button, and —

The Centaurian bit his lip in embarrassment, but said nothing.

But Tan Porus, himself, did not laugh. To tease the soldier was one thing; to humiliate him, quite another. With a bound, he was on a chair and laid his small hand on the other's massive shoulder.

'No offense, my friend – a little lesson, that is all. Fight the subhumanoids and the hostile environments of fifty worlds. Dare space in a leaky rattletrap of a ship. Defy whatever dangers you wish. But never, *never* offend a psychologist. He might get angry in *earnest* the next time.'

Arn bent his head back and laughed – a gigantic roar of mirth that shook the room with its earthquakelike lustiness.

'Your advice is well taken, psychologist. Burn me with an atomo, if I don't think you're right.' He strode from the room with his shoulders still heaving with suppressed laughter.

Porus hopped off the chair and turned to face the board.

'This is an interesting race of Humanoids we have stumbled upon, colleagues.'

'Ah,' said Obel, dryly, 'the great Porus feels bound to come to his pupil's defense. Your digestion seems to have improved, since you feel yourself capable of swallowing Haridin's report.'

Haridin, standing, head bowed, in the corner, reddened angrily, but did not move.

Porus frowned, but his voice kept to its even tone. 'I do, and the report, if properly analyzed, will give rise to a revolution in the science. It is a psychological gold mine; and Homo Sol, the find of the millenium.'

'Be specific, Tan Porus,' drawled someone. 'Your tricks are all very well for a Centaurian blockhead, but we remain unimpressed.'

The fiery little Rigellian emitted a gurgle of anger. He shook one tiny fist in the direction of the last speaker.

'I'll be more specific, Inar Tubal, you hairy space bug.' Prudence and anger waged a visible battle within him. 'There is more to a Humanoid than you think – certainly far more than you mental cripples can understand. Just to show you what you don't know, you desiccated group of fossils, I'll undertake to show you a bit of psycho-technology that'll knock the guts right out of you. Panic, morons, panic! Worldwide *panic*!'

There was an awful silence. 'Did you say world-wide panic?' stuttered Frian Obel, his green skin turning gray. 'Panic?'

'Yes, you parrot. Give me six months and fifty assistants and I'll show you a world of Humanoids in panic.'

Obel attempted vainly to answer. His mouth worked in a heroic attempt to remain serious – and failed. As though by signal, the entire board dropped its dignity and leaned back in a single burst of laughter.

'I remember,' gasped Inar Tubal of Sirius, his round face streaked with tears of pure joy, 'a student of mine who once claimed to have discovered a stimulus that would induce world-wide panic. When I checked his results, I came across an ex-

24

ponent with a misplaced decimal point. He was only ten orders of magnitude out of the way. How many decimal points have you misplaced, Colleague Porus?'

'What of Kraut's Law, Porus, which says you can't panic more than five Humanoids at a time? Shall we pass a resolution repealing it? And maybe the atomic theory as well, while we're about it?' and Semper Gor of Capella cackled gleefully.

Porus climbed onto the table and snatched Obel's gavel. 'The next one who laughs is getting this over his empty head.' There was sudden silence.

'I'm taking fifty assistants,' shouted the green-eyed Rigellian, 'and Joselin Arn is taking me to Sol. I want five of you to come with me – Inar Tubal, Semper Gor and any three others – so that I can watch their stupid faces when I've done what I said I would.' He hefted the gavel, threateningly. 'Well?'

Frian Obel gazed at the ceiling placidly. 'All right, Porus. Tubal, Gor, Helvin, Prat and Winson can go with you. At the end of the specified time, we'll witness world-wide panic which will be very gratifying – or we'll watch you eat your words, and how much more gratifying *that* would be.' And with that, he chuckled very quietly to himself.

Tan Porus stared thoughtfully out the window. Terrapolis, capital city of Earth, sprawled beneath him to the very edge of the horizon. Its muted roar reached even to the half-mile height at which he stood.

There was something over that city, invisible and intangible but none the less real. Its presence was only too evident to the small psychologist. The choking cloak of dank fear that spread over the metropolis beneath was one of his own weaving – a horrible cloak of dark uncertainty, that clutched with clammy fingers at the hearts of Mankind and stopped short – just short – of actual panic.

The roar of the city had voices in it, and the voices were tiny ones of fear.

The Rigellian turned away in disgust. 'Hey, Haridin,' he roared.

The young Arcturian turned away from the televisor. 'Calling me, boss?'

'What do you think I'm doing? Talking to myself? What's the latest from Asia?'

'Nothing new. The stimuli just aren't strong enough. The yellow men seem to be more stolid of disposition than the white dominants of America and Europe. I've sent out orders not to increase the stimuli, though.'

'No, they mustn't,' agreed Porus. 'We can't risk *active* panic.' He ruminated in silence. 'Listen, we're about through. Tell them to hit a few of the big cities – they're more susceptible – and quit.'

He turned to the window again. 'Space, what a world – what a world! An entirely new branch of psychology has opened up – one we never dreamed of. Mob psychology, Haridin, mob psychology.' He shook his head impressively.

'There's lots of suffering, though, boss,' muttered the younger man. 'This passive panic has completely paralyzed trade and commerce. The business life of the entire planet is stagnant. The poor government is helpless – they don't know what's wrong.'

'They'll find out – when I'm ready. And, as for the suffering – well, I don't like it, either, but it's all a means to an end, a damned important end.'

There followed a short silence, and then Porus' lips twitched into a nasty smile. 'Those five nitwits returned from Europe yesterday, didn't they?'

Haridin smiled in turn and nodded vigorously. 'And hopping sore! Your predictions have checked to the fifth decimal place. They're fit to be tied.'

'Good! I'm only sorry I can't see Obel's face right now, after the last message I sent him. And, incidentally' – his voice dropped lower – 'what's the latest on *them*?'

Haridin raised two fingers. 'Two weeks, and they'll be here.'

'Two weeks ... two weeks,' gurgled Porus jubilantly. He rose and made for the door. 'I think I'll find my dear, dear colleagues and pass the time of day.'

The five scientists of the board looked up from their notes and fell into an embarrassed silence as Porus entered.

The latter smiled impishly. 'Notes satisfactory, gentlemen? Found some fifty or sixty fallacies in my fundamental assumptions, no doubt?'

Hybron Prat of Alpha Cepheus rumpled the gray fuzz he called hair. 'I don't trust the unholy tricks this crazy mathematical notation of yours plays.'

The Rigellian emitted a short bark of laughter. 'Invent a better, then. So far, it's done a good job of handling reactions, hasn't it?'

There was an unmusical chorus of throat-clearings but no definite answer.

'Hasn't it?' thundered Porus.

'Well, what if it has,' returned Kim Winson, desperately. 'Where's your panic? All this is well and good. These Humanoids are cosmic freaks, but where's the big show you were going to put on? Until you break Kraut's Law, this entire exhibition of yours isn't worth a pinhead meteor.'

'You're beaten, gentlemen, you're beaten,' crowed the small master psychologist. 'I've proven my point – this passive panic is as impossible according to classic psychology as the active form. You're trying to deny facts and save face now, by harping on a technicality. Go home; go home, gentlemen, and hide under the bed.'

Psychologists are only human. They can analyze the motives that drive them, but they are the slave of those motives just as much as the commonest mortal of all. These galaxy-famous psychologists writhed under the lash of wounded pride and shattered vanity, and their blind stubbornness was the mechanical reaction due therefrom. They knew it was and they knew Porus knew it was – and that made it all the harder.

Inar Tubal stared angrily from red-rimmed eyes. 'Active panic or nothing, Tan Porus. That's what you promised, and that's what we'll have. We want the letter of the bond or, by space and time, we'll balk at any technicality. Active panic or we report failure!'

Porus swelled ominously and, with a tremendous effort, spoke quietly. 'Be reasonable, gentlemen. We haven't the equipment to handle active panic. We've never come up against this superform they have here on Earth. What if it gets beyond control?' He shook his head violently.

'Isolate it, then,' snarled Semper Gor. 'Start it up and put it out. Make all the preparations you want, but do it!'

'If you can,' grunted Hybron Prat.

But Tan Porus had *his* weak point. His brittle temper lay in splintered shards about him. His agile tongue blistered the atmosphere and inundated the sullen psychologist with wave after wave of concentrated profanity.

'Have your way, vacuumheads! Have your way and to outer

space with you!' He was breathless with passion. 'We'll set it off right here in Terrapolis as soon as all the men are back home. Only you'd all better get from under!'

And with one last parting snarl, he stalked from the room.

Tan Porus parted the curtains with a sweep of his hand, and the five psychologists facing him averted their eyes. The streets of Earth's capital were deserted of civilian population. The ordered tramp of the military patrolling the highways of the city sounded like a dirge. The wintry sky hung low over the scene of strewn bodies – and silence; the silence that follows an orgy of wild destruction.

'It was touch and go for a few hours there, colleagues.' Porus' voice was tired. 'If it had passed the city limits, we could never have stopped it.'

'Horrible, horrible!' muttered Hybron Prat. 'It was a scene a psychologist would have given his right arm to witness – and his life to forget.'

'And these are Humanoids!' groaned Kim Winson.

Semper Gor rose to his feet in sudden decision. 'Do you see the significance of this, Porus? These Earthmen are sheer uncontrolled atomite. They can't be handled. Were they twice the technological geniuses they are, they would be useless. With their mob psychology, their mass panics, their superemotionalism, they simply won't fit into the Humanoid picture.'

Porus raised an eyebrow. 'Comet gas! Individually, we are as emotional as they are. They carry it into mass action and we don't; that's the only difference.'

'And that's enough!' exclaimed Tubal. 'We've made our decision, Porus. We made it last night, at the height of the ... the ... of *it*. The Solar System is to be left to itself. It is a plague spot and we want none of it. As far as the Galaxy is concerned, Homo Sol will be placed in strict quarantine. That is final!'

The Rigellian laughed softly. 'For the Galaxy, it may be final. But for Homo Sol?'

Tubal shrugged. 'They don't concern us.'

Porus laughed again. 'Say, Tubal. Just between the two of us, have you tried a time integration of Equation 128 followed by expansion with Karolean tensors?'

'No-o. I can't say I have.'

'Well, then, just glance up and down these calculations and

enjoy yourself.'

The five scientists of the board grouped themselves about the sheets of paper Porus had handed them. Expressions changed from interest to bewilderment and then to something approaching panic.

Naru Helvin tore the sheets across with a spasmodic movement. 'It's a lie,' he screeched.

'We're a thousand years ahead of them now, and by that time we'll be advanced another two hundred years!' Tubal snapped. 'They won't be able to do anything against the mass of the Galaxy's people.'

Tan Porus laughed in a monotone, which is hard to do, but very unpleasant to hear. 'You still don't believe mathematics. That's in your behaviour pattern, of course. All right, let's see if experts convince you – as they should, unless contact with these off-normal Humanoids has twisted you. Joselin – Joselin Arn – come in here!'

The Centaurian commander came in, saluted automatically, and looked expectant.

'Can one of your ships defeat one of the Sol ships in battle, if necessary?'

Arn grinned sourly. 'Not a chance, sir. These Humanoids break Kraut's Law in panic – and also in fighting. We have a corps of experts manning our ships; these people have a single crew that functions as a unit, without individuality. They manifest a form of fighting – panic, I imagine, is the best word. Every individual on a ship becomes an organ of the ship. With us, as you know, that's impossible.

'Furthermore, this world's a mass of mad geniuses. They have, to my certain knowledge, taken no less than twenty-two interesting but useless gadgets they saw in the Thalsoon Museum when they visited us, turned 'em inside out and produced from them some of the most unpleasant military devices I've seen. You know of Julmun Thill's gravitational line tracer? Used – rather ineffectively – for spotting ore deposits before the modern electric potential method came in?

'They've turned it – somehow – into one of the deadliest automatic fire directors it's been my displeasure to see. It will automatically lay a gun or projector on a completely invisible target in space, air, water or rock, for that matter.'

'We,' said Tan Porus, gleefully, 'have far greater fleets than they. We could overwhelm them, could we not?'

Joselin Arn shook his head. 'Defeat them now – probably. It wouldn't be overwhelming, though, and I wouldn't bet on it too heavily. Certainly wouldn't invite it. The trouble is, in a military way, this collection of gadget maniacs invent things at a horrible rate. Technologically, they're as unstable as a wave in water; our civilization is more like a sanddune. I've seen their ground-car plants install a complete plant of machine tools for production of a new model of automobile – and rip it out in six months because it's completely obsolete!

'Now we've come in contact with their civilization briefly. We've learned the methods of one new civilization to add to our previous two hundred and eighty-odd – a small percentage advantage. They've added one new civilization to their previous one – a one-hundred-percent advance!'

'How about,' Porus asked gently, 'our military position if we simply ignore them completely for two hundred years?'

Joselin Arn gave an explosive little laugh. '*If* we could – which means *if* they'd let us – I'd answer offhand and with assurance. They're all I'd care to tackle right now. Two hundred years of exploring the new tracks suggested by their brief contact with us and they'd be doing things I can't imagine. Wait two hundred years and there won't be a battle; there'll be an annexation.'

Tan Porus bowed formally. 'Thank you, Joselin Arn. That was the result of my mathematical work.'

Joselin Arn saluted and left the room.

Turning to the five thoroughly paralyzed scientists, Porus went on: 'And I hope these learned gentlemen still react in a vaguely Humanoid way. Are you convinced that it is not up to us to decide to end all intercourse with this race? We may – but they won't!

'Fools' – he spat out the word – 'do you think I'm going to waste time arguing with you? I'm laying down the law, do you understand? Homo Sol *shall* enter the Federation. They are going to be trained into maturity in two hundred years. And I'm not asking you; *I'm telling you!*' The Rigellian stared up at them truculently.

'Come with me!' he growled brusquely.

They followed in tame submission and entered Tan Porus'

sleeping quarters. The little psychologist drew aside a curtain and revealed a life-size painting.

'Make anything of that?'

It was the portrait of an Earthman, but of such an Earthman as none of the psychologists had yet seen. Dignified and sternly handsome, with one hand stroking a regal beard, and the other holding the single flowing garment that clothed him, he seemed personified majesty.

'That's Zeus,' said Porus. 'The primitive Earthmen created him as the personification of storm and lightning.' He whirled upon the bewildered five. 'Does it remind you of anybody?'

'Homo Canopus?' ventured Helvin uncertainly.

For a moment, Porus' face relaxed in momentary gratification and then it hardened again. 'Of course,' he snapped. 'Why do you hesitate about it? That's Canopus to the life, down to the full yellow beard.'

Then: 'Here's something else.' He drew another curtain.

The portrait was of a female, this time. Full-bosomed and wide-hipped she was. An ineffable smile graced her face and her hands seemed to caress the stalks of grain that sprang thickly about her feet.

'Demeter!' said Porus. 'The personification of agricultural fertility. The idealized mother. Whom does *that* remind you of?'

There was no hesitation this time. Five voices rang out as one: 'Homo Betelgeuse!'

Tan Porus smiled in delight. 'There you have it. Well?'

'Well?' said Tubal.

'Don't you see?' The smile faded. 'Isn't it clear? Nitwit! If a hundred Zeuses and a hundred Demeters were to land on Earth as part of a "trade mission," and turned out to be trained psychologists – *Now* do you see?'

Semper Gor laughed suddenly. 'Space, time and little meteors. Of course! The Earthmen would be putty in the hands of their own personifications of storm and motherhood come to life. In two hundred years – why, in two hundred years, we could do anything.'

'But this so-called trade mission of yours, Porus,' interposed Prat. 'How would you get Homo Sol to accept it in the first place?'

Porus cocked his head to one side. 'Dear Colleague Prat,' he murmured, 'do you suppose that I created the passive panic just for the show – or just to gratify five woodenheads? This passive panic paralyzed industry, and the Terrestrial government is faced with revolution – another form of mob action that could use investigation. Offer them Galactic trade and eternal prosperity and do you think they'd jump at it? Has matter mass?'

The Rigellian cut short the excited babble that followed with an impatient gesture. 'If you've nothing more to ask, gentlemen, let's begin our preparations to leave. Frankly, I'm tired of Earth, and, more than that, I'm blasted anxious to get back to that squid of mine.'

He opened the door and shouted down the corridor: 'Hey, Haridin! Tell Arn to have the ship ready in six hours. We're leaving.'

'But ... but —' The chorus of puzzled objections crystallized into sudden action as Semper Gor dashed at Porus and snatched him back as he was on the point of leaving. The little Rigellian struggled vainly in the other's powerful grasp.

'Let go!'

'We've endured enough, Porus,' said Gor, 'and now you'll just calm down and behave like a Humanoid. Whatever you say, we're not leaving until we're finished. We've got to arrange with the Terrestrial government concerning the trade mission. We've got to secure approval of the board. We've got to pick our psychologist. We've got to —'

Here Porus, with a sudden jerk, freed himself. 'Do you suppose for one moment that I would wait for your precious board to start to begin to commence to consider doing something about the situation in two or three decades?

'Earth agreed to my terms unconditionally a month ago. The squad of Canopans and Betelgeusans set sail five months ago, and landed day before yesterday. It was only with their help that we managed to stop yesterday's panic – though you never suspected it. You probably thought you did it yourself. Today, gentlemen, they have the situation in full control and your services are no longer needed. We're going home.'

THE END

'Homo Sol' has a plot of a sort that particularly appealed to

Campbell. Although the human beings in the story are far behind the other intelligences of the Galaxy, it is clear that there is something special about them, that they have an unusual ability to move ahead very quickly, and that everyone else had better watch out for them.

Campbell liked stories in which human beings proved themselves superior to other intelligences, even when those others were further advanced technologically. It pleased him to have human beings shown to possess a unique spirit of daring, or a sense of humor, or a ruthless ability to kill when necessary, that always brought them victory over other intelligences, even against odds.

I sometimes got the uncomfortable notion, however, that this attitude reflected Campbell's feelings on the smaller, Earth scale. He seemed to me to accept the natural superiority of Americans over non-Americans, and he seemed automatically to assume the picture of an American as one who was of northwest European origin.

I cannot say that Campbell was racist in any evil sense of the term. I cannot recall any act of his that could be construed as unkind, and certainly he never, *not once*, made me feel uncomfortable over the fact that I was Jewish. Nevertheless, he did seem to take for granted, somehow, the stereotype of the Nordic white as the true representative of Man the Explorer, Man the Darer, Man the Victor.

I argued with him strenuously on the subject, or as violently as I dared, and in years to come our relationship was to be as nearly strained as it could be (considering our mutual affection, and all that I owed him) over the civil rights issue. I was on the liberal side of the issue, he on the conservative, and our minds never met on that subject.

All this had an important bearing on my science fiction work. I did not like Campbell's attitude concerning humanity vis-à-vis other intelligences and it took two revisions of 'Homo Sol' before Campbell could move me close enough to what he wanted. Even then, he inserted several paragraphs, here and there, without consulting me, in the final version.

I tried to avoid such a situation in future. One way out was to depart from the traditions of those writers who wove plots against the gigantic web of entire galaxies containing many intelligences – notably those of E. E. Smith and of Campbell himself. Instead, I began to think of stories involving a galaxy populated by human intelligences only.

This came to fruit, soon enough, in the 'Foundation' series. Undoubtedly the Smith–Campbell view makes more sense. It is almost certain that among the hundreds of billions of worlds in a large galaxy there ought to be hundreds or even thousands of different intelligent species. That there should be only one, ourselves, as I postulated, is most unlikely.

Some science fiction critics (notably Sam Moskowitz) have given me credit for inventing the human-only galaxy, as though it were some kind of literary advance. Others may have thought privately (I have never heard it stated openly) that I had only human intelligences in my galaxy because I lacked the imagination to think up extraterrestrials.

But the fact is that I was only trying to avoid a collision with Campbell's views; I did not want to set up a situation in which I would be forced to face the alternatives of adopting Campbell's views when I found them repugnant and failing to sell a story (which I also found repugnant).

On March 25, 1940, the day I put through my final submission of 'Homo Sol,' I went on to visit Fred Pohl at his office. He told me that the response to 'Half-Breed' had been such that he felt justified in asking for a sequel. It was the first time I had ever been requested to write a specific story with acceptance virtually guaranteed in advance.

I spent April and May working on the sequel, 'Half-Breeds on Venus,' and submitted it to Pohl on June 3. On June 14, he accepted it. The story was ten thousand words long, the longest I had ever sold up to that time. What's more, Pohl's magazines were doing so well that his budget had been increased and he was able to pay me five eighths of a cent a word for it – $62.50.

It appeared in the issue of *Astonishing* that reached the stands on October 24, 1940, two years almost to a day since my first sale. This was a red-letter day for me, too, since it was the first time that the cover painting on a magazine was ever taken from one of my stories. I had 'made the cover.'

The title of the story and my name were on the cover in bold letters. It was a flattering indication that my name could be counted on to sell magazines by this time.

10: Half-Breeds on Venus

The damp, somnolent atmosphere stirred violently and shrieked aside. The bare plateau shook three times as the heavy egg-shaped projectiles shot down from outer space. The sound of the landing reverberated from the mountains on one side to the lush forest on the other, and then all was silent again.

One by one, three doors clanged open, and human figures stepped out in hesitant single file. First slowly, and then with impatient turbulence, they set first foot upon the new world, until the space surrounding the ships was crowded.

A thousand pairs of eyes gazed upon the prospect and a thousand mouths chattered excitedly. And in the other-world wind, a thousand crests of foot-high white hair swayed gracefully.

The Tweenies had landed on Venus!

Max Scanlon sighed wearily, 'Here we are!'

He turned from the porthole and slumped into his own special arm-chair. 'They're as happy as children – and I don't blame them. We've got a new world – one all for ourselves – and that's a great thing. But just the same, there are hard days ahead of us. I am almost afraid! It is a project so lightly embarked upon, but one so hard to carry out to completion.'

A gentle arm stole about his shoulder and he grasped it tightly, smiling into the soft, blue eyes that met his. 'But *you're* not afraid, are you, Madeline?'

'Certainly not!' And then her expression grew sadder, 'If only father had come with us. You – you know that he meant more to us than to the others. We were the – the first he took under his wing, weren't we?'

There was a long silence after that as each fell into deep thought.

Max sighed, 'I remember him that day forty years ago – old suit, pipe, everything. He took me in. *Me,* a despised half-

Astonishing Stories, December 1940
Copyright © 1940 by Fictioneers, Inc.
Copyright renewed © 1967 by Isaac Asimov

breed! And – and he found you for me, Madeline!'

'I know,' there were tears in her eyes. 'But he's still with us, Max, and always will be – here, and there.' Her hand crept first to her own heart and then to Max's.

'Hey, there, Dad, catch her, catch her!'

Max whirled at the sound of his elder son's voice, just in time to catch up the little bundle of flying arms and legs that catapulted into him.

He held her gravely up before him, 'Shall I give you to your papa, Elsie? He wants you.'

The little girl kicked her legs ecstatically. 'No, no. I want *you*, grand-daddy. I want you to give me a piggy-back and come out with grandmamma to see how nice everything is.'

Max turned to his son, and motioned him sternly away, 'Depart, despised father, and let old grand-dad have a chance.'

Arthur laughed and mopped a red face, 'Keep her, for Heaven's sake. She's been leading me and the wife a merry chase outside. We had to drag her back by the dress to keep her from running off into the forest. Didn't we, Elsie?'

Elsie, thus appealed to, suddenly recalled a past grievance. 'Grand-daddy, tell him to let me see the pretty trees. He doesn't want me to.' She wriggled from Max's grasp and ran to the porthole. 'See them, grand-daddy, see them. It's all trees outside. It's not black anymore. I hated it when it was black, didn't you?'

Max leaned over and ruffled the child's soft, white hair gravely, 'Yes, Elsie, I hated it when it was black. But it isn't black anymore, and it won't ever be black again. Now go run to grandmamma. She'll get some cake specially for you. Go ahead, run!'

He followed the departing forms of his wife and granddaughter with smiling eyes, and then, as they turned to his son, they became serious once more.

'Well, Arthur?'

'Well, dad, what now?'

'There's no time to waste, son. We've got to start building immediately – underground!'

Arthur snapped into an attentive attitude, 'Underground!' He frowned his dismay.

'I know, I know. I said nothing of this previously, but it's got

36

to be done. At all costs we must vanish from the face of the System. There are Earthmen on Venus – purebloods. There aren't many, it's true, but there are some. They mustn't find us – at least, not until we are prepared for whatever may follow. *That* will take years.'

'But father, *underground*! To live like moles, hidden from light and air. I don't like that.'

'Oh, nonsense. Don't overdramatize. We'll *live* on the surface – but the city; the power-stations, the food and water reserves, the laboratories – all that must be below and impregnable.'

The old Tweenie gestured the subject away with impatience, 'Forget that, anyway. I want to talk about something else – something we've discussed already.'

Arthur's eyes hardened and he shifted his glance to the ceiling. Max rose and placed his hands upon his son's brawny shoulders.

'I'm past sixty, Arthur. How long I have yet to live, I don't know. In any case, the best of me belongs to the past and it is better that I yield the leadership to a younger, more vigorous person.'

'Dad, that's sentimental bosh and you know it. There isn't one of us that's fit to wipe your shoes and no one is going to listen for a second to any plan of appointing a successor while you're still alive.'

'I'm not going to ask them to listen. It's done – and you're the new leader.'

The younger man shook his head firmly, 'You can't make me serve against my will.'

Max smiled whimsically, 'I'm afraid you're dodging responsibility, son. You're leaving your poor old father to the strains and hardships of a job beyond his aged strength.'

'Dad!' came the shocked retort. 'That's not so. You know it isn't. You —'

'Then prove it. Look at it this way. Our race needs *active* leadership, and I can't supply it. I'll always be here – while I live – to advise you and help you as best I can, but from now on, *you* must take the initiative.'

Arthur frowned and the words came from him reluctantly, 'All right, then. I take the job of field commander. But remember, *you're* commander-in-chief.'

'Good! And now let's celebrate the occasion.' Max opened a cupboard and withdrew a box, from which he abstracted a pair of cigars. He sighed, 'The supply of tobacco is down to the vanishing point and we won't have any more until we grow our own, but – we'll smoke to the new leader.'

Blue smoke curled upwards and Max frowned through it at his son, 'Where's Henry?'

Arthur grinned, 'Dunno! I haven't seen him since we landed. I can tell you with whom he is, though.'

Max grunted, 'I know that, too.'

'The kid's making hay while the sun shines. It won't be many years now, Dad, before you'll be spoiling a second set of grandchildren.'

'If they're as good as the three of my first set, I only hope I live to see the day.'

And father and son smiled affectionately at each other and listened in silence to the muted sound of happy laughter from the hundreds of Tweenies outside.

Henry Scanlon cocked his head to one side, and raised his hand for silence, 'Do you hear running water, Irene?'

The girl at his side nodded, 'Over in that direction.'

'Let's go there, then. A river flashed by just before we landed and maybe that's it.'

'All right, if you say so, but I think we ought to be getting back to the ships.'

'What for?' Henry stopped and stared. 'I should think you'd be glad to stretch your legs after weeks on a crowded ship.'

'Well, it might be dangerous.'

'Not here in the highlands, Irene. Venusian highlands are practically a second Earth. You can see this is forest and not jungle. Now if we were in the coastal regions —' He broke off short, as if he had just remembered something. 'Besides, what's there to be afraid of? *I'm* with you, aren't I?' And he patted the Tonite gun at his hip.

Irene repressed a sudden smile and shot an arch glance at her strutting companion, 'I'm quite aware that you're with me. *That's* the danger.'

Henry's chest deflated with an audible gasp. He frowned. '*Very* funny – And I on my best behavior, too.' He drifted away, brooded sulkily awhile, and then addressed the trees in a distant manner, 'Which reminds me that tomorrow is Daphne's birthday. I've promised her a present.'

'Get her a reducing belt,' came the quick retort. 'Fat thing!'

'Who's fat? Daphne? Oh – I wouldn't say so.' He considered matters carefully, one thoughtful eye upon the young girl at his side. 'Now my description of her would be – shall we say – "pleasingly plump," or, maybe, "comfortably upholstered." '

'She's *fat*,' Irene's voice was suddenly a hiss, and something very like a frown wrinkled her lovely face, 'and her eyes are green.' She swung on ahead, chin high, and superbly conscious of her own little figure.

Henry hastened his steps and caught up, 'Of course, I prefer skinny girls any day.'

Irene whirled on him and her little fists clenched, 'I'm not skinny, you incredibly stupid ape.'

'But Irene, who said I meant you?' His voice was solemn, but his eyes were laughing.

The girl reddened to the ears and turned away, lower lip trembling. The smile faded from Henry's eyes and was replaced by a look of concern. His arm shot out hesitantly and slipped about her shoulder.

'Angry, Irene?'

The smile that lit her face of a sudden was as brilliant as the sparkling sheen of her silvery hair in the bright sun.

'No,' she said.

Their eyes met and, for a moment, Henry hesitated – and found that he who hesitates is lost; for with a sudden twist and a smothered laugh, Irene was free once more.

Pointing through a break in the trees, she cried, 'Look, a lake!' and was off at a run.

Henry scowled, muttered something under his breath and ran after.

The scene was truly Earthly. A rapids-broken stream wound its way through banks of slender-trunked trees and then spread into a placid lake some miles in width. The brooding quiet was unbroken save by the muffled beat that issued from the throat-bags of the frilled lizards that nested in the upper reaches of the trees.

The two Tweenies – boy and girl – stood hand in hand upon the bank and drank in the beauty of the scene.

Then there was a muffled splash near by and Irene shrank

into the encircling arms of her companion.

'What's the matter?'

'N-nothing. Something moved in the water, I think.'

'Oh, imagination, Irene.'

'No. I *did* see something. It came up and – oh, goodness, Henry, don't squeeze so tightly —'

She almost lost her balance as Henry suddenly dropped her altogether and jerked at his Tonite gun.

Immediately before them, a dripping green head lifted out of the water and regarded them out of wide-set, staring goggle-eyes. Its broad lipless mouth opened and closed rapidly, but not a sound issued forth.

Max Scanlon stared thoughtfully at the rugged foot-hills ahead and clasped his hands behind his back.

'You think so, do you?'

'Certainly, Dad,' insisted Arthur, enthusiastically. 'If we burrow under these piles of granite, all Earth couldn't get at us. It wouldn't take two months to form the entire cavern, with our unlimited power.'

'Hmph! It will require care!'

'It will get it!'

'Mountainous regions are quake regions.'

'We can rig up enough stat-rays to hold up all Venus, quakes or no quakes.'

'Stat-rays eat up energy wholesale, and a breakdown that will leave us energyless would mean the end.'

'We can hook up five separate power-houses – as foolproof as we can make them. All five won't break down at once.'

The old Tweenie smiled. 'All right, son. I see you've got it planned thoroughly. Go ahead! Start whenever you want – and remember, it's all up to you.'

'Good! Let's get back to the ships.' They picked their way gingerly down the rocky slope.

'You know, Arthur,' said Max, stopping suddenly, 'I've been thinking about those stat-beams.'

'Yes?' Arthur offered his arm, and the two resumed their walk.

'It's occurred to me that if we could make them two-dimensional in extent and curve them, we'd have the perfect defense, as long as our energy lasted – a stat-field.'

40

'You need four-dimensional radiation for that, Dad – nice to think about but can't be done.'

'Oh, is that so? Well, listen to this —'

What Arthur was to listen to remained hidden, however – for that day at least. A piercing shout ahead jerked both their heads upward. Up towards them came the bounding form of Henry Scanlon, and following him, at a goodly distance and a much more leisurely pace, came Irene.

'Say, Dad, I had a devil of a time finding you. Where were you?'

'Right here, son. Where were you?'

'Oh, just around. Listen, Dad. You know those amphibians the explorers talk about as inhabiting the highland lakes of Venus, don't you? Well, we've located them, lots of them, a regular convoy of them. Haven't we, Irene?'

Irene paused to catch her breath and nodded her head, 'They're the cutest things, Mr. Scanlon. All green.' She wrinkled her nose laughingly.

Arthur and his father exchanged glances of doubt. The former shrugged. 'Are you sure you haven't been seeing things? I remember once, Henry, when you sighted a meteor in space, scared us all to death, and then had it turn out to be your own reflection in the port glass.'

Henry, painfully aware of Irene's snicker, thrust out a belligerent lower lip, 'Say, Art, I guess you're looking for a shove in the face. And I'm old enough to give it to you, too.'

'Whoa there, quiet down,' came the peremptory voice of the elder Scanlon, 'and you, Arthur, had better learn to respect your younger brother's dignity. Now here, Henry, all Arthur meant was that these amphibians are as shy as rabbits. No one's ever caught more than a glimpse of them.'

'Well, we have, Dad. Lots of them. I guess they were attracted by Irene. No one can resist her.'

'I know *you* can't,' and Arthur laughed loudly.

Henry stiffened once more, but his father stepped between. 'Grow up, you two. Let's go and see these amphibians.'

'This is amazing,' exclaimed Max Scanlon. 'Why, they're as friendly as children, I can't understand it.'

Arthur shook his head, 'Neither can I, Dad. In fifty years, no explorer has ever gotten a good look at one, and here they are – thick as flies.'

Henry was throwing pebbles into the lake. 'Watch this, all of you.'

A pebble curved its way into the water, and as it splashed six green forms turned a back somersault and slid smoothly below the surface. With no time for a breath between, one was up again and the pebble arced back to fall at Henry's feet.

The amphibians were crowding closer in ever increasing numbers now, approaching the very edge of the lake, where they grasped at the coarse reeds on the bank and stared goggle-eyed at the Tweenies. Their muscular webbed legs could be seen below the surface of the water, moving back and forth with lazy grace. Without cessation, the lipless mouths opened and closed in a queer, uneven rhythm.

'I think they're talking, Mr. Scanlon,' said Irene, suddenly.

'It's quite possible,' agreed the old Tweenie, thoughtfully. 'Their brain-cases are fairly large, and they may possess considerable intelligence. If their voice boxes and ears are tuned to sound waves of higher or lower range than our own, we would be unable to hear them – and that might very well explain their soundlessness.'

'They're probably discussing us as busily as we are them,' said Arthur.

'Yes, and wondering what sort of freaks we are,' added Irene.

Henry said nothing. He was approaching the edge of the lake with cautious steps. The ground grew muddy beneath his feet, and the reeds thick. The group of amphibians nearest turned anxious eyes toward him, and one or two loosened their hold and slipped silently away.

But the nearest held his ground. His wide mouth was clamped tight; his eyes were wary – but he did not move.

Henry, paused, hesitated, and then held out his hand, 'Hiya, Phib!'

The 'Phib' stared at the outstretched hand. Very cautiously, his own webbed forelimb stretched out and touched the Tweenie's fingers. With a jerk, they were drawn back, and the Phib's mouth worked in soundless excitement.

'Be careful,' came Max's voice from behind. 'You'll scare him that way. His skin is terribly sensitive and dry objects must irritate him. Dip your hand in the water.'

Slowly, Henry obeyed. The Phib's muscles tensed to escape at the slighest sudden motion, but none came. Again the Tweenie's hand was held out, dripping wet this time.

For a long minute, nothing happened, as the Phib seemed to debate within itself the future course of action. And then, after two false starts and hasty withdrawals, fingers touched again.

'Ataphib,' said Henry, and clasped the green hand in his own.

A single, startled jerk followed and then a lusty return of pressure to an extent that numbed the Tweenie's fingers. Evidently encouraged by the first Phib's example, his fellows were crowding close now, offering hosts of hands.

The other three Tweenies slushed up through the mud now, and offered wetted hands in their turn.

'That's funny,' said Irene. 'Everytime I shake hands I seem to keep thinking of hair.'

Max turned to her, 'Hair?'

'Yes, ours. I get a picture of long, white hair, standing straight up and shining in the sun.' Her hand rose unconsciously to her own smooth tresses.

'Say!' interrupted Henry suddenly, 'I've been noticing that, too, now that you mention it. Only when I shake hands, though.'

'How about you, Arthur?' asked Max.

Arthur nodded once, his eyebrows climbing.

Max smiled and pounded fist into palm. 'Why, it's a primitive sort of telepathy – too weak to work without physical contact and even then capable of delivering only a few simple ideas.'

'But why hair, dad?' asked Arthur.

'Maybe it's our hair that attracted them in the first place. They've never seen anything like it and – and – well, who can explain their psychology?'

He was down on his knees suddenly, splashing water over his high crest of hair. There was a frothing of water and a surging of green bodies as the Phibs pressed closer. One green paw passed gently through the stiff white crest, followed by excited, if noiseless, chattering. Struggling among themselves for favored vantage-points, they competed for the privilege of touching the hair until Max, for sheer weariness, was forced to rise again.

'They're probably our friends for life now,' he said. 'A pretty queer set of animals.'

It was Irene, then, who noticed the group of Phibs a hundred yards from shore. They paddled quietly, making no effort to approach closer. 'Why don't *they* come?' she asked.

She turned to one of the foremost Phibs and pointed, making frantic gestures of dubious meaning. She received only solemn stares in return.

'That's not the way, Irene,' admonished Max, gently. He held out his hand, grasped that of a willing Phib and stood motionless for a moment. When he loosed his grip, the Phib slid into the water and disappeared. In a moment, the laggard Phibs were approaching shore slowly.

'How did you do it?' gasped Irene.

'Telepathy! I held on tightly and pictured an isolated group of Phibs and a long hand stretching out over the water to shake theirs.' He smiled gently, 'They are quite intelligent, or they would not have understood so readily.'

'Why, they're females,' cried Arthur, in sudden breathless astonishment. 'By all that's holy – they suckle their young!'

The newcomers were slenderer and lighter in color than the others. They advanced shyly, urged on by the bolder males and held out timid hands in greeting.

'Oh-h,' Irene cried in sudden delight. 'Look at this!'

She was down on her knees in the mud, arms outstretched to the nearest female. The other three watched in fascinated silence as the nervous she-Phib clasped its tiny armful closer to its breast.

But Irene's arms made little inviting gestures, 'Please, please. It's so cute. I won't hurt him.'

Whether the Phib mother understood is doubtful, but with a sudden motion, she held out a little green bundle of squirming life and deposited it in the waiting arms.

Irene rose, squealing with delight. Little webbed feet kicked aimlessly and round frightened eyes stared at her. The other three crowded close and watched it curiously.

'It's the *dearest* little thing, it is. Look at its funny little mouth. Do you want to hold it, Henry?'

Henry jumped backwards as if stung, 'Not on your life! I'd probably drop it.'

44

'Do you get any thought images, Irene?' asked Max, thoughtfully.

Irene considered and frowned her concentration, 'No-o. It's too young, mayb – oh, *yes*! It's – it's —' She stopped, and tried to laugh. 'It's *hungry*!'

She returned the little baby Phib to its mother, whose mouth worked in transports of joy and whose muscular arms clasped the little mite close. The tiny Phib swiveled its little green head to bend one last goggling look at the creature that had held it for an instant.

'Friendly creatures,' said Max, 'and intelligent. They can keep their lakes and rivers. We'll take the land and won't interfere with them.'

A lone Tweenie stood on Scanlon Ridge and his field-glass pointed at the Divide ten miles up the hills. For five minutes, the glass did not waver and the Tweenie stood like some watchful statue made of the same rock as formed the mountains all about.

And then the field-glass lowered, and the Tweenie's face was a pale thin-lipped picture of gloom. He hastened down the slope to the guarded, hidden entrance to Venustown.

He shot past the guards without a word and descended into the lower levels where solid rock was still being puffed into nothingness and shaped at will by controlled blasts of superenergy.

Arthur Scanlon looked up and with a sudden premonition of disaster, gestured the Disintegrators to a halt.

'What's wrong, Sorrell?'

The Tweenie leant over and whispered a single word into Arthur's ear.

'Where?' Arthur's voice jerked out hoarsely.

'On the other side of the ridge. They're coming through the Divide now in our direction. I spotted the blaze of sun on metal and —' he held up his field-glass significantly.

'Good Lord!' Arthur rubbed his forehead distractedly and then turned to the anxiously-watching Tweenie at the controls of the Disinto. 'Continue as planned! No change!'

He hurried up the levels to the entrance, and snapped out hurried orders, 'Triple the guard immediately. No one but me or those with me, are to be permitted to leave. Send out men to round up any stragglers outside immediately and order them to keep within shelter and make so unnecessary sound.'

Then, back again through the central avenue to his father's quarters.

Max Scanlon looked up from his calculations and his grave forehead smoothed out slowly.

'Hello, son. Is anything wrong? Another resistant stratum?'

'No, nothing like that.' Arthur closed the door carefully and lowered his voice. 'Earthmen!'

For a moment, Max made no movement. The expression on his face froze for an instant, and then, with a sudden exhalation, he slumped in his chair and the lines in his forehead deepened wearily.

'Settlers?'

'Looks so. Sorrell said women and children were among them. There were several hundred in all, equipped for a stay – and headed in this direction.'

Max groaned, 'Oh, the luck, the luck! All the vast empty spaces of Venus to choose and they come here. Come, let's get a firsthand look at this.'

They came through the Divide in a long, snaky line. Hard-bitten pioneers with their pinched work-worn women and their carefree, half-barbarous, wilderness-bred children. The low, broad 'Venus Vans' joggled clumsily over the untrodden ways, loaded down with amorphous masses of household necessities.

The leaders surveyed the prospect and one spoke in clipped, jerky syllables, 'Almost through, Jem. We're out among the foothills now.'

And the other replied slowly, 'And there's good new growing-land ahead. We can stake out farms and settle down.' He sighed, 'It's been tough going this last month. I'm glad it's over!'

And from a ridge ahead – the last ridge before the valley – the Scanlons, father and son, unseen dots in the distance, watched the newcomers with heavy hearts.

'The one thing we could not prepare for – and it's happened.'

Arthur spoke slowly and reluctantly, 'They are few and unarmed. We can drive them out in an hour.' With sudden fierceness, 'Venus is *ours*!'

46

'Yes, we can drive them out in an hour – in ten minutes. But they would return, in thousands, and armed. We're not ready to fight all Earth, Arthur.'

The younger man bit his lip and words were muttered forth half in shame, 'For the sake of the race, Father – we could kill them all.'

'Never!' exclaimed Max, his old eyes flashing. '*We* will not be the first to strike. If we kill, we can expect no mercy from Earth; and we will deserve none.'

'But, Father, what else? We can expect no mercy from Earth as it is. If we're spotted, – if they ever suspect our existence, our whole hegira becomes pointless and we lose out at the very beginning.'

'I know. I know.'

'We can't change now,' continued Arthur, passionately. 'We've spent months preparing Venustown. How could we start over?'

'We can't,' agreed Max, tonelessly. 'To even attempt to move would mean sure discovery. We can only —'

'Live like moles after all. Hunted fugitives! Frightened refugees! Is that it?'

'Put it any way you like – but we must hide, Arthur, and bury ourselves.'

'Until —?'

'Until I – or we – perfect a curved two-dimensional stat-beam. Surrounded by an impermeable defense, we can come out into the open. It may take years; it may take one week. I don't know.'

'And every day we run the risk of detection. Any day the swarms of purebloods can come down upon us and wipe us out. We've got to hang on by a hair day after day, week after week, month after month —'

'We've *got* to.' Max's mouth was clamped shut, and his eyes were a frosty blue.

Slowly, they went back to Venustown.

Things were quiet in Venustown, and eyes were turned to the topmost level and the hidden exits. Out there was air and the sun and space – and Earthmen.

They had settled several miles up the river-bed. Their rude houses were springing up. Surrounding land was being cleared.

47

Farms were being staked out. Planting was taking place.

And in the bowels of Venus, eleven hundred Tweenies shaped their home and waited for an old man to track down the elusive equations that would enable a stat-ray to spread in two dimensions and curve.

Irene brooded somberly as she sat upon the rocky ledge and stared ahead to where the dim gray light indicated the existence of an exit to the open. Her shapely legs swung gently back and forth and Henry Scanlon, at her side, fought desperately to keep his gaze focussed harmlessly upon air.

'You know what, Henry?'

'What?'

'I'll bet the Phibs could help us.'

'Help us do what, Irene?'

'Help us get rid of the Earthmen.'

Henry thought it over carefully, 'What makes you think that?'

'Well, they're pretty clever – cleverer than we think. Their minds are altogether different, though, and maybe they could fix it. Besides – I've just got a feeling.' She withdrew her hand suddenly, 'You don't have to hold it, Henry.'

Henry swallowed, 'I – I thought you had a sort of unsteady seat there – might fall, you know.'

'Oh!' Irene looked down the terrific three-foot drop. 'There's something in what you say. It does look pretty high here.'

Henry decided he was in the presence of a hint, and acted accordingly. There was a moment's silence while he seriously considered the possibility of her feeling a bit chilly – but before he had quite decided that she probably was, she spoke again.

'What I was going to say, Henry, was this. Why don't we go out and see the Phibs?'

'Dad would take my head off if I tried anything like that.'

'It would be a lot of fun.'

'Sure, but it's dangerous. We can't risk anyone seeing us.'

Irene shrugged resignedly, 'Well, if you're afraid, we'll say no more about it.'

Henry gasped and reddened. He was off the ledge in a bound, 'Who's afraid? When do you want to go?'

'Right now, Henry. Right this very minute.' Her cheeks flushed with enthusiasm.

'All right then. Come on.' He started off at a half-run, dragging her along. – And then a thought occurred to him and he stopped short.

He turned to her fiercely, '*I'll* show you if I'm afraid.' His arms were suddenly about her and her little cry of surprise was muffled effectively.

'Goodness,' said Irene, when in a position to speak once more. 'How thoroughly *brutal*!'

'Certainly. I'm a very well-known brute,' gasped Henry, as he uncrossed his eyes and got rid of the swimming sensation in his head. 'Now let's get to those Phibs; and remind me, when I'm president, to put up a memorial to the fellow who invented kissing.'

Up through the rock-lined corridor, past the backs of outward-gazing sentries, out through the carefully camouflaged opening, and they were upon the surface.

The smudge of smoke on the southern horizon was grim evidence of the presence of man, and with that in mind, the two young Tweenies slithered through the underbrush into the forest and through the forest to the lake of the Phibs.

Whether in some strange way of their own the Phibs sensed the presence of friends, the two could not tell, but they had scarcely reached the banks when approaching dull-green smudges beneath water told of the creatures' coming.

A wide, goggle-eyed head broke the surface, and, in a second, bobbing frogheads dotted the lake.

Henry wet his hand and seized the friendly forelimb outstretched to him.

'Hi there, Phib.'

The grinning mouth worked and made its soundless answer.

'Ask him about the Earthmen, Henry,' urged Irene. Henry motioned impatiently.

'Wait a while. It takes time. I'm doing the best I can.'

For two slow minutes, the two, Tweenie and Phib, remained motionless and stared into each other's eyes. And then the Phib broke away and, at some silent order, every lake-creature vanished, leaving the Tweenies alone.

Irene stared for a moment, nonplussed, 'What happened?'

Henry shrugged, 'I don't know. I pictured the Earthmen and he seemed to know who I meant. Then I pictured Earthmen fighting us and killing us – and he pictured a lot of us and only a few of them and another fight in which we killed them. But then I pictured us killing them and then a lot more of *them* coming – hordes and hordes – and killing us and then —'

But the girl was holding her hands to her tortured ears, 'Oh, my goodness. No wonder the poor creature didn't understand. I wonder he didn't go crazy.'

'Well, I did the best I could,' was the gloomy response. 'This was all your nutty idea, anyway.'

Irene got no further with her retort than the opening syllable, for in a moment the lake was crowded with Phibs once more. 'They've come back,' she said instead.

A Phib pushed forward and seized Henry's hand while the others crowded around in great excitement. There were several moments of silence and Irene fidgeted.

'Well?' she said.

'Quiet, please. I don't get it. Something about big animals, or monsters, or —' His voice trailed away, and the furrow between his eyes deepened into painful concentration.

He nodded, first abstractedly, then vigorously.

He broke away and seized Irene's hands. 'I've got it – and it's the perfect solution. We can save Venustown all by ourselves, Irene, with the help of the Phibs – if you want to come to the Lowlands with me tomorrow. We can take along a pair of Tonite pistols and food supplies and if we follow the river, it oughtn't to take us more than two or three days there and the same time back. What do you say, Irene?'

Youth is not noted for forethought. Irene's hesitation was for effect only, 'Well – maybe we shouldn't go ourselves, but – but I'll go – with you.' There was the lightest accent on the last word.

Ten seconds later, the two were on their way to Venustown, and Henry was wondering, if on the whole, it weren't better to put up *two* memorials to the fellow who invented kissing.

The flickering red-yellow of the fire sent back ruddy highlights from Henry's lordly crest of hair and cast shifting shadows upon his brooding face.

It was hot in the Lowlands, and the fire made it worse, yet Henry huddled close and kept an anxious eye upon the sleeping form of Irene on the other side. The teeming life of the

Venusian jungle respected fire, and the flames spelt safety.

They were three days from the plateau now. The stream had become a lukewarm, slowly-moving river, the shores of which were covered with the green scum of algae. The pleasant forests had given way to the tangled, vine-looped growths of the jungle. The mingled sounds of life had grown in volume and increased to a noisy crescendo. The air became warmer and damper; the ground swampier; the surroundings more fantastically unfamiliar.

And yet there was no real danger – of that, Henry was convinced. Poisonous life was unknown on Venus, and as for the tough-skinned monsters that lorded the jungles, the fire at night and the Phibs during day would keep them away.

Twice the ear-splitting shriek of a Centosaur had sounded in the distance and twice the sound of crashing trees had caused the two Tweenies to draw together in fear. Both times, the monsters had moved away again.

This was the third night out, and Henry stirred uneasily. The Phibs seemed confident that before morning they could start their return trip, and somehow the thought of Venustown was rather attractive. Adventure and excitement are fine and with every passing hour the glory of his scintillating bravery grew in Irene's eyes – which was wonderful – but still Venustown and the friendly Highlands were nice to think about.

He threw himself on his stomach and gazed morosely into the fire, thinking of his twenty years of age – almost twenty years.

'Why, heck,' he tore at the rank grass beneath. 'It's about time I was thinking of getting *married*.' And his eye strayed involuntarily to the sleeping form beyond the fire.

As if in response, there was a flickering of eyelids and a vague stare out of deep blue eyes.

Irene sat up and stretched.

'I can't sleep at all,' she complained, brushing futilely at her white hair. 'It's so hot.' She stared at the fire distastefully.

Henry's good humor persisted. 'You slept for hours – and snored like a trombone.'

Irene's eyes snapped wide open, 'I did not!' Then, with a voice vibrant with tragedy, 'Did I?'

'No, of course not!' Henry howled his laughter, stopping only at the sudden, sharp contact between the toe of Irene's shoe and the pit of his own stomach. 'Ouch,' he said.

'Don't speak to me anymore, *Mister* Scanlon!' was the girl's frigid remark.

It was Henry's turn to look tragic. He rose in panicky dismay and took a simple step toward the girl. And then he froze in his tracks at the ear-piercing shriek of a Centosaur. When he came to himself, he found his arms full of Irene.

Reddening, she disentangled herself, and then the Centosaurian shriek sounded again, from another direction, – and there she was, right back again.

Henry's face was pale, in spite of his fair armful. 'I think the Phibs have snared the Centosaurs. Come with me and I'll ask them.'

The Phibs were dim blotches in the gray dawn that was breaking. Rows and rows of strained, abstracted individuals were all that met the eye. Only one seemed to be unoccupied and when Henry rose from the handclasp, he said, 'They've got three Centosaurs and that's all they can handle. We're starting back to the Highlands right now.'

The rising sun found the party two miles up the river. The Tweenies, hugging the shore, cast wary eyes toward the bordering jungle. Through an occasional clearing, vast gray bulks could be made out. The noise of the reptilian shrieks was almost continuous.

'I'm sorry I brought you, Irene,' said Henry. 'I'm not so sure now that the Phibs can take care of the monsters.'

Irene shook her head. 'That's all right, Henry. I *wanted* to come. Only – I wish we had thought of letting the Phibs bring the beasts themselves. They don't need us.'

'Yes, they do! If a Centosaur gets out of control, it will make straight for the Tweenies and they'd never get away. We've got the Tonite guns to kill the 'saurs with if the worst comes to the worst —' His voice trailed away and he glanced at the lethal weapon in his hand and derived but cold comfort thereform.

The first night was sleepless for both Tweenies. Somewhere, unseen in the backness of the river, Phibs took shifts and their telepathic control over the tiny brains of the gigantic, twenty-legged Centosaurs maintained its tenuous hold. Off in the jungle, three hundred-ton monsters howled impatiently against the force that drove them up the river side against their will and raved impotently against the unseen barrier that prevented them from approaching the stream.

By the side of the fire, a pair of Tweenies, lost between mountainous flesh on one side and the fragile protection of a telepathic web on the other, gazed longingly towards the Highlands some forty miles off.

Progress was slow. As the Phibs tired, the Centosaurs grew balkier. But gradually, the air grew cooler. The rank jungle growth thinned out and the distance to Venustown shortened.

Henry greeted the first signs of familiar temperate-zone forest with a tremulous sigh of relief. Only Irene's presence prevented him from discarding his role of heroism.

He felt pitifully eager for their quixotic journey to be over, but he only said, 'It's practically all over but the shouting. And you can bet there'll be shouting, Irene. We'll be heroes, you and I.'

Irene's attempt at enthusiasm was feeble. 'I'm tired, Henry. Let's rest.' She sank slowly to the ground, and Henry, after signalling the Phibs, joined her.

'How much longer, Henry?' Almost without volition, she found her head nestling wearily against his shoulder.

'One more day, Irene. Tomorrow this time, we'll be back.' He looked wretched, 'You think we shouldn't have tried to do this ourselves, don't you?'

'Well, it seemed a good idea at the time.'

'Yes, I know,' said Henry. 'I've noticed that I get lots of ideas that seem good at the time, but sometimes they turn sour.' He shook his head philosophically, 'I don't know why, but that's the way it is.'

'All I know,' said Irene, 'is that I don't care if I never move another step in my life. I wouldn't get up now —'

Her voice died away as her beautiful blue eyes stared off toward the right. One of the Centosaurs stumbled into the waters of a small tributary to the stream they were following. Wallowing in the water, his huge serpentine body mounted on the ten stocky pairs of legs, glistened horribly. His ugly head weaved towards the sky and his terrifying call pierced the air. A second joined him.

Irene was on her feet. 'What are you waiting for, Henry. Let's go! Hurry!'

Henry gripped his Tonite gun tightly and followed.

Arthur Scanlon gulped savagely at his fifth cup of black coffee and, with an effort, brought the Audiomitter into optical focus. His eyes, he decided, were becoming entirely too balky. He rubbed them into red-rimmed irritation and cast a glance over his shoulder at the restlessly sleeping figure on the couch.

He crept over to her and adjusted the coverlet.

'Poor Mom,' he whispered, and bent to kiss the pale lips. He turned to the Audiomitter and clenched a fist at it, 'Wait till I get you, you crazy nut.'

Madeline stirred, 'Is it dark yet?'

'No,' lied Arthur with feeble cheerfulness. "He'll call before sundown, Mom. You just sleep and let me take care of things. Dad's upstairs working on that stat-field and he says he's making progress. In a few days everything will be all right.' He sat silently beside her and grasped her hand tightly. Her tired yes closed once more.

The signal light blinked on and, with a last look at his mother, he stepped out into the corridor, 'Well!'

The waiting Tweenie saluted smartly, 'John Barno wants to say that it looks as if we are in for a storm.' He handed over an official report.

Arthur glanced at it peevishly, 'What of that? We've had plenty so far, haven't we? What do you expect of Venus?'

'This will be a particularly bad one, from all indications. The barometer has fallen unprecedentedly. The ionic concentration of the upper atmosphere is at an unequalled maximum. The Beulah River has overflowed its banks and is rising rapidly.'

The other frowned. 'There's not an entrance to Venustown that isn't at least fifty yards above river level. As for rain – our drainage system is to be relied upon.' He grimaced suddenly, 'Go back and tell Barno that it can storm for my part – for forty days and forty nights if it wants to. Maybe it will drive the Earthmen away.'

He turned away, but the Tweenie held his ground, 'Beg pardon sir, but that's not the worst. A scouting party today —'

Arthur whirled. 'A scouting party? Who ordered one to be sent out?'

'Your father, sir. They were to make contact with the Phibs, – I don't know why.'

54

'Well, go on.'

'Sir, the Phibs could not be located.'

And now, for the first time, Arthur was startled out of his savage ill-humor, 'They were gone?'

The Tweenie nodded. 'It is thought that they have sought shelter from the coming storm. It is that which causes Barno to fear the worst.'

'They say rats desert a sinking ship,' murmured Arthur. He buried his head in trembling hands. 'God! Everything at once! Everything at once!'

The darkening twilight hid the pall of blackness that lowered over the mountains ahead and emphasized the darting flashes of lightning that flickered on and off continuously.

Irene shivered, 'It's getting sort of windy and chilly, isn't it?'

'The cold wind from the mountains. We're in for a storm, I guess,' Henry assented absently. 'I think the river is getting wider.'

A short silence, and then, with suddenly vivacity, 'But look, Irene, only a few more miles to the lake and then we're practically at the Earth village. It's almost over.'

Irene nodded, 'I'm glad for all of us – and the Phibs, too.'

She had reason for the last statement. The Phibs were swimming slowly now. An additional detachment had arrived the day before from upstream, but even with those reinforcements, progress had slowed to a walk. Unaccustomed cold was nipping the multi-legged reptiles and they yielded to superior mental force more and more reluctantly.

The first drops fell just after they had passed the lake. Darkness had fallen, and in the blue glare of the lightning the trees about them were ghostly specters reaching swaying fingers toward the sky. A sudden flare in the distance marked the funeral pyre of a lightning-hit tree.

Henry paled. 'Make for the clearing just ahead. At a time like this, trees are dangerous.'

The clearing he spoke of composed the outskirts of the Earth village. The rough-hewn houses, crude and small against the fury of the elements, showed lights here and there that spoke of human occupancy. And as the first Centosaur stumbled out from between splintered trees, the storm suddenly burst in all its fury.

The two Tweenies huddled close. 'It's up to the Phibs,' screamed Henry, dimly heard above the wind and rain. 'I hope they can do it.'

The three monsters converged upon the houses ahead. They moved more rapidly as the Phibs called up every last line of mental power.

Irene buried her wet head in Henry's equally wet shoulder, 'I can't look! Those houses will go like matchsticks. Oh, the poor people!'

'No, Irene, no. They've stopped!'

The Centosaurs pawed vicious gouges out of the ground beneath and their screams rang shrill and clear above the noise of the storm. Startled Earthmen rushed from their cabins.

Caught unprepared – most having been roused from sleep – and faced with a Venusian storm and nightmarish Venusian monsters, there was no question of organized action. As they stood, carrying nothing but their clothes, they broke and ran.

There was the utmost confusion. One or two, with dim attempts at presence of mind, took wild, ineffectual pot-shots at the mountains of flesh before them – and then ran.

And when it seemed that all were gone, the giant reptiles surged forward once more and where once had been houses, there were left only mashed splinters.

'They'll never come back, Irene, they'll never come back.' Henry was breathless at the success of his plan. 'We're heroes now, and —' His voice rose to a hoarse shriek, 'Irene, get back! Make for the trees!'

The Centosaurian howls had taken on a deeper note. The nearest one reared onto his two hindmost pairs of legs and his great head, two hundred feet above ground, was silhouetted horribly against the lightning. With a rumbling thud, he came down on all feet again and made for the river – which under the lash of the storm was now a raging flood.

The Phibs had lost control!

Henry's Tonite gun flashed into quick action as he shoved Irene away. She, however, backed away slowly and brought her own gun into line.

The ball of purple light that meant a hit blazed into being and the nearest Centosaur screamed in agony as its mighty tail threshed aside the surrounding trees. Blindly, the hole where once a leg had been gushing blood, it charged.

A second glare of purple and it was down with an earth-shaking thud, its last shriek reaching a crescendo of shrill frightfulness.

But the other two monsters were crashing toward them. They blundered blindly toward the source of the power that had held them captive almost a week; driving violently with all the force of their mindless hate to the river. And in the path of the Juggernauts were the two Tweenies.

The boiling torrent was at their backs. The forest was a groaning wilderness of splintered trees and ear-splitting sound.

Then, suddenly, the report of Tonite guns sounded from the distance. Purple glares – a flurry of threshing – spasmodic shrieking – and then a silence in which even the wind, as if overawed by recent events, held its peace momentarily.

Henry yelled his glee and performed an impromptu war-dance. 'They've come from Venustown, Irene,' he shouted. 'They've got the Centosaurs and everything's finished! We've saved the Tweenies!'

It happened in a breath's time. Irene had dropped her gun and sobbed her relief. She was running to Henry and then she tripped – and the river had her.

'Henry!' The wind whipped the sound away.

For one dreadful moment, Henry found himself incapable of motion. He could only stare stupidly, unbelievingly, at the spot where Irene had been, and then he was in the water. He plunged into the surrounding backness desperately.

'Irene!' He caught his breath with difficulty. The current drove him on.

'*Irene!*' No sound but the wind. His efforts at swimming were futile. He couldn't even break surface for more than a second at a time, his lungs were bursting.

'*Irene!*' There was no answer. Nothing but rushing water and darkness.

And then something touched him. He lashed out at it in-stinctively, but the grip tightened. He felt himself borne up into the air. His tortured lungs breathed in gasps. A grinning Phib face stared into his and after that there was nothing but con-fused impressions of cold, dark wetness.

He became aware of his surroundings by stages. First, that he was sitting on a blanket under the trees, with other blankets wrapped tightly about him. Then, he felt the warm radiation of the heat-lamps upon him and the illumination of Atomo bulbs. People were crowding close and he noticed that it was no longer raining.

He stared about him hazily and then, 'Irene!'

She was beside him, as wrapped up as he, and smiling feebly, 'I'm all right, Henry. The Phibs dragged me back, too.'

Madeline was bending over him and he swallowed the hot coffee placed to his lips. 'The Phibs have told us of what you two have helped them do. We're all proud of you, son – you and Irene.'

Max's smile transfigured his face into the picture of paternal pride, 'The psychology you used was perfect. Venus is too vast and has too many friendly areas to expect Earthmen to return to places that have shown themselves to be infested with Centosaurs – not for a good long while. And when they *do* come back, we shall have our stat-field.'

Arthur Scanlon hurried up out of the gloom. He thwacked Henry on the shoulder and then wrong Irene's hand. 'Your guardian and I,' he told her, 'are fixing up a celebration for day after tomorrow, so get good and rested. It's going to be the greatest thing you ever saw.'

Henry spoke up, 'Celebration, huh? Well, I'll tell you what you can do. After it's over, you can announce an engagement.'

'An engagement?' Madeline sat up and looked interested. 'What do you mean?'

'An engagement – to be married,' came the impatient answer. 'I'm old enough, I suppose. Today proves it!'

Irene's eyes bent in furious concentration upon the grass, 'With whom, Henry?'

'Huh? With *you*, of course. Gosh, who else could it be?'

'But you haven't asked me.' The words were uttered slowly and with great firmness.

For a moment Henry flushed, and then his jaws grew grim, 'Well, I'm not going to. I'm telling you! And what are you going to do about it?'

He leaned close to her and Max Scanlon chuckled and motioned the others away. On tip-toes, they left.

A dim shape hobbled into view and the two Tweenies separated in confusion. They had forgotten the others.

But it wasn't another Tweenie. 'Why – why, it's a Phib!' cried Irene.

He limped his ungainly way across the wet grass, with the inexpert aid of his muscular arms. Approaching, he flopped wearily on his stomach and extended his forearms.

His purpose was plain. Irene and Henry grasped a hand apiece. There was silence a moment or two and the Phib's great eyes glinted solemnly in the light of the Atomo lamps. Then there was a sudden squeal of embarrassment from Irene and a shy laugh from Henry. Contact was broken.

'Did you get the same thing I did?' asked Henry.

Irene was red, 'Yes, a long row of little baby Phibs, maybe fifteen —'

'Or twenty,' said Henry.

'– with *long white hair!*'

THE END

The story, not surprisingly, reflects my personal situation at the time. I had gone to a boys' high school and to a boys' college. Now that I was in graduate school, however, the surroundings were, for the first time, coeducational.

In the fall of 1939, I discovered that a beautiful blond girl had the desk next to mine in the laboratory of my course in synthetic organic chemistry. Naturally I was attracted.

I persuaded her to go out with me on simple dates, the very first being on my twentieth birthday, when I took her to Radio City Music Hall. For five months, I mooned after her with feckless romanticism.

At the end of the school year, though, she had earned her master of arts degree and, having decided not to go on for her doctorate, left school and took a job in Wilmington, Delaware, leaving me behind, woebegone and stricken.

I got over it, of course, but while she was still at school I wrote 'Half-Breeds on Venus.' Of all the stories I had yet written, it was the most heavily boy-and-girl. The heroine's name was Irene, which was the name of my pretty blond lab neighbor.

Merely having a few dates on the hand-holding level did not, however, perform the magic required to make me capable of handling passion in literature, and I continued to use girls sparingly in later stories – and a good thing, too, I think.

The success of 'Half-Breeds on Venus' made the notion of writing sequels generally seem a good idea. A sequel to a successful story must, after all, be a reasonably sure sale. So even while I was working on 'Half-Breeds on Venus,' I suggested to Campbell that I write a sequel to 'Homo Sol.'

Campbell's enthusiasm was moderate, but he was willing to look at such a sequel if I were to write it. I did write it as soon as 'Half-Breeds on Venus' was done and called it 'The Imaginary.' Although it used one of the chief characters of 'Homo Sol,' the human-nonhuman confrontation was absent, which probably didn't help it as far as Campbell was concerned. I submitted it to him on June 11, and received it back – a rejection, sequel or no sequel – on June 19.

Pohl rejected it, too. Tremaine read it with more sympathy and was thinking of taking it for *Comet*, I heard, but that magazine ceased publication and the story was back on the market. Actually, I retired it, but two years later I sold it to Pohl's magazine after all – but at a time when Pohl was no longer editor.

But though I had my troubles and didn't click every time, or even right away, I did manage to make $272 during my first year as a graduate student, and that was an enormous help.

11 : The Imaginary

The telecaster flashed its fitful signal, while Tan Porus sat by complacently. His sharp, green eyes glittered their triumph, and his tiny body was vibrant with excitement. Nothing could have better indicated the greatness of the occasion than his extraordinary position – Tan Porus had his feet on the desk!

The 'caster glowed into life and a broad Arcturian countenance frowned fretfully out at the Rigellian psychologist.

'Do you have to drag me here straight from bed, Porus? It's the middle of the night!'

'It's broad daylight in this part of the world, Final. But I've got something to tell you that'll make you forget all about sleep.'

Gar Final, editor of the J.G.P. – *Journal of Galactic Psychology* – allowed a look of alertness to cross his face. Whatever Tan Porus's faults – and Arcturus knew they were many – he had never issued a false alarm. If he said something was in the air, it was not merely great – it was colossal!

It was quite evident that Porus was enjoying himself. 'Final,' he said, 'the next article I send to your rag is going to be the greatest thing you've ever printed.'

Final was impressed. 'Do you really mean what you say?' he asked idiotically.

'What kind of a stupid question is that? Of course I do. Listen —' There followed a dramatic silence, while the tenseness on Final's face reached painful proportions. Then came Porus's husky whisper – 'I've solved the problem of the squid!'

Of course the reaction was exactly what Porus had expected. There was a blow-up at the other end, and for thirty interesting seconds the Rigellian was surprised to learn that the staid and respectable Final had a blistering vocabulary.

Porus's squid was a by-word throughout the galaxy. For two years now, he had been fussing over an obscure Draconian animal that persisted in going to sleep when it wasn't supposed to. He had set up equations and torn them down with a regu-

Super Science Stories, November 1942

larity that had become a standing joke with every psychologist in the Federation – and none had explained the unusual reaction. Now Final had been dragged from bed to be told that the solution had been reached – and that was all.

Final ripped out a concluding phrase that all but put the 'caster out of commission.

Porus waited for the storm to pass and then said calmly, 'But do you know how I solved it?'

The other's answer was an indistinct mumble.

The Rigellian began speaking rapidly. All traces of amusement had left his face and, after a few sentences, all traces of anger left Final's.

The Arcturian's expression became one of wide-eyed interest. 'No?' he gasped.

'Yes!'

When Porus had finished, Final raced madly to put in rush calls to the printers to delay publication of the coming issue of the J.G.P. for two weeks.

Furo Santins, head of the math department of the University of Arcturus, gazed long and steadily at his Sirian colleague.

'No, no, you're wrong! His equations were legitimate. I checked them myself.'

'Mathematically, yes,' retorted the round-faced Sirian. 'But psychologically they had no meaning.'

Santins slapped his high forehead. 'Meaning! Listen to the mathematician talk. Great space, man, what have mathematics to do with meaning? Mathematics is a tool and as long as it can be manipulated to give proper answers and to make correct predictions, actual meaning has no significance. I'll say this for Tan Porus – most psychologists don't know enough mathematics to handle a slide-rule efficiently, but he knows his stuff.'

The other nodded doubtfully, 'I guess so. I guess so. But using imaginary quantities in psychological equations stretches my faith in science just a little bit. Square root of minus one!'

He shuddered....

The seniors' lounge in Psychology Hall was crowded and a-buzz with activity. The rumor of Porus's solution to the now-classic problem of the squid had spread fast, and conversation touched on nothing else.

At the center of the thickest group was Lor Haridin. He was young, with but newly acquired Senior status. But as Porus's assistant he was, under present conditions, master of the situation.

'Look, fellows – just exactly what it's all about I don't know. That's the old man's secret. All I can tell you is that I've got the general idea as to how he solved it.'

The others squeezed closer. 'I hear he had to make up a new mathematical notation for the squid,' said one, 'like that time we had trouble with the humanoids of Sol.'

Lor Haridin shook his head. 'Worse! What made him think of it, I can't imagine. It was either a brainstorm or a nightmare, but anyway he introduced imaginary quantities – the square root of minus one.'

There was an awful silence and then someone said, 'I don't believe it!'

'Fact!' was the complacent reply.

'But it doesn't make sense. What can the square root of minus one represent, psychologically speaking? Why, that would mean' – he was doing rapid calculation in his head, as were most of the others – 'that the neural synapses were hooked up in neither more nor less than four dimensions!'

'Sure,' broke in another. 'I suppose that if you stimulate the squid today, it will react yesterday. That's what an imaginary would mean. Comet gas! That's what *I* say.'

'That's why you're not the man Tan Porus is,' said Haridin. 'Do you suppose he cares how many imaginaries there are in the intermediate steps if they all square out into minus one in the final solution. All he's interested in is that they give him the proper sign in the answer – an answer which will explain that sleep business. As for its physical significance, what matter? Mathematics is only a tool, anyway.'

The others considered silently and marveled.

Tan Porus sat in his stateroom aboard the newest and most luxurious interstellar liner and gazed at the young man before him happily. He was in amazing good humour and, for perhaps the first time in his life, did not mind being interviewed by the keen, efficient employees of the Ether Press.

The Ethereporter on his side wondered in silence at the affability of the scientist. From bitter experience, he had found out that scientists, as a whole, detested reporters – and that psychologists, in particular, thought it fun to practice a bit of applied psych on them and to induce killingly amusing – to others – reactions.

He remembered the time that the old fellow from Canopus had convinced him that arboreal life was the greatest good. It had taken twenty men to drag him down from the tree-tops and an expert psychologist to bring him back to normal.

But here was the greatest of them all, Tan Porus, actually answering questions like a normal human being.

'What I would like to know now, Professor,' said the reporter, 'is just what this imaginary quantity is all about. That is,' he interposed hastily, 'not the mathematics of it – we'll take your word on that – but just a general idea that the ordinary humanoid can picture. For instance, I've heard that the squid has a four-dimensional mind.'

Porus groaned, 'Oh, Rigel! Four-dimensional poppycock! To tell the honest truth, that imaginary I used – which seems to have caught the popular fancy – probably indicates nothing more than some abnormality in the squid's nervous system, but just what, I don't know. Certainly, to the gross methods of ecology and micro-physiology, nothing unusual has been found. No doubt, the answer would lie in the atomic physics of the creature's brain, but there I have no hope.' There was a trace of disdain in his voice. 'The atomic physicists are too far behind the psychologists to expect them to catch up at this late date.'

The reporter bore down furiously on his stylus. The next day's headline was clear in his mind: *Noted Psychologist Blasts Atomic Physicists!*

Also, the headline of the day after: *Indignant Physicists Denounce Noted Psychologist!*

Scientific feuds were great stuff for the Ether Press, particularly that between psychologists and physicists, who, it was well known, hated each other's guts.

The reporter glanced up brightly. 'Say, Professor, the humanoids of the galaxy are very interested, you know, in the private lives of you scientists. I hope you don't mind if I ask you a few questions about your trip home to Rigel IV.'

'Go ahead,' said Porus, genially. 'Tell them it's the first time I'm getting home in two years. I'm sort of looking forward to it. Arcturus is just a bit too yellow for my eyes and the furniture you have here is too big.'

'It's true, isn't it, that you have a wife at home?'

Porus coughed. 'Hmm, yes. Sweetest little woman in the galaxy. I'm looking forward to seeing her, too. Put that down.'

The reporter put it down. 'How is it you didn't bring her to Arcturus with you?'

Some of the geniality left the Rigellian's face. 'I like to be alone when I work. Women are all right – in their place. Besides, my idea of a vacation is one by myself. Don't put that down.'

The reporter didn't put it down. He gazed at the other's little form with open admiration. 'Say, Prof, how did you ever get her to stay home, though? I wish you'd tell me the secret.' Then, with a wealth of feeling he added, 'I could use it!'

Porus laughed. 'I tell you, son. When you're an ace psychologist, you're master in your own home!'

He motioned the interview to an end and then suddenly grasped the other by the arm. His green eyes were piercingly sharp. 'And listen, son, that last remark doesn't go into the story, you know.'

The reporter paled and backed away. 'No, sir; no, sir! We've got a little saying in our profession that goes: "Never monkey around with a psychologist, or he'll make a monkey of *you*."'

'Good! I can do it literally, you know, if I have to.'

The young press employee ducked out hastily after that, wiped the cold perspiration from his brow and left with his story. For a moment, towards the last, he had felt himself hanging on the ragged edge. He made a mental note to refuse all future interviews with psychologists – unless they raised his pay.

Tens of billions of miles out, the pure white orb of Rigel had reached Porus's eyes, and something in his heart uplifted him.

Type B reaction – nostalgia; conditioned reflex through association of Rigel with happy scenes of youth —

Words, phrases, equations spun through his keen brain, but he was happy in spite of them. And in a little while, the human triumphed over the psychologist and Porus abandoned analysis for the superior joy of uncritical happiness.

He sat up past the middle of the sleep period two nights

before the landing to catch first glimpse of Hanlon, fourth planet of Rigel, his home world. Some place on that world, on the shores of a quiet sea, was a little two-story house. A little house – not those giant structures fit only for Arcturians and other hulking humanoids.

It was the summer season now and the house would be bathed in the pearly light of Rigel, and after the harsh yellow-red of Arcturus, how restful that would be.

And – he almost shouted in his joy – the very first night he was going to insist on gorging himself with broiled *tryptex*. He hadn't tasted it for two years, and his wife was the best hand at *tryptex* in the system.

He winced a little at the thought of his wife. It *had* been a dirty trick, getting her to stay home the last two years, but it had had to be done. He glanced over the papers before him once more. There was just a little nervousness in his fingers as they shuffled the sheets. He had spent a full day in calculating her reactions at first seeing him after two years' absence and they were not pleasant.

Nina Porus was a woman of untamed emotions, and he would have to work quickly and efficiently.

He spotted her quickly in the crowd. He smiled. It was nice to see her, even if his equations did predict long and serious storms. He ran over his initial speech once more and made a last-minute change.

And then she saw him. She waved frantically and broke from the forefront of the crowd. She was on Tan Porus before he was aware of it and, in the grip of her affectionate embrace, he went limp with surprise.

That wasn't the reaction to be expected at all! Something was wrong!

She was leading him dexterously through the crowd of reporters to the waiting stratocar, talking rapidly along the way.

'Tan Porus, I thought I'd never live to see you again. It's so good to have you with me again; you have absolutely no idea. Everything here at home is just fine, of course, but it isn't quite the same without you.'

Porus's green eyes were glazed. This speech was entirely uncharacteristic of Nina. To the sensitive ears of a psycholo-

66

gist, it sounded little short of the ravings of a maniac. He had not even the presence of mind to grunt at proper intervals. Frozen mutely in his seat, he watched the ground rush downwards and heard the air shriek backwards as they headed for their little house by the sea.

Nina Porus prattled on gaily – the one normal aspect of her conversation being her ability to uphold both ends of a dialogue with smooth efficiency.

'And, of course, dear, I've fixed up an entire *tryptex*, broiled to a turn, garnished with *sarnees*. And, oh yes, about that affair last year with that new planet – Earth, do you call it? I was so proud of you when I heard about it. I said —'

And so on and on, until her voice degenerated into a meaningless conglomeration of sounds.

Where were her tears? Where were the reproaches, the threats, the impassioned self-pity?

Tan Porus roused himself to one great effort at dinner. He stared at the steaming dish of *tryptex* before him with an odd lack of appetite and said, 'This reminds me of the time at Arcturus when I dined with the President Delegate —'

He went into details, dilating on the gayety and abandon of the affair, waxing lyrical over his own enjoyment of it, stressing, almost unsubtly, the fact that he had not missed his wife, and finally, in one last wild burst of desperation, mentioning casually the presence of a surprising number of Rigellian females in the Arcturian system.

And through it all, his wife sat smiling. 'Wonderful, darling,' she'd say. 'I'm so glad you enjoyed yourself. Eat your *tryptex*.'

But Porus did not eat his *tryptex*. The mere thought of food nauseated him. With one lingering stare of dismay at his wife, he arose with what dignity he could muster and left for the privacy of his room.

He tore up the equations furiously and hurled himself into a chair. He seethed with anger, for evidently something had gone wrong with Nina. Terribly wrong! Even interest in another man – and for just a moment that had occurred to him as a possible explanation – would not cause such a revolution in character.

He tore at his hair. There was some hidden factor more startling than that – but what it was he had no idea. At that moment Tan Porus would have given the sum total of his worldly possessions to have his wife enter and make one – just one – attempt to snatch his scalp off, as of old.

And below, in the dining room, Nina Porus allowed a crafty gleam to enter her eye.

Lor Haridin put down his pen and said, 'Come in!'

The door opened, and his friend, Eblo Ranin, entered, brushed off a corner of the desk and sat down.

'Haridin, I've got an idea.' His voice was uncommonly like a guilty whisper.

Haridin gazed at him suspiciously.

'Like the time,' he said, 'you set up the booby trap for old man Obel?'

Ranin shuddered. He had spent two days hiding in the ventilator shaft after that brilliant piece of work. 'No, this is legitimate. Listen, Porus left you in charge of the squid, didn't he?'

'Oh, I see what you're getting at. It's no go. I can feed the squid, but that's all. If I as much as clapped my hands at it to induce a color-change tropism, the boss would throw a fit.'

'To space with him! He's parsecs away, anyway.' Ranin drew forth a two-month-old copy of the J.G.P. and folded the cover back. 'Have you been following Livell's experiments at Procyon U.? You know – magnetic fields applied with and without ultra-violet radiation.'

'Out of my field,' grunted Haridin. 'I've heard of it, but that's all. What about it?'

'Well, it's a type E reaction which gives, believe it or not, a strong Fimbal Effect in practically every case, especially in the higher invertebrates.'

'Hmm!'

'Now, if we could try it on this squid, we could —'

'No, no, no, no!' Haridin shook his head violently. 'Porus would break me. Great stars and little meteors, *how* he would break me!'

'Listen, you nut – Porus can't tell you what to do with the squid. It's Frian Obel that has final say. He's head of the Psychological Board, not Porus. All you have to do is to apply for his permission and you'll get it. Just between us, since that Homo Sol affair last year, he can't stand the sight of Porus anyway.'

Haridin weakened. 'You ask him.'

Ranin coughed. 'No. On the whole, perhaps I'd better not. He's sort of got a suspicion that I set that booby trap, and I'd rather keep out of his way.'

'Hmm. Well – all right!'

Lor Haridin looked as if he had not slept well for a week – which shows that sometimes appearances are not deceiving. Eblo Ranin regarded him with patient kindliness and sighed.

'Look! Will you please sit down? Santin said he would have the final results in today, didn't he?'

'I know, I know, but it's humiliating. I spent seven years on higher math. And now I make a stupid mistake and can't even find it!'

'Maybe it's not there to find.'

'Don't be silly. The answer is just impossible. It must be impossible. It must be.' His high forehead creased. 'Oh, I don't know what to think.'

He continued his concentrated attempt to wear out the nap of the rug beneath and mused bitterly. Suddenly he sat down.

'It's those time integrals. You can't work with them, I tell you. You look 'em up in a table, taking half an hour to find the proper entry, and they give you seventeen possible answers. You have to pick the one that makes sense, and – Arcturus help me! – either they all do, or none do! Run up against eight of them, as we do in this problem, and we've got enough permutations to last us the rest of our life. Wrong answer! It's a wonder I lived through it at all.'

The look he gave the fat volume of Helo's *Tables of Time Integrals* did not sear the binding, to Ranin's great surprise.

The signal light flashed, and Haridin leaped to the door.

He snatched the package from the messenger's hand and ripped open the wrappings frantically.

He turned to the last page and stared at Santin's final note:

'Your calculations are correct. Congratulations – and won't this knock Porus's head right off his shoulders! Better get in touch with him at once.'

Ranin read it over the other's shoulder, and for one long minute the two gazed at each other.

'I was right,' whispered Haridin, eyes bulging. 'We've found something in which the imaginary doesn't square out. We've

69

got a predicted reaction which includes an imaginary quantity!'

The other swallowed and brushed aside his stupefaction with an effort. 'How do you interpret it?'

'Great space! How in the galaxy should I know? We've got to get Porus, that's all.'

Ranin snapped his fingers and grabbed the other by the shoulders. 'Oh, no, we won't. This is our big chance. If we can carry this through, we're made for life.' He stuttered in his excitement. 'Arcturus! Any psychologist would sell his life twice over to have our opportunity right now.'

The Draconian squid crawled placidly about, unawed by the huge solenoid that surrounded its tank. The mass of tangled wires, the current leads, the mercury-vapor lamp up above meant nothing to it. It nibbled contentedly at the fronds of the sea fern about it and was at peace with the world.

Not so the two young psychologists. Eblo Ranin scurried through the complicated set-up in a last-minute effort at checking everything. Lor Haridin helped him in intervals between nail-biting.

'Everything's set,' said Ranin, and swabbed wearily at his damp brow. 'Let her shoot!'

The mercury-vapor lamp went on and Haridin pulled the window curtains together. In the cold red-less light, two green tinted faces watched the squid closely. It stirred restlessly, its warm pink changing to a dull black in the mercury light.

'Turn on the juice,' said Haridin hoarsely.

There was a soft click, and that was all.

'No reaction?' questioned Ranin, half to himself. And then he held his breath as the other bent closer.

'Something's happening to the squid. It seems to glow a bit – or is it my eyes?'

The glow became perceptible and then seemed to detach itself from the body of the animal and take on a spherical shape of itself. Long minutes passed.

'It's emitting some sort of radiation, field, force – whatever you want to call it – and there seems to be expansion with time.'

There was no answer, and none was expected. Again they waited and watched.

And then Ranin emitted a muffled cry and grasped Haridin's elbow tightly. 'Crackling comets, what's it doing?'

The globular glowing sphere of whatever it was had thrust out a pseudopod. A gleaming little projection touched the swaying branch of the sea-fern, and where it touched the leaves turned brown and withered!

'Shut off the current!'

The current clicked off; the mercury-vapor lamp went out; the shades were parted and the two stared at each other nervously.

'What was it?'

Haridin shook his head. 'I don't know. It was something definitely insane. I never saw anything like it.'

'You never saw an imaginary in a reaction equation before, either, did you? As a matter of fact, I don't think that expanding field was any known form of energy at —'

His breath came out in one long whistling exhalation and he retreated slowly from the tank containing the squid. The mollusc was motionless, but around it half the fern in the tank hung sere and withered.

Haridin gasped. He pulled the shades and in the gloom, the globe of glowing haze bulked through half the tank. Little curving tentacles of light reached toward the remaining fern and one pulsing thread extended through the glass and was creeping along the table.

That fright in Ranin's voice rendered it a cracked, scarcely-understood sound.

'It's a lag reaction. Didn't you test it by Wilbon's Theorem?'

'How could I?' The other's heart pumped madly and his dry lips fought to form words. 'Wilbon's Theorem didn't make sense with an imaginary in the equation. I let it go.'

Ranin sped into action with feverish energy. He left the room and was back in a moment with a tiny, squealing, squirrel-like animal from his own lab. He dropped it in the path of the thread of light stealing along the table, and held it there with a yard rule.

The glowing thread wavered, seemed to sense the presence of life in some horribly blind way, and lunged toward it. The little rodent squealed once, a high-pitched shriek of infinite torture, and went limp. In two seconds it was a shriveled, shrunken travesty of its former self.

Ranin swore and dropped the rule with a sudden yell, for the thread of light – a bit brighter, a bit thicker – began creeping up the wood toward him.

'Here,' said Haridin, 'let's end this!' He yanked a drawer open and withdrew the chromium-plated Tonite gun within. Its sharp thin beam of purple light lunged forward toward the squid and exploded in blazing, soundless fury against the edge of the sphere of force. The psychologist shot again and again, and then compressed the trigger to form one continuous purple stream of destruction that ceased only when power failed.

And the glowing sphere remained unharmed. It engulfed the entire tank. The ferns were brown masses of death.

'Get the Board,' yelled Ranin. 'It's beyond us entirely!'

There was no confusion – humanoids in the mass are simply not subject to panic, if you don't count the half-genius, half-humanoid inhabitants of the planets of Sol – and the evacuation of the University grounds was carried out smoothly.

'One fool,' said old Mir Deana, ace physicist of Arcturus U., 'can ask more questions than a thousand wise men can answer.' He fingered his scraggly beard and his button nose sniffed loudly in disdain.

'What do you mean by that?' questioned Frian Obel sharply. His green Vegan skin darkened angrily.

'Just that, by analogy, one cosmic fool of a psychologist can make a bigger mess than a thousand physicists can clear up.'

Obel drew in his breath dangerously. He had his own opinion of Haridin and Ranin, but no lame-brain psysicist could —

The plump figure of Qual Wynn, university president, came charging down upon them. He was out of breath and spoke between puffs.

'I've gotten in touch with the Galactic Congress and they're arranging for evacuation of all Eron, if necessary.' His voice became pleading. 'Isn't there anything that can be done?'

Mir Deana sighed, 'Nothing – yet! All we know is this: the squid is emitting some sort of pseudo-living radiatory field which is not electromagnetic in character. Its advance cannot be stopped by anything we have yet tried, material or vacuum. None of our weapons affect it, for within the field the ordinary attributes of space-time apparently don't hold.'

The president shook a worried head. 'Bad, bad! You've sent for Porus, though?' He sounded as though he were clutching at a last straw.

'Yes,' scowled Frian Obel. 'He's the only one that really knows that squid. If he can't help us, no one can.' He stared off toward the gleaming white of the university buildings, where the grass over half the campus was brown stubble and the trees blasted ruins.

'Do you think,' said the president, turning to Deana once more, 'that the field can span interplanetary space?'

'Sizzling novae, I don't know what to think!' Deana exploded, and he turned pettishly away.

There was a thick silence of utter gloom.

Tan Porus was sunk in deep apathy. He was unaware of the brilliant coruscations of color overhead. He didn't hear a sound of the melodious tones that filled the auditorium.

He knew only one thing – that he had been talked into attending a concert. Concerts above all were anathema to him, and in twenty years of married life he had steered clear of them with a skill and ease that only the greatest psychologist of them all could have shown. And now —

He was startled out of his stupor by the sudden discordant sounds that arose from the rear.

There was a rush of ushers to the exit where the disturbance originated, a waving of protesting uniformed arms and then a strident voice: 'I am here on urgent business direct from the Galactic Congress on Eron, Arcturus. Is Tan Porus in the audience?'

Tan Porus was out of his seat with a bound. Any excuse to leave the auditorium was nothing short of heaven-sent.

He ripped open the communication handed him by the messenger and devoured its contents. At the second sentence, his elation left him. When he was finished, he raised a face in which only his darting green eyes seemed alive.

'How soon can we leave?'

'The ship is waiting now.'

'Come, then.'

He took one step forward and stopped. There was a hand on his elbow.

'Where are you going?' asked Nina Porus. There was hidden steel in her voice.

Tan Porus felt stifled for a moment. He foresaw what would happen. 'Darling, I must go to Eron immediately. The fate of a world, of the whole galaxy perhaps, is at stake. You don't know how important it is. I tell you —'

'All right, go! And I'll go with you.'

The psychologist bowed his head.

'Yes, dear!' he said. He sighed.

The psychological board hemmed and hawed as one man and then stared dubiously at the large-scale graph before them.

'Frankly, gentlemen,' said Tan Porus, 'I don't feel too certain about it myself, but – well, you've all seen my results, and checked them too. And it is the only stimulus that will yield a canceling reaction.'

Frian Obel fingered his chin nervously. 'Yes, the mathematics is clear. Increase of hydrogen-ion activity past pH3 would set up a Demane's Integral and that — But listen, Porus, we're not dealing with space-time. The math might not hold – perhaps nothing will hold.'

'It's our only chance. If we were dealing with normal space-time, we could just dump in enough acid to kill the blasted squid or fry it with a Tonite. As it is, we have no choice but to take our chances with —'

Loud voices interrupted him. 'Let me through, I say! I don't care if there are ten conferences going on!'

The door swung open and Qual Wynn's portly figure made its entrance. He spied Porus and bore down upon him. 'Porus, I tell you I'm going crazy. Parliament is holding me, as university president, responsible for all this, and now Deana says that —' He sputtered into silence and Mir Deana, standing composedly behind him, took up the tale.

'The field now covers better than one thousand square miles and its rate of increase is growing steadily. There seems to be no doubt now that it can span interplanetary space if it wishes to do so – interstellar as well, if given the time.'

'You hear that? You hear that?' Wynn was fairly dancing in his anxiety. 'Can't you do something? The galaxy is doomed, I tell you, doomed!'

74

'Oh, keep your tunic on,' groaned Porus, 'and let *us* handle this.' He turned to Deana. 'Didn't your physicist stooges conduct some clumsy investigations as to the speed of penetration of the field through various substances?'

Deana nodded stiffly.

'Penetration varies, in general, inversely with density. Osmium, iridium and platinum are the best. Lead and gold are fair.'

'Good! That checks! What I'll need then is an osmium-plated suit with a lead-glass helmet. And make both plating and helmet good and thick.'

Qual Wynn stared horrified. 'Osmium plating! Osmium! By the great nebula, think of the expense.'

'I'm thinking,' said Porus frostily.

'But they'll charge it to the university; they'll —' He recovered with difficulty as the somber stares of the assembled psychologists fastened themselves upon him. 'When do you need it?' he muttered weakly.

'You're really going, yourself?'

'Why not?' asked Porus, clambering out of the suit.

Mir Deana said, 'The lead-glass headpiece will hold off the field not longer than an hour and you'll probably be getting partial penetration in much shorter time. I don't know if you can do it.'

'*I'll* worry about that.' He paused, and then continued uncertainly. 'I'll be ready in a few minutes. I'd like to speak to my wife first – alone.'

The interview was a short one. It was one of the very few occasions that Tan Porus forgot that he was a psychologist, and spoke as his heart moved him, without stopping to consider the natural reaction of the one spoken to.

One thing he did know – by instinct rather than thought – and that was that his wife would not break down or go sentimental on him; and there he was right. It was only in the last few seconds that her eyes fell and her voice quavered. She tugged a handkerchief from her wide sleeve and hurried from the room.

The psychologist stared after her and then stooped to pick up the thin book that had fallen as she had removed the handkerchief. Without looking at it, he placed it in the inner pocket of his tunic.

He smiled crookedly. 'A talisman!' he said.

Tan Porus's gleaming one-man cruiser whistled into the 'death field.' The clammy sensation of desolation impressed itself upon him at once.

He shrugged. 'Imagination! Mustn't get nervy now.'

There was the vaguest glitter – a sparkle that was felt rather than seen – in the air about him. And then it invaded the ship itself, and, looking up, the Rigellian saw the five Eronian rice-birds he had brought with him lying dead on the floor of their cage, huddled masses of bedraggled feathers.

'The "death field" is in,' he whispered. It had penetrated the steel hull of the cruiser.

The cruiser bumped to a rather unskillful landing on the broad university athletic field, and Tan Porus, an incongruous figure in the bulky osmium suit, stepped out. He surveyed his depressing surroundings. From the brown stubble underfoot to the glimmering haze that hid the normal blue of the sky, all seemed – dead.

He entered Psychology Hall.

His lab was dark; the shades were still drawn. He parted them and studied the squid's tank. The water replenisher was still working, for the tank was full. However, that was the only normal thing about it. Only a few dark-brown, ragged strands of rot were left of what had once been sea-fern. The squid itself lay inertly upon the floor of the tank.

Tan Porus sighed. He felt tired and numbed. His mind was hazy and unclear. For long minutes he stared about him un-seeingly.

Then, with an effort, he raised the bottle he held and glanced at the label – 12 molar hydrochloric acid.

He mumbled vaguely to himself. 'Two hundred cc. Just dump the whole thing in. That'll force the pH down – if only hydrogen ion activity means something here.'

He was fumbling with the glass stopper, and – suddenly – laughing. He had felt exactly like this the one and only time he had ever been drunk.

He shook the gathering cobwebs from his brain. 'Only got a few minutes to do – to do what? I don't know – something anyway. Dump this thing in. Dump it in. Dump! Dump!

Dumpety-dump!' He was mumbling a silly popular song to himself as the acid gurgled its way into the open tank.

Tan Porus felt pleased with himself and he laughed. He stirred the water with his mailed fist and laughed some more. He was still singing that song.

And then he became aware of a subtle change in environment. He fumbled for it and stopped singing. And then it hit him with the suddenness of a downpour of cold water. *The glitter in the atmosphere had gone!*

With a sudden motion, he unclasped the helmet and cast it off. He drew in long breaths of air, a bit musty, but unkilling.

He had acidified the water of the tank, and destroyed the field at its source. Chalk up another victory for the pure mathematics of psychology!

He stepped out of his osmium suit and stretched. The pressure on his chest reminded him of something. Withdrawing the booklet his wife had dropped, he said, 'The talisman came through!' and smiled indulgently at his own whimsy.

The smile froze as he saw for the first time the title upon the book.

The title was *Intermediate Course in Applied Psychology – Volume 5.*

It was as if something large and heavy had suddenly fallen onto Porus's head and driven understanding into it. *Nina had been boning up on applied psych for two whole years.*

This was the missing factor. He could allow for it. He would have to use triple time integrals, but —

He threw the communicator switch and waited for contact. 'Hello! This is Porus! Come on in, all of you! The death field is gone! I've beaten the squid.' He broke contact and added triumphantly, '– and my wife!'

Strangely enough – or, perhaps, not so strangely – it was the latter feat that pleased him more.

THE END

The chief interest to me in 'The Imaginary' is that it foreshadows 'psychohistory' that was to play such a big role in the 'Foundation' series. It was in this story and in its predecessor, 'Homo Sol,' that for the first time I treated psychology as a mathematically refined science.

It was about time that I made another stab at *Unknown*, and I did so with a story called 'The Oak,' which, as I recall, was something about an oak tree that served as an oracle and delivered ambiguous statements. I submitted it to Campbell on July 16, 1940, and it was promptly rejected.

One of the bad things about writing for *Unknown* was that the magazine was one of a kind. If *Unknown* rejected a story, there was no place else to submit it. It was possible to try *Weird Tales*, a magazine that was older than any science fiction magazine, but it dealt with old-fashioned, creaky horror tales and paid very little to boot. I wasn't really interested in trying to get into it. (And besides, they rejected both 'Life Before Birth' and 'The Oak' when I submitted them.)

Still, July 29, 1940, was a turning point in my career, although, of course, I had no way of telling it. I had up to that point written twenty-two stories in twenty-five months. Of these I had sold (or was to sell) thirteen, while nine never sold at all and no longer exist. The record wasn't abysmal but neither was it great – let's call it mediocre.

However, as it happened, except for two short-short stories that were special cases, I never again wrote a science fiction story I could never sell. I had found the range.

But not *Campbell's* range particularly. In August I wrote 'Heredity,' which I submitted to Campbell on August 15, and which he rejected two weeks later. Fortunately, Pohl snapped it up at once.

12: Heredity

Dr. Stefansson fondled the thick sheaf of typewritten papers that lay before him, 'It's all here, Harvey – twenty-five years of work.'

Mild-mannered Professor Harvey puffed idly at his pipe, 'Well, your part is over – and Markey's, too, on Ganymede. It's up to the twins, themselves, now.'

A short ruminative silence, and then Dr. Stefansson stirred uneasily, 'Are you going to break the news to Allen soon?'

The other nodded quietly, 'It will have to be done before we get to Mars, and the sooner the better.' He paused, then added in a tightened voice, 'I wonder how it feels to find out after twenty-five years that one has a twin brother whom one has never seen. It must be a damned shock.'

'How did George take it?'

'Didn't believe it at first, and I don't blame him. Markey had to work like a horse to convince him it wasn't a hoax. I suppose I'll have as hard a job with Allen.' He knocked the dottle from his pipe and shook his head.

'I have half a mind to go to Mars just to see those two get together,' remarked Dr. Stefansson wistfully.

'You'll do no such thing, Stef. This experiment's taken too long and means too much to have you ruin it by any such fool move.'

'I know, I know! Heredity versus environment! Perhaps at last the definite answer.' He spoke half to himself, as if repeating an old, familiar formula, 'Two identical twins, separated at birth; one brought up on old, civilized Earth, the other on pioneer Ganymede. Then, on their twenty-fifth birthday brought together for the first time on Mars – God! I wish Carter had lived to see the end of it. They're *his* children.'

'Too bad! – But we're alive, and the twins. To carry the experiment to its end will be our tribute to him.'

There is no way of telling, at first seeing the Martian branch

Astonishing Stories, April 1941
Copyright © 1941 by Fictioneers, Inc.
Copyright renewed © 1969 by Isaac Asimov

of Medicinal Products, Inc., that it is surrounded by anything but desert. You can't see the vast underground caverns where the native fungi of Mars are artificially nurtured into huge blooming fields. The intricate transportation system that connects all parts of the square miles of fields to the central building is invisible. The irrigation system; the air-purifiers; the drainage pipes, are all hidden.

And what one sees is the broad squat red-brick building and Martian desert, rusty and dry, all about.

That had been all George Carter had seen upon arriving via rocket-taxi, but him, at least, appearances had not deceived. It would have been strange had it done so, for his life on Ganymede had been oriented in its every phase towards eventual general managership of that very concern. He knew every square inch of the caverns below as well as if he had been born and raised in them himself.

And now he sat in Professor Lemuel Harvey's small office and allowed just the slightest trace of uneasiness to cross his impassive countenance. His ice-blue eyes sought those of Professor Harvey.

'This – this twin brother o' mine. He'll be here soon?'

Professor Harvey nodded, 'He's on his way over right now.'

George Carter uncrossed his knees. His expression was almost wistful, 'He looks a lot like me, d'ya rackon?'

'Quite a lot. You're identical twins, you know.'

'Hmm! Rackon so! Wish I'd known him all the time – on Ganny!' He frowned, 'He's lived on Airth all's life, huh?'

An expression of interest crossed Professor Harvey's face. He said briskly, 'You dislike Earthmen?'

'No, not exactly,' came the immediate answer. 'It's just the Airthmen are tenderfeet. All of 'm I know are.'

Harvey stifled a grin, and conversation languished.

The door-signal snapped Harvey out of his reverie and George Carter out of his chair at the same instant. The professor pressed the desk-button and the door opened.

The figure on the threshold crossed into the room and then stopped. The twin brothers faced each other.

It was a tense, breathless moment, and Professor Harvey sank into his soft chair, put his finger-tips together and watched keenly.

The two stood stiffly erect, ten feet apart, neither making a move to lessen the distance. They made a curious contrast – a contrast all the more marked because of the vast similarity between the two.

Eyes of frozen blue gazed deep into eyes of frozen blue. Each saw a long, straight nose over full, red lips pressed firmly together. The high cheekbones were as prominent in one as in the other, the jutting, angular chin as square. There was even the same, odd half-cock of one eyebrow in twin expressions of absorbed, part-quizzical interest.

But with the face, all resemblance ended. Allen Carter's clothes bore the New York stamp on every square inch. From his loose blouse, past his dark purple knee breeches, salmon-colored cellulite stockings, down to the glistening sandals on his feet, he stood a living embodiment of latest Terrestrial fashion.

For a fleeting moment, George Carter was conscious of a feeling of ungainliness as he stood there in his tight-sleeved, close-necked shirt of Ganymedan linen. His unbuttoned vest and his voluminous trousers with their ends tucked into high-laced, heavy-soled boots were clumsy and provincial. Even *he* felt it – for just a moment.

From his sleeve-pocket Allen removed a cigarette case – it was the first move either of the brothers had made – opened it, withdrew a slender cylinder of paper-covered tobacco that spontaneously glowed into life at the first puff.

George hesitated a fraction of a second and his subsequent action was almost one of defiance. His hand plunged into his inner vest pocket and drew therefrom the green, shriveled form of a cigar made of Ganymedan greenleaf. A match flared into flame upon his thumbnail and for a long moment, he matched, puff for puff, the cigarette of his brother.

And then Allen laughed – a queer, high-pitched laugh, 'Your eyes are a little closer together, I think.'

'Rackon 'tis, maybe. Y'r hair's fixed sort o' different.' There was faint disapproval in his voice. Allen's hand went self-consciously to his long, light-brown hair, carefully curled at the ends, while his eyes flickered over the carelessly-bound queue into which the other's equally long hair was drawn.

'I suppose we'll have to get used to each other. – I'm willing to try.' The Earth twin was advancing now, hand outstretched.

George smiled, 'Y' bet. 'At goes here, too.'

The hands met and gripped.

'Y'r name's All'n, huh?' said George.

'And yours is George, isn't it?' answered Allen.

And then for a long while they said nothing more. They just looked – and smiled as they strove to bridge the twenty-five year gap that separated them.

George Carter's impersonal gaze swept over the carpet of low-growing purple blooms that stretched in plot-path bordered squares into the misty distance of the caverns. The newspapers and feature writers might rhapsodize over the 'Fungus Gold' of Mars – about the purified extracts, in yields of ounces to acres of blooms, that had become indispensable to the medical profession of the System. Opiates, purified vitamins, a new vegetable specific against pneumonia – the blooms were worth their weight in gold, almost.

But they were merely blooms to George Carter – blooms to be forced to full growth, harvested, baled and shipped to the Aresopolis labs hundreds of miles away.

He cut his little ground car to half-speed and leant furiously out the window, 'Hi y' mudcat there. Y' with the dairty face. Watch what y'r doing – keep the domned water in the channel.'

He drew back and the ground car leapt ahead once more. The Ganymedan muttered viciously to himself, 'These domned men about here are wairse than useless. So many machines t' do their wairk for 'm they give their brains a pairmenent vacation. I rackon.'

The ground car came to a halt and he clambered out. Picking his way between the fungus plots, he approached the clustered group of men about the spider-armed machine in the plotway ahead.

'Well, here I am. What is 't, All'n?'

Allen's head bobbed up from behind the other side of the machine. He waved at the men about him, 'Stop it for a second!' and leaped toward his twin.

'George, it works. It's slow and clumsy, but it works. We can improve it now that we've got the fundamentals down. And in no time at all, we'll be able to —'

'Now wait a while, All'n. On Ganny, we go slow. Y' live long, that way. What y' got there?'

Allen paused and swabbed at his forehead. His face shone with grease, sweat and excitement. 'I've been working on this thing ever since I finished college. It's a modification of something we have on Earth – but it's no end improved. It's a mechanical bloom picker.'

He had fished a much-folded square of heavy paper from his pocket and talked steadily as he spread it on the plotway before them, 'Up to now, bloom-picking has been the bottle-neck of production, to say nothing of the 15 to 20% loss due to picking under- and over-ripe blooms. After all, human eyes are only human eyes, and the blooms — Here, look!'

The paper was spread flat and Allen squatted before it. George leaned over his shoulder, with frowning watchfulness.

'You see. It's a combination of fluoroscope and photo-electric cell. The ripeness of the bloom can be told by the state of the spores within. This machine is adjusted so that the proper circuit is tripped upon the impingement of just that combination of light and dark formed by ripe spores within the bloom. On the other hand, this second circuit – but look, it's easier to show you.'

He was up again, brimming with enthusiasm. With a jump, he was in the low seat behind the picker and had pulled the lever.

Ponderously, the picker turned toward the blooms and its 'eye' travelled sideways six inches above the ground. As it passed each fungus bloom, a long spidery arm shot out, lop-ping it cleanly half an inch from the ground and depositing it neatly in the downward-sloping slide beneath. A pile of blooms formed behind the machine.

'We can hook on a binder, too, later on. Do you notice those blooms it doesn't touch? Those are unripe. Just wait till it comes to an over-ripe one and see what it does.'

He yelled in triumph a moment later when a bloom was torn out and dropped on the spot.

He stopped the machine. 'You see? In a month, perhaps, we can actually start putting it to work in the fields.'

George Carter gazed sourly upon his twin, 'Take more 'n a month, I rackon. It'll take foraver, more likely.'

'What do you mean, forever. It just has to be sped up —'

'I don't care if 't just has t' be painted pairple. 'Tisn't going t' appear on *my* fields.'

'*Your* fields?'

'Yup, mine,' was the cool response. 'I've got veto pow'r here same as you have. Y' can't do anything 'thout my say-so – and y' won't get it f'r this. In fact, I want y' t' clear that thing out o' here, altogether. Got no use f'r 't.'

Allen dismounted and faced his brother, 'You agreed to let me have this plot to experiment on, veto-free, and I'm holding you to that agreement.'

'All right, then. But keep y'r domned machine out o' the rest o' the fields.'

The Earthman approached the other slowly. There was a dangerous look in his eyes. 'Look, George, I don't like your attitude – and I don't like the way you're using your veto power. I don't know what you're used to running on Ganymede, but you're in the big time now, and there are a lot of provincial notions you'll have to get out of your head.'

'Not unless I want to. And if y' want t' have 't out with me, we'd batter go t' y'r office. Spatting before the men 'd be bad for discipline.'

The trip back to Central was made in ominous silence. George whistled softly to himself while Allen folded his arms and stared with ostentatious indifference at the narrow, twisting plotway ahead. The silence persisted as they entered the Earthman's office. Allen gestured shortly toward a chair and the Ganymedan took it without a word. He brought out his ever-present green-leaf cigar and waited for the other to speak.

Allen hunched forward upon the edge of his seat and leaned both elbows on his desk. He began with a rush.

'There's lots to this situation, George, that's a mystery to me. I don't know why they brought up you on Ganymede and me on Earth, and I don't know why they never let us know of each other, or made us co-managers now with veto-power over one another – but I do know that the situation is rapidly growing intolerable.

'This corporation needs modernization, and you know that. Yet you've been wielding that veto-power over every trifling advance I've tried to initiate. I don't know just what your viewpoint is, but I've a suspicion that you think you're still living on Ganymede. If you're still in the sticks, – I'm warning you – get out of them fast. I'm from Earth, and this corporation is going to be run with Earth efficiency and Earth organization. Do you understand?'

George puffed odorous tobacco at the ceiling before answering, but when he did, his eyes came down sharply, and there was a cutting edge to his voice.

'Airth, is it? Airth efficiency, no less? Well, All'n, I like ye. I can't help it. Y'r so much like me, that disliking y' would be like disliking myself, I rackon. I hate t' say this, but y're upbringing's all wrong.'

His voice became sternly accusatory, 'Y'r an Airthman. Well, look at y'. An Airthman's but half a man at best, and naturally y' lean on machines. But d' y' suppose *I* want the corporation to be run by machines – just *machines*? What're the *men* t' do?'

'The men run the machines,' came the clipped, angry response.

The Ganymedan rose, and a fist slammed down on the desk, 'The machines run the men, and y' know it. Fairst, y' use them; then y' depend on them; and finally y'r slaves t' them. Over on y'r pracious Airth, it was machines, machines, machines – and as a result, what *are* y'? I'll tell y'. Half a man!'

He drew himself up, 'I still like y'. I like y' well enough t' wish y'd lived on Gannie with me. By Jupe 'n' domn, 'twould have made a man o' y'.'

'Finished?' said Allen.

'Rackon so!'

'Then I'll tell you something. There's nothing wrong with you that a life time on a decent planet wouldn't have fixed. As it is, however, you belong on Ganymede. I'd advise you to go back there.'

George spoke very softly, 'Y'r not thinking o' taking a punch at me, are y'?'

'No. I couldn't fight a mirror image of myself, but if your face were only a little different, I would enjoy splashing it about the premises a bit.'

'Think y' could do it – an Airthman like you? Here, sit down. We're both getting a bit too excited, I rackon. Nothing'll be settled *this* way.'

He sat down once more, puffed vainly at his dead cigar, and tossed it into the incinerator chute in disgust.

'Where's y'r water?' he grunted.

Allen grinned with sudden delight, 'Would you object to having a machine supply it?'

'Machine? What d' y' mean?' The Ganymedan gazed about him suspiciously.

'Watch! I had this installed a week ago.' He touched a button on his desk and a low click sounded below. There was the sound of pouring water for a second or so and then a circular metal disk beside the Earthman's right hand slid aside and a cup of water lifted up from below.

'Take it,' said Allen.

George lifted it gingerly and drank it down. He tossed the empty cup down the incinerator shaft, then stared long and thoughtfully at his brother, 'May I see this water feeder o' y'rs?'

'Surely. It's just under the desk. Here, I'll make room for you.'

The Ganymedan crawled underneath while Allen watched uncertainly. A brawny hand was thrust out suddenly and a muffled voice said, 'Hand me a screwdriver.'

'Here! What are you going to do?'

'Nothing. Nothing 't all. Just want t' investigate this contraption.'

The screw-driver was handed down and for a few minutes there was no other sound than an occasional soft scraping of metal on metal. Finally, George withdrew a flushed face and adjusted his wrinkled collar with satisfaction.

'Which button do I press for the water?'

Allen gestured and the button was pressed. The gurgling of water sounded. The Earthman stared in mystification from his desk to his brother and back again. And then he became aware of a moistness about his feet.

He jumped, looked downwards and squawked in dismay, 'Why, damn you, what have you done?' A snaky stream of water wriggled blindly out from under the desk and the pouring sound of water still continued.

George made leisurely for the door, 'Just short-caircuited it. Here's y'r screw-driver; fix 't up again.' And just before he slammed the door, 'So much f'r y'r pracious machines. They go wrong at the wrong times.'

The sounder was buzzily insistent and Allen Carter opened one eye peevishly. It was still dark.

With a sigh, he lifted one arm to the head of his bed and put the Audiomitter into commission.

The treble voice of Amos Wells of the night shift squawked excitedly at him. Allen's eyes snapped open and he sat up.

'You're crazy!' But he was plunging into his breeches even as he spoke. In ten seconds, he was careening up the steps three at a time. He shot into the main office just behind the charging figure of his twin brother.

The place was crowded; – its occupants in a jitter.

Allen brushed his long hair out of his eyes, 'Turn on the turret searchlight!'

'It's on,' said someone helplessly.

The Earthman rushed to the window and looked out. The yellow beam reached dimly out a few feet and ended in a muddy murkiness. He pulled at the window and it lifted upwards grittily a few inches. There was a whistle of wind and a tornado of coughing from within the room. Allen slammed it down again and his hands went at once to his tear-filled eyes.

George spoke between sneezes, 'We're not located in the sandstorm zone. This can't be one.'

'It is,' asserted Wells in a squeak. 'It's the worst I've ever seen. Started full blast from scratch just like that. It caught me flat-footed. By the time I closed off all exits to above, it was too late.'

'Too late!' Allen withdrew his attention from his sand-filled eyes and snapped out the words, 'Too late for what?'

'Too late for our rolling stock. Our rockets got it worst of all. There isn't one that hasn't its propulsives clogged with sand. And that goes for our irrigation pumps and the ventilating system. The generators below are safe but everything else will have to be taken apart and put together again. We're stalled for a week at least. Maybe more.'

There was a short, pregnant silence, and then Allen said, 'Take charge, Wells. Put the men on double shift and tackle the irrigation pumps first. They've got to be in working order inside of twenty-four hours, or half the crop will dry up and die on us. Here – wait, I'll go with you.'

He turned to leave, but his first footstep froze in midair at the sight of Michael Anders, communications officer, rushing up the stairs.

'What's the matter?'

Anders spoke between gasps, 'The damned planet's gone crazy. There's been the biggest quake in history with its center not ten miles from Aresopolis.'

There was a chorus of 'What?' and a ragged follow-up of blistering imprecations. Men crowded in anxiously; – many had relatives and wives in the Martian metropolis.

Anders went on breathlessly, 'It came all of a sudden. Aresopolis is in ruins and fires have started. There aren't any details but the transmitter at our Aresopolis labs went dead five minutes ago.'

There was a babel of comment. The news spread out into the furthest recesses of Central, and excitement waxed to dangerously panicky proportions. Allen raised his voice to a shout.

'Quiet, everyone. There's nothing we can do about Aresopolis. We've got our own troubles. This freak storm is connected with the quake some way – and that's what *we* have to take care of. Everyone back to his work now – and work fast. They'll be needing us at Aresopolis damned soon.' He turned to Anders, 'You! Get back to that receiver and don't knock off until you've gotten in touch with Aresopolis again. Coming with me, George?'

'No, rackon not,' was the response. 'Y' tend t' y'r machines. I'll go down with Anders.'

Dawn was breaking, a dusky, lightless dawn, when Allen Carter returned to Central. He was weary – weary in mind and body – and looked it. He entered the radio room.

'Things are a mess. If —'

There was a 'Shhh' and George waved frantically. Allen fell silent. Anders bent over the receiver, turning tiny dials with nervous fingers.

Anders looked up. 'It's no use, Mr. Carter. Can't get them.'

'All right. Stay here and keep y'r ears open. Let me know if anything turns up.'

He walked out, hooking an arm underneath his brother's and dragging the latter out.

'When c'n we get out the next shipment, All'n?'

'Not for at least a week. We haven't a thing that'll either roll or fly for days, and it will be even longer before we can start

88

harvesting again.'

'Have we any supplies on hand now?'

'A few tons of assorted blooms – mainly the red-purples. The Earth shipment last Tuesday took off almost everything.'

George fell into a reverie.

His brother waited a moment and did sharply, 'Well, what's on your mind? What's the news from Aresopolis?'

'Domned bad! The quake's leveled three-fourths o' Aresopolis and the rest's pretty much gutted with fire, I rackon. There 're fifty thousand that'll have t' camp out nights. – That's no fun in Martian autumn weather with the Airth gravity system broken down.'

Allen whistled, 'Pneumonia!'

'And common colds and influenza and any o' half doz'n diseases t' say nothing o' people bairnt. – Old Vincent is raising cain.'

'Wants blooms?'

'He's only got a two-day supply on hand. He's *got* t' have more.'

Both were speaking quietly, almost with indifference, with the vast understatement that is all that makes great crises bearable.

There was a pause and then George spoke again, 'What the best we c'n do?'

'Not under a week – not if we kill ourselves to do it. If they could send over a ship as soon as the storm dies down, we might be able to send what we have as a temporary supply until we can get over with the rest.'

'Silly even t' think o' that. The Aresopolis port is just ruins. They haven't a ship t' their names.'

Again silence. Then Allen spoke in a low, tense voice, 'What are you waiting for? What's that look on your face for?'

'I'm waiting f'r y' t' admit y'r domned machines have failed y' in the fairest emairgency we've had t' meet.'

'Admitted,' snarled the Earthman.

'Good! And now it's up t' me t' show y' what human ingenuity can do.' He handed a sheet of paper to his brother, 'There's a copy of the message I sent Vincent.'

Allen looked long at his brother and slowly read the pencilled scribbling.

'Will deliver all we have on hand in thirty-six hours. Hope it will keep you going the few days until we can get a real shipment out. Things are a little rough out here.'

'How are you going to do it?' demanded Allen, upon finishing.

'I'm trying to show y',' answered George, and Allen realized for the first time that they had left Central and were out in the caverns.

George led the way for five minutes and stopped before an object bulking blackly in the dimness. He turned on the section lights and said, 'Sand truck!'

The sand truck was not an imposing object. With the low driving car in front and the three squat, open-topped freight-cars behind it, presented a picture of obsolete decrepitude. Fifteen years ago, it had been relegated to the dust-heap by the sand-sleds and rocket-freights.

The Ganymedan was speaking, 'Checked it an hour ago, m'self, and 'tis still in wairking order. It has shielded bearings, air conditioning unit f'r the driving car and an intairnal combustion engine.'

The other looked up sharply. There was an expression of distaste on his face. 'You mean it burns chemical fuel.'

'Yup! Gas'line. That's why I like it. Reminds me o' Ganymede. On Gannie, I had a gas engine that —'

'But wait a while. We haven't any of that gasoline.'

'No, rackon not. But we got lots o' liquid hydrocarbons round the place. How about Solvent D? That's mostly octane. We've got tanks o' it.'

Allen said, 'That's so; – but the truck holds only two.'

'I know it. I'm one.'

'And I'm the other.'

George grunted, 'I rackond y'd say that – but this isn't going t' be a push-button machine job. Rackon y'r up t' it – Airthman?'

'I reckon I am – Gannie.'

The sun had been up some two hours before the sand-truck's engine whirred into life, but outside, the murk had become, if anything, thicker.

The main driveway within the caverns was ahum with activity. Grotesque figures with eyes peering through the thick glass of improvised air-helmets stepped back as the truck's broad,

90

sand-adapted wheels began their slow turn. The three cars behind had been piled high with purple blooms, canvas covers had been thrown over them and bound down tightly – and now the signal was given to open the doors.

The lever was jerked downwards and the double doors separated with sand-clogged protests. Through a gray whirl of inblown sand, the truck made its way outwards, and behind it sand-coated figures brushed at their air-helmets and closed the doors again.

George Carter, inured by long Ganymedan custom, met the sudden gravity change as they left the protective Gravitor fields of the caverns, with a single long-drawn breath. His hands held steady upon the wheels. His Terrestrial brother, however, was in far different condition. The hard nauseating knot into which his stomach tied itself loosened only very gradually, and it was a long time before his irregular stertorous breathing approached anything like normality again.

And throughout, the Earthman was conscious of the other's side-long glance and of just a trace of a smile about the other's lips.

It was enough to keep the slightest moan from issuing forth, though his abdominal muscles cramped and icy perspiration bathed his face.

The miles clicked off slowly, but the illusion of motionlessness was almost as complete as that in space. The surroundings were gray – uniform, monotonous and unvarying. The noise of the engine was a harsh purr and the clicking of the air-purifier behind like a drowsy tick. Occasionally, there was an especially strong gust of wind, and a patter of sand dashed against the window with a million tiny, separate pings.

George kept his eye strictly upon the compass before him. The silence was almost oppressive.

And then the Ganymedan swivelled his head, and growled, 'What's wrong with the domned vent'lator?'

Allen squeezed upward, head against the low top, and then turned back, pale-faced, 'It's stopped.'

'It'll be hours 'fore the storm's over. We've got t' have air till then. Crawl in back there and start it again.' His voice was flat and final.

'Here,' he said, as the other crawled over his shoulder into

91

the back of the car. 'Here's the tool-kit. Y've got 'bout twenty minutes 'fore the air gets too foul t' breathe. 'Tis pretty bad now.'

The clouds of sand hemmed in closer and the dim yellow light above George's head dispelled only partially the darkness within.

There was the sound of scrambling from behind him and then Allen's voice, 'Damn this rope. What's it doing here?' There was a hammering and then a disgusted curse.

'This thing is choked with rust.'

'Anything else wrong?' called out the Ganymedan.

'Don't know. Wait till I clear it out.' More hammering and an almost continuous harsh, scraping sound followed.

Allen backed into his seat once more. His face dripped rusty perspiration and a swab with the back of an equally damp, rust-covered hand did it no good.

'The pump is leaking like a punctured kettle, now that the rust's been knocked loose. I've got it going at top speed, but the only thing between it and a total breakdown is a prayer.'

'Start praying,' said George, bruskly. 'Pray for a button to push.'

The Earthman frowned, and stared ahead in sullen silence.

At four in the afternoon, the Ganymedan drawed, 'Air's beginning t' thin out, looks like.'

Allen snapped to alertness. The air was foul and humid within. The ventilator behind swished sibilantly between each click and the clicks were spacing themselves further apart. It wouldn't hold out much longer now.

'How much ground have we covered?'

' 'Bout a thaird o' the distance,' was the reply. 'How 'r y' holding out?'

'Well enough,' Allen snapped back. He retired once more into his shell.

Night came and the first brilliant stars of a Martian night peeped out when with a last futile and long-sustained swi-i-is-s-sh, the ventilator died.

'Domn!' said George. 'I can't breathe this soup any longer, anyway. Open the windows.'

The keenly cold Martian wind swept in and with it the last

traces of sand. George coughed as he pulled his woolen cap over his ears and turned on the heaters.

'Y' can still taste the grit.'

Allen looked wistfully up into the skies, 'There's Earth – with the moon hanging right onto her tail.'

'Airth?' repeated George with fine contempt. His finger pointed horizonwards, 'There's good old Jupe for y'.'

And throwing back his head, he sang in a full-throated baritone:

> *'When the golden orb o' Jove*
> *Shines down from the skies above,*
> *Then my spirit longs to go*
> *To that happy land I know,*
> *Back t' good, old* Ganyme-e-e-e-ede.'

The last note quavered and broke, and quavered and broke again and still again in an ever increasing rapidity of tempo until its vibrating ululation pierced the air about ear-shatteringly.

Allen stared at his brother wide-eyed, 'How did you do that?'

George grinned, 'That's the Gannie quaver. Didn't y' ever hear it before?'

The Earthman shook his head, 'I've heard *of* it, but that's all.'

The other became a bit more cordial, 'Well, o' course y' can only do it in a thin atmosphere. Y' should hear me on Gannie. I c'd shake y' right off y'r chair when I'm going good. Here! Wait till I gulp down some coffee, and then I'll sing y' vairse twenty-four o' the "Ballad o' Ganymede."'

He took a deep breath:

> *'There's a fair-haired maid I love*
> *Standing in the light o' Jove*
> *And she's waiting there for me-e-e-e-e.*

Then —'

Allen grasped him by the arm and shook him. The Ganymedan choked into silence.

'What's the matter?' he asked sharply.

'There was a thumping sound on the roof just a second ago. There's something up there.'

George stared upwards, 'Grab the wheel. I'll go up.' Allen shook his head, 'I'm going myself. I wouldn't trust myself

93

running this primitive contraption.'

He was out on the running board the next instant.

'Keep her going,' he shouted, and threw one foot up onto the roof.

He froze in that position when he became aware of two yellow slits of eyes staring hard into his. It took not more than a second for him to realize that he was face to face with a *keazel*, a situation which for discomfort is about on a par with the discovery of a rattlesnake in one's bed back on Earth.

There was little time for mental comparisons of his position with Earth predicaments, however, for the *keazel* lunged forward, its poisonous fangs agleam in the starlight.

Allen ducked desperately and lost his grip. He hit the sand with a slow-motion thud and the cold, scaly body of the Martian reptile was upon him.

The Earthman's reaction was almost instinctive. His hand shot out and clamped down hard upon the creature's narrow muzzle.

In that position, beast and man stiffened into breathless statuary. The man was trembling and within him his heart pounded away with hard rapidity. He scarcely dared move. In the unaccustomed Martian gravity, he found he could not judge the movements of his limbs. Muscles knotted almost of their own accord and legs swung when they ought not to.

He tried to lie still – and think.

The *keazel* squirmed, and from its lips, clamped shut by earth muscles, issued a tremendous whine. Allen's hand grew slick with perspiration and he could feel the beast's muzzle turn a bit within his palm. He clamped harder, panic-stricken. Physically, the *keazel* was no match for an Earthman, even a tired, frightened, gravity-unaccustomed Earthman – but one bite, anywhere, was all that was needed.

The *keazel* jerked suddenly; its back humped and its legs threshed. Allen held on with both hands and *could* not let go. He had neither gun or knife. There was no rock on the level desert sands to crack its skull against. The sand-truck had long since disappeared into the Martian night, and he was alone – alone with a *keazel*.

In desperation, he twisted. The *keazel*'s head bent. He could hear its breath whistling forth harshly – and again there was

94

that low whine.

Allen writhed above it and clamped knees down upon its cold, scaly abdomen. He twisted the head, further and further. The *keazel* fought desperately, but Allen's Earthly biceps maintained their hold. He could almost sense the beast's agony in the last stages, when he called up all his strength, – and something snapped.

And the beast lay still.

He rose to his feet, half-sobbing. The Martin night wind knifed into him and the perspiration froze on his body. He was alone in the desert.

Reaction set in. There was an intense buzzing in his ears. He found it difficult to stand. The wind was biting – but somehow he didn't feel it any more.

The buzzing in his ears resolved itself into a voice – a voice calling weirdly through the Martian wind.

'All'n, where are y'? Domn y', y' tanderfoot, where are y'? All'n! *All'n!*'

New life swept into the Earthman. He tossed the *keazel*'s carcass onto his shoulders and staggered on towards the voice.

'Here I am, G-Gannie. Right here.'

He stumbled blindly into his brother's arms.

George began harshly, 'Y' blasted Airthman, can't y' even keep y'r footing on a sandtruck moving at ten miles per? Y' might've —'

His voice died away in a semi-gurgle.

Allen said tiredly, 'There was a *keazel* on the roof. He knocked me off. Here, put it somewhere. There's a hundred dollar bonus for every *keazel* skin brought in to Aresopolis.'

He had no clear recollection of anything for the next half hour. When things straightened out, he was in the truck again with the taste of warm coffee in his mouth. The engine was rumbling once more and the pleasant warmth of the heaters surrounded him.

George sat next to him silently, eyes fixed on the desert ahead. But once in a while, he cleared his throat and shot a lightning glance at his brother. There was a queer look in his eyes.

Allen said, 'Listen, I've got to keep awake – and you look half dead yourself – so how about teaching me that "Gannie quaver" of yours. That's bound to wake the dead.'

The Ganymedan stared even harder and then said gruffly, 'Sure, watch m' Adam's apple while I do 't again.'

The sun was half-way to zenith when they reached the canal.

An hour before dawn there had come the crackling sound of hoarfrost beneath the heavy wheels and that signified the end of the desert area and the approach of the canal oasis. With the rising of the sun, the crackling disappeared and the softening mud underneath slowed the sand-adapted truck. The pathetic clumps of gray-green scrub that dotted the flat landscape were the first variant to eternal red sand since the two had started on their journey.

And then Allen had learned forward and grasped his brother by the arm, 'Look, there's the canal itself right ahead.'

The 'canal' – a small tributary of the mighty Jefferson Canal – contained a mere trickle of water at this season of the year. A dirty winding line of dampness, it was, and little more. Surrounding it on both sides were the boggy areas of black mud that were to fill up into a rushing ice-cold current an Earth-year hence.

The sand-truck nosed gingerly down the gentle slope, weaving a tortuous path among the sparsely-strewn boulders brought down by the spring's torrents and left there as the sinking waters receded.

It slopped through the mud and splashed clumsily through the puddles. It jounced noisily over rocks, muddied itself past the hubs as it made its way through the murky mid-stream channel and then settled itself for the upward pull out.

And then, with a suddenness that tossed the two drivers out of their seats, it sideslipped, made one futile effort to proceed onwards and thereafter refused to budge.

The brothers scrambled out and surveyed the situation. George swore lustily, voice more thickly accented than ever.

'B' Jupe 'n' domn, we're in a pickled situation f'r fair. 'Tis wallowing in the mud there like a blasted pig.'

Allen shoved his hair back wearily, 'Well, don't stand there looking at it. We're still a hundred miles or better from Aresopolis. We've got to get it out of there.'

'Sure, but how?' His imprecations dropped to sibilant breathings as he reached into the truck for the coil of rope in the

96

back. He looked at it doubtfully.

'Y' get in here, All'n, and when I pull, press down with y'r foot on that pedal.'

He was tying the rope to the front axle even as he spoke. He played it out behind him as he slogged out through ankledeep mud, and stretched it taut.

'All right, now, *give*!' he yelled. His face turned purple with effort as his back muscles ridged. Allen, within the car, pressed the indicated pedal to the floor, heard a loud roar from the engine and a spinning whir from the back wheels. The truck heaved once, and then sank back.

''Tis no use,' George called. 'I can't get a footing. If the ground were dry, I c'd do it.'

'If the ground were dry, we wouldn't be stuck,' retorted Allen. 'Here, give me that rope.'

'D' y' think y' can do it, if *I* can't?' came the enraged cry, but the other had already left the car.

Allen had spied the large, deep-bedded boulder from the truck, and it was with relief that he found it to be within reaching distance of the rope. He pulled it taut and tossed its free end about the boulder. Knotting it clumsily, he pulled, and it held.

His brother leaned out of the car window, as he made his way, back, with one lumped Ganymedan fist agitating the air.

'Hi, y' nitwit. What're y' doing? D' y' expect that overgrown rock t' pull us out?'

'Shut up,' yelled back Allen, 'and feed her the gas when I pull.'

He paused midway between boulder and truck and seized the rope.

'*Give!*' he shouted in his turn, and with a sudden jerk pulled the rope toward him with both hands.

The truck moved; its wheels caught hold. For a moment it hesitated with the engine blasting ahead full speed, and George's hands trembling upon the wheel. And then it went over. And almost simultaneously, the boulder at the other end of the taut rope lifted out of the mud with a liquid smacking sound and went over on its side.

Allen slipped the noose off it and ran for the truck.

'Keep her going,' he shouted, and hopped onto the running board, rope trailing.

'How did y' do that?' asked George, eyes round with awe.

'I haven't got the energy to explain it now. When we get to Aresopolis and after we've had a good sleep, I'll draw the triangle of forces for you, and show you what happened. No muscles were involved. Don't look at me as if I were Hercules.'

George withdrew his gaze with an effort, 'Triangle o' forces, is it? I never heard o' it, but if *that's* what it c'n do, education's a great thing.'

'Comet-gas! Is any coffee left?' He stared at the last thermos-bottle, shook it near his ear dolefully, and said, 'Oh, well, let's practice the quaver. It's almost as good and I've practically got it perfected.'

He yawned prodigiously, 'Will we make it by nightfall?'

'Maybe!'

The canal was behind them now.

The reddening sun was lowering itself slowly behind the Southern Range. The Southern Range is one of the two 'mountain chains' left on Mars. It is a region of hills; ancient, time-worn, eroded hills behind which lies Aresopolis.

It possesses the only scenery worth mentioning on all Mars and also the golden attribute of being able, through the updrafts along its sides to suck an occasional rain out of the desiccated Martian atmosphere.

Ordinarily, perhaps, a pair from Earth and Ganymede might have idled through this picturesque area, but this was definitely not the case with the Carter twins.

Eyes, puffed for lack of sleep, glistened once more at the sight of hills on the horizon. Bodies, almost broken for sheer weariness, tensed once more when they rose against the sky.

And the truck leaped ahead, – for just behind the hills lay Aresopolis. The road they traveled was no longer a rule-edge straight one, guided by the compass, over table-top-flat land. It followed narrow, twisting trails over rocky ground.

They had reached Twin Peaks, then, when there was a sudden sputter from the motor, a few halting coughs and then silence.

Allen sat up and there was weariness and utter disgust in his voice, 'What's wrong with this everlastingly-to-be-damned machine now?'

His brother shrugged, 'Nothing that I haven't been expecting for the last hour. We're out o' gas. Doesn't matter at all. We're at Twin Peaks – only ten miles fr'm the city. We c'n get there in an hour, and then they c'n send men out here for the blooms.'

'Ten miles in an hour!' protested Allen. 'You're crazy.' His face suddenly twisted at an agonizing thought, 'My God! We can't do it under three hours and it's almost night. No one can last that long in a Martian night. George, we're —'

George was pulling him out of the car by main force, 'By Jupe 'n' domn, All'n, don't let the tenderfoot show through *now*. We c'n do it in an hour, I tell y'. Didn't y' ever try running under sub-normal gravity? It's like flying. Look at me.'

He was off, skimming the ground closely, and proceeding in ground-covering leaps that shrank him to a speck up the mountain side in a moment.

He waved, and his voice came thinly, 'Come on!'

Allen started, – and sprawled at the third wild stride, arms flailing and legs straddled wide. The Ganymedan's laughter drifted down in heartless gusts.

Allen rose angrily and dusted himself. At an ordinary walk, he made his way upwards.

'Don't get sore, All'n,' said George. 'It's a knack, and I've had practice on Gannie. Just pretend y'r running along a feather bed. Run rhythmically – a sort o' very slow rhythm – and run close t' the ground; don't leap high. Like this. Watch me!'

The Earthman tried it, eyes on his brother. His first few uncertain strides became surer and longer. His legs stretched and his arms swung as he matched his brother, step for step.

George shouted encouragement and speeded his pace, 'Keep lower t' the ground, All'n. Don't leap 'fore y'r toes hit the ground.'

Allen's eyes shone and, for the moment, weariness was forgotten, 'This is great! It *is* like flying – or like springs on your shoes.'

'Y' ought t' have lived on Gannie with me. We've got special fields f'r subgravity races. An expairt racer c'n do forty miles an hour at times – and I c'n do thirty-five myself. – O' course, the gravity there's a bit lower than here on Mars.'

Long hair streamed backwards in the wind and skin reddened at the bittercold air that blew past. The ruddy patches of sunlight traveled higher and higher up the slopes, lingered briefly upon the very summits and went out altogether. The short Martian twilight started upon its rapidly darkening career. The Evening Star – Earth – was already glimmering brightly, its attendant moon somewhat closer than the night previous.

The passing minutes went unheeded by Allen. He was too absorbed by the wonderful new sensation of sub-gravity running, to do anything more than follow his brother. Even the increasing chilliness scarcely registered upon his consciousness.

It was George, then, upon whose countenance a tiny, puckered uneasiness grew into a vast, panicky frown.

'Hi, All'n, hold up!' he called. Leaning backward, he brought himself to a short, hopping halt full of grace and ease. Allen tried to do likewise, broke his rhythm and went forward upon his face. He rose with loud reproaches.

The Ganymedan turned a deaf ear to them. His gaze was sombre in the dusk, 'D' y' know where we are, All'n?'

Allen felt a cold constriction about his windpipe as he stared about him quickly. Things looked different in semi-darkness, but they looked more different than they ought. It was impossible for things to be *so* different.

'We should've sighted Old Baldy by now, shouldn't we have?' he quavered.

'We sh'd've sighed him long ago,' came the hard answer. ''Tis that domned quake. Landslides must've changed the trails. The peaks themselves must've been screwed up —' His voice was thin-edged, 'Allen, 'tisn't any use making believe. We're dead lost.'

For a moment, they stood silently – uncertainly. The sky was purple and the hills retreated into the night. Allen licked bluechilled lips with a dry tongue.

'We can't be but a few miles away. We're bound to stumble on the city if we look.'

'Consider the situation, Airthman,' came the savage, shouted answer, ''Tis night, Martian night. The temperature's down past zero and plummeting every minute. We haven't any time t' look; – we've got t' go straight there. If we're not there in half an hour, we're not going t' get there at all.'

Allen knew that well, and mention of the cold increased his consciousness of it. He spoke through chattering teeth as he drew his heavy, fur-lined coat closer about him.

'We might build a fire!' The suggestion was a half-hearted one, muttered indistinctly, and fallen upon immediately by the other.

'With what?' George was beside himself with sheer disappointment and frustration. 'We've pulled through this far, and now we'll prob'ly freeze t' death within a mile o' the city. C'mon, keep running. It's a hundred-t'-one chance.'

But Allen pulled him back. There was a feverish glint in the Earthman's eye, 'Bonfires!' he said irrelevantly. 'It's a possibility. Want to take a chance that might do the trick?'

'Nothin' else t' do,' growled the other. 'But hurry. Every minute I —'

'Then run with the wind – and keep going.'

'Why?'

'Never mind why. Do what I say – run with the wind!'

There was no false optimism in Allen as he bounded through the dark, stumbling over loose stones, sliding down declivities, – always with the wind at his back. George ran at his side, a vague, formless blotch in the night.

The cold was growing more bitter, but it was not quite as bitter as the freezing pang of apprehension gnawing at the Earthman's vitals.

Death is unpleasant!

And then they topped the rise, and from George's throat came a loud 'B' Jupe 'n' domn!' of triumph.

The ground before them, as far as the eye could see, was dotted by bonfires. Shattered Aresopolis lay ahead, its homeless inhabitants making the night bearable by the simple agency of burning wood.

And on the hilly slopes, two weary figures slapped each other on the backs, laughed wildly and pressed half-frozen, stubbly cheeks together for sheer, unadulterated joy.

They were there at last!

The Aresopolis lab, on the very outskirts of the city, was one of the few structures still standing. Within, by makeshift light, haggard chemists were distilling the last drops of extract.

Without, the city's police-force remnants were clearing desperate way for the precious flasks and vials as they were distributed to the various emergency medical centres set up in various regions of the bonfire-pocked ruins that were once the Martian metropolis.

Old Hal Vincent supervised the process and his faded eyes ever and again peered anxiously into the hills beyind, watching hopefully but doubtfully for the promised cargo of blooms.

And then two figures reeled out of the darkness and collapsed to a halt before him.

Chill anxiety clamped down upon him, 'The blooms! Where are they? Have you got them?'

'At Twin Peaks,' gasped Allen. 'A ton of them and better in a sand-truck. Send for them.'

A group of police grind-cars set off before he had finished, and Vincent exclaimed bewilderedly, 'A sand-truck? Why didn't you send it in a ship? What's wrong with you out there, anyway? Earthquake —'

He received no direct answer. George had stumbled toward the nearest bonfire with a beatific expression on his worn face.

'Ahhh, 'tis warm!' Slowly, he folded and dropped, asleep before he hit the ground.

Allen coughed gaspingly, 'Huh! The Gannie tenderfoot! Couldn't – ulp – take it!'

And the ground came up and hit him in the face.

Allen woke with the evening sun in his eyes and the odor of frying bacon in his nostrils. George shoved the frying pan toward him and said between gigantic, wolfing mouthfuls, 'Help yourself.'

He pointed to the empty sand-truck outside the labs, 'They got the stuff all right.'

Allen fell to, quietly. George wiped his lips with the back of his hand and said, 'Say, All'n, how 'd y' find the city? I've been sitting here trying t' figure it all out.'

'It was the bonfires,' came the muffled answer. 'It was the only way they could get heat, and fires over square miles of land create a whole section of heated air, which rises, causing the cold surrounding air of the hills to sweep in.' He suited his words with appropriate gestures. 'The wind in the hills was heading for the city to replace warm air and we followed the wind. – Sort of a natural compass, pointing to where we wanted to go.'

George was silent, kicking with embarrassed vigor at the ashes of the bonfire of the night before.

'Lis'n, All'n, I've had y' a'wrong. Y' were an Airthman tanderfoot t' me till—' He paused, drew a deep breath and exploded with, 'Well, by Jupe 'n' domn, y'r my twin brother and I'm proud o' it. All Airth c'dn't drown out the Carter blood in y'.'

The Earthman opened his mouth to reply but his brother clamped one palm over it. 'Y' keep quiet, till I'm finished. After we get back, y' can fix up that mechanical picker or anything else y' want. I drop my veto. If Airth and machines c'n tairn out y'r kind o' man, they're all right. But just the same,' there was a trace of wistfulness in his voice, 'y' got t' admit that everytime the machines broke down – from irrigation-trucks and rocket-ships to ventilators and sand-trucks – 'twas men who had t' pull through in spite o' all that Mars could do.'

Allen wrenched his face from out behind the restraining palm.

'The machines do their best,' he said, but not too vehemently.

'Sure, but that's all they *can* do. When the emairgency comes, a man's got t' do a damn lot better than his best or he's a goner.'

The other paused, nodded and gripped the other's hand with sudden fierceness, 'Oh, we're not so different. Earth and Ganymede are plastered thinly over the outside of us, but inside —'

He caught himself.

'Come on, let's give out with that old Gannie quaver.'

And from the two fraternal throats tore forth a shrieking eldritch yell such as the thin, cold Martian air had seldom before carried.

THE END

I got the cover again with 'Heredity.'

In connection with that story, I remember best a comment I received from a young fellow named Scott Feldman (who was then still in his teens but who was later, as Scott Meredith, to become one of the most important literary agents in the business). He disapproved of the story because I introduced two characters at the start who disappeared from the story and were never heard of again.

Once that was pointed out to me, it seemed to me that this was indeed a major flaw, and I wondered why neither Campbell nor Pohl had specifically pointed it out. I never quite had the courage to ask, however.

But it did cause me to look at my stories more closely thereafter, and to realize again that writing isn't all inspiration and free flow. You do have to ask yourself pretty mechanical questions, such as, 'What do I do with this character now that I've taken the trouble to make use of him?'

By the time Campbell was rejecting, and Pohl accepting 'Heredity,' I was writing 'History.' The same thing happened. I submitted it to Campbell on September 13. It was rejected, and, eventually, Pohl took it.

Ullen's lank arm pushed the stylus carefully and painstakingly across the paper; his near-sighted eyes blinked through thick lenses. The signal light flashed twice before he answered.

He turned a page, and called out, 'Is dat you, Johnnie? Come in, please.'

He smiled gently, his thin, Martian face alight with pleasure.

'Sit down, Johnnie – but first lower de window-shade. De glare of your great Eard sun is annoying. Ah, dat's good, and now sid down and be very, very quiet for just a little while, because I am busy.'

John Brewster shifted a pile of ill-stacked papers and seated himself. He blew the dust from the edges of an open book in the next chair and looked reproachfully on the Martian historian.

'Are you still poking around these musty old things? Don't you get tired?'

'Please, Johnnie,' Ullen did not look up, 'you will lose de page. Dat book dere is William Stewart's "Hitlerian Era" and it is very hard to read. So many words he uses which he doesn't explain.'

His expression as it focussed upon Johnnie was one of frowning petulance, '*Never* do dey explain deir terms. It is so unscientific. On Mars, before we even start, we say, "Dis is a list of all definitions of terms to be used." How oderwise can people talk sensibly? Hmp! You *crazy* Eardmen.'

'Oh, nuts, Ullen – forget it. Why don't you *look* at me. Don't you even notice anything?'

The Martian sighed, removed his glasses, cleaned them thoughtfully and carefully replaced them. He stared impersonally at Johnnie, 'Well, I dink it is new clothes you are wearing. It is not so?'

'New clothes! Is *that* all you can say, Ullen? This is a *uniform*. I'm a member of the Home Defense.' He rose to his feet, a picture of boyish exuberance.

Super Science Stories, March 1941
Copyright © 1941 by Fictioneers, Inc.
Copyright renewed © 1968 by Isaac Asimov

'What is dis "Home Defense"?' asked Ullen languidly.

Johnnie gulped and sat down helplessly, 'You know, I really think you haven't heard that Earth and Venus have been at war for the last week. I'll bet money you haven't.'

'I've been busy.' He frowned and pursed his thin, bloodless lips, 'On Mars, dere is no war – at least, dere isn't any more. Once, we used to fight, but dat was long ago. Once we were scientists, too, and *dat* was long ago. Now, dere are only a few of us – and we do not fight. Dere is no happiness dat way.' He seemed to shake himself, and spoke more briskly, 'Tell me, Johnnie, do you know where it is I can find what it means, dis "national honor?" It holds me back. I can't go furder unless I can understand it.'

Johnnie rose to his full height and glittered in the spotless green of the Terrestrial Service. He laughed with fond indulgence. 'You're hopeless, Ullen, – you old coot. Aren't you going to wish me luck? I'm hitting space tomorrow.'

'Oh, is dere danger?'

There was a squawk of laughter, 'Danger? What do you think?'

'Well, den, to seek danger – it is foolish. Why do you do it?'

'You wouldn't understand, Ullen. Just wish me luck and say you hope I come through whole.'

'Cer-tain-ly! I don't want *anyone* to die.' He slipped his hand into the strong fist held out to him. 'Take care of yourself, Johnnie – and wait, before you go, bring me Stewart's book. Everything is so heavy here on Eard. Heavy, heavy, – and de words have no definitions.'

He sighed, and was back at his books as Johnnie slipped quietly out of the room.

'Dese barbarous people,' he muttered sleepily to himself. 'War! Dey dink dat by killing —' His voice died away and merged into a slurred mumble as his eyes followed creeping finger across the page.

' "From the very moment of the union of the Anglo-Saxon world into a single governmental entity and even as far back as the spring of 1941, it was evident that the doom of —" '

'Dese crazy Eardmen!'

Ullen leaned heavily upon his crutches on the steps of the

University library and one thin hand shielded his watering eyes from the terrible Earthly sun.

The sky was blue, cloudless, – undisturbed. Yet somewhere up above, beyond the planet's airy blanket, steel-sided ships were veering and sparking in vicious combat. And down upon the city were falling the tiny 'Drops of Death,' the highly-publicized radioactive bombs that noiselessly and inexorably ate out a fifteen foot crater wherever they fell.

The city's population was herding into the shelters and burying themselves inside the deep-set leaden cells. Upstaring, silent, anxious, they streamed past Ullen. Uniformed guards invested some sort of order into the gigantic flight, steering the stragglers and speeding the laggards.

The air was filled with barked orders.

'Hit the shelter, Pop. Better get going. You can't stand there, you know.'

Ullen turned to the guard who addressed him and slowly brought his wandering thoughts to bear upon the situation.

'I am sorry, Eardman – but I cannot move very fast on your huge world.' He tapped one crutch upon the marble flags beneath. 'Dings are so heavy. If I were to crowd in wid de rest, I would be crushed.'

He smiled gently down from his lank height, and the guard rubbed a stubby chin, 'All right, pop, I can fix that. It *is* tough on you Marsies at that. – Here, hold those crutches up out of the way.'

With a heave, he cradled the Martian, 'Hold your legs close to my body, because we're going to travel fast.'

His bulky figure pressed through the line of Earthmen. Ullen shut his eyes as the rapid motion under supernormal gravity stirred his stomach into rebellion. He opened them once again in the dim recesses of the low-ceilinged shelter.

The guard set him down carefully and adjusted the crutches beneath Ullen's armpits, 'O.K. Pop. Take care of yourself.'

Ullen took in his surroundings and hobbled to one of the low benches at the near end of the shelter. From behind him came the sombre clang of the thick, leaden door.

The Martian historian fished a worn tablet from his pocket and scribbled slow notes. He disregarded the excited babble that

107

arose about him and the scraps of heated talk that filled the air thickly.

And then he scratched at his furrowed forehead with the stub end of his pencil, meeting the staring eyes of the man sitting next to him. He smiled abstractedly and returned to his notes.

'You're a Martian, aren't you?' His neighbor spoke in quick, squeaky tones. 'I don't like foreigners much, but I've got nothing special against Marsies. These Veenies, now, they —'

Ullen's soft tones interrupted him. 'Hate is all wrong, I dink. Dis war is a great annoyance – a great one. It interferes wid my work and you Eardmen ought to stop it. Is it not so?'

'You can bet your hide we're going to stop it,' came the emphatic reply. 'We're going to bash their planet inside out – and the dirty Veenies with it.'

'You mean attack deir cities like dis?' The Martian blinked owlishly in thought, 'You dink dat would be best?'

'Damn it, yes. It —'

'But look.' Ullen placed a skeleton finger in one palm and continued in gentle argument. 'Would it not be easier to get de ships demselves by de fall-apart weapon? – Don't you dink so? Or is it dat de Venus people, dey have de screens?'

'What weapon, did you say?'

Ullen ruminated carefully, 'I suppose dat isn't de name *you* call it by – but I don't know about weapons, anyway. We call it on Mars de "*skellingbeg*" and dat means in English "fall-apart weapon." Now you know?'

There was no direct answer unless a vague under-breath mutter could be called one. The Earthman pushed away from his companion and stared at the opposite wall in a fidget.

Ullen sensed the rebuff and shrugged one shoulder wearily, 'It is not dat I care much about de whole ding. It is only dat de war is a big bodder. It should be ended.' He sighed, 'But I don't care!'

His fingers had just begun manipulating the pencil once more in its travels across the open tablet on his lap, when he looked up again.

'Tell me, please, what is de name of dat country where Hitler died. Your Eard names, dey are so complicated sometimes. I dink it begins wid an M.'

His neighbor ripped him open with a stare and walked away.

108

Ullen's eyes followed him with a puzzled frown.

And then the all-clear signal sounded.

'Oh, yes,' said Ullen. 'Madagascar! Such a silly name!'

Johnnie Brewster's uniform was war-worn now; a bit more wrinkled about the neck and shoulders, a trance more worn at knees and elbows.

Ullen ran his finger along the angry scar that ran the length of Johnnie's right fore-arm, 'It hurts no more, Johnnie?'

'Nuts! A scratch! I got the Veenie that did that. He's chasing dreams in the moon now.'

'You were in de hospital long, Johnnie?'

'A week!' He lit a cigarette, pushed some of the mess off the Martian's desk and seated himself. 'I've spent the rest of the time with my family, though I did get around to visiting you, you see.'

He leaned over and poked an affectionate hand at the Martian's leathery cheek, 'Aren't you going to say you're glad to see me?'

Ullen removed his glasses and peered at the Earthman, 'Why, Johnnie, are you so uncertain dat I am glad to see you, dat you require I should say it in words?' He paused, 'I'll make a note of dat. You silly Eardmen must always be telling each oder dese simple dings – and den you don't believe it anyway. On Mars —'

He was rubbing his glasses methodically, as he spoke, and now he replaced them, 'Johnnie, don't you Eardmen have de "fall-apart" weapon? I met a person once in de raid shelter and he didn't know what I was talking about.'

Johnnie frowned, 'I don't either, for that matter. Why do you ask?'

'Because it seems strange dat you should have to fight so hard dese Venus men, when dey don't seem to have de screens to stop it wid. Johnnie, I want de war should be over. It makes me all de time stop my work to go to a shelter.'

'Hold on, now, Ullen. Don't sputter. What is this "fall-apart" weapon? A disintegrator? What do you know about it?'

'I? I know nodding about it at all. I dought you knew – dat's why I asked. Back on Mars, in our histories, dey talk about using dat kind of weapon in our old wars. But we don't know nodding about weapons any more. Anyway, dey're so silly, because de oder side always dinks of someding which protects against it, and den everyding is de same as always. – Johnnie, do you suppose you could go down to de desk and ask for a copy of Higginboddam's "Beginnings of Space Travel?" '

The Earthman clenched his fists and shook them impotently, 'Ullen, you damned Martian pedant – don't you understand that this is important? Earth is at war? War! War! *War!*'

'Well, den, stop de war.' There was irritation in Ullen's voice. 'Dere is no peace and quiet anywheres on Eard. I wish I had dis library – Johnnie, be careful. Please, what are you doing? You're hurting me.'

'I'm sorry, Ullen, but you've got to come with me. We're going to see about this.' Johnnie had the feebly protesting Martian wedged into the wheel-chair and was off with a rush, before he had finished the sentence.

A rocket-taxi was at the bottom of the Library steps, and together chauffeur and Spaceman lifted the chair inside. With a comet-tail of smoke, they were off.

Ullen moaned softly at the acceleration, but Johnnie ignored him. 'Washington in twenty minutes, fellow,' he said to the driver, 'and ignore the signal beams.'

The starched secretary spoke in a frozen monotone, 'Admiral Korsakoff will see you now.'

Johnnie wheeled and stamped out the last cigarette butt. He shot a hasty glance at his watch and grunted.

At the motion of the wheel-chair, Ullen roused himself out of a troubled sleep. He adjusted his glasses, 'Did dey let us in finally, Johnnie?'

'Sh!'

Ullen's impersonal stare swept over the rich furnishings of the room, the huge maps of Earth and Venus on the wall, the imposing desk in the center. It lingered upon the pudgy, bearded figure behind this desk and then came to rest upon the lanky, sandy-haired man at his side.

The Martian attempted to rise from the chair in sudden eagerness, 'Aren't you Dr. Dorning? I saw you last year at Princeton. You remember me, don't you? Dey gave me at dat time, my honorary degree.'

Dr. Thorning had advanced and shook hands vigorously,

'Certainly. You spoke then on Martian historical methods, didn't you?'

'Oh, you remember. I'm glad! But dis is a great opportunity for me, meeting you. Tell me, as a scientist, what would be your opinion of my deory dat de social insecurity of de Hitlerian Era was de direct cause for de lag —'

Dr. Thorning smiled, 'I'll discuss it with you later, Dr. Ullen. Right now, Admiral Korsakoff wants information from you, with which we hope to end the war.'

'Exactly,' Korsakoff spoke in clipped tones as he met Ullen's mild gaze. 'Although a Martian, I presume you favor the victory of the principles of freedom and justice over the foul practices of Venusian tyranny.'

Ullen stared uncertainly, 'Dat sounds familiar – but I don't dink about it much. You mean, maybe, de war should end?'

'With victory, yes.'

'Oh, "victory," dat is just a silly word. History proves dat a war decided on military superiority only lays de groundwork for future wars of retaliation and revenge. I refer you to a very good essay on de subject by a James Calkins. It was published all de way back in 2050.'

'My dear sir!'

Ullen raised his voice in bland indifference to Johnnie's urgent whisperings. 'Now to end de war – really end it – you should say to de plain people of Venus, "It is unnecessary to fight. Let us just talk" —'

There was the slam of fist on desk and a muttered oath of frightful import. 'For God's sakes, Thorning, get what you want out of him. I give you five minutes.'

Thorning stifled his chuckle, 'Dr. Ullen, we want you to tell us what you know about the disintegrator.'

'Disintegrator?' Ullen put a puzzled finger to his cheek.

'The one you told Lieutenant Brewster of.'

'Ummmm— Oh! You mean de "fall-apart" weapon. I don't know nodding about it. De Martian historians mention it some times, but none of dem *know* about it – de technical side, dat is.'

The sandy-haired physicist nodded patiently, 'I know, I know. But what do they say? What kind of a weapon is it?'

'Well, de way dey talk about it, it makes de metals to fall to

111

pieces. What is it you call de ding dat holds metals togedder, now?'

'Intra-molecular forces?'

Ullen frowned and then spoke thoughtfully, 'Maybe. I forgot what de Martian word is – except dat it's long. Anyway, dis weapon, it makes dis force dat holds de metals togedder not to exist anymore and it all falls apart in a powder. But it only works on de dree metals, iron, cobalt and – uh – de odder one!'

'Nickel,' prompted Johnnie, softly.

'Yes, yes, nickel!'

Thorning's eyes glittered, 'Aha, the ferromagnetic elements. There's an oscillating magnetic field mixed up in this, or I'm a Veenie. How about it, Ullen?'

The Martian sighed, 'Such crazy Eard words. – Let's see now, most of what I know about de weapon is from de work of Hogel Beg. It was – I'm pretty sure – in his "Cultural and Social History of de Dird Empire." It was a huge work in twenty-four volumes, but I always dought it was radder mediocre. His technique in de presentation of —'

'Please,' said Thorning, 'the weapon —'

'Oh, yes, *dat*!' He hitched himself higher in his chair and grimaced with the effort. 'He talks about electricity and it goes back and ford very fast – *very* fast, and its pressure —' He paused hopelessly, and regarded the scowling visage of the bearded Admiral naively, 'I *dink* de word is pressure, but I don't know, because it is hard to translate. De Martian word is "*cranstad.*" Does dat help?'

'I think you mean "potential," Dr. Ullen!' Thorning sighed audibly.

'Well, if you say so. Anyway, dis "potential" changes also *very* fast and de two changes are synchronized somehow along wid magnetism dat – uh – shifts and dat's all I know about it.' He smiled uncertainly, 'I would like to go back now. It would be all right now, wouldn't it?'

The Admiral vouchsafed no answer, 'Do you make anything out of that mess, Doctor?'

'Damned little,' admitted the physicist, 'but it gives me a lead or two. We might try getting hold of this Beg's book, but there's not much hope. It will simply repeat what we've just heard. Dr. Ullen, are there any scientific works on your planet?'

112

The Martian saddened, 'No, Dr. Dorning, dey were all de-stroyed during de Kalynian reaction. On Mars, we doroughly disbelieve in science. History has shown dat it comes from science no happiness.' He turned to the young Earthman at his side, 'Johnnie, let us go now, please.'

Korsakoff dismissed the two with a wave of the hand.

Ullen bent carefully over the closely-typed manuscript and inserted a word. He glanced up brightly at Johnnie Brewster, who shook his head and placed a hand on the Martian's arm. His brow furrowed more deeply.

'Ullen,' he said harshly, 'You're in trouble.'

'Eh? I? In trouble? Why, Johnnie, dat is not so. My book is coming along famously. De whole first volume, it is completed and, but for a bit of polishing, is ready for de printers.'

'Ullen, if you can't give the government definite information on the disintegrator, I won't answer for the consequences.'

'But I told all I knew —'

'It won't do. It's not enough. You've got to remember more, Ullen, you've *got* to.'

'But knowledge where dere is none is impossible to have – dat is an axiom.' Ullen sat upright in his seat, propping him-self on a crutch.

'I know it,' Johnnie's mouth twisted in misery, 'but you've got to understand.

'The Venusians have control of space; our Asteroid garri-sons have been wiped out, and last week Phobos and Deimos fell. Communications between Earth and Luna are broken and God knows how long the Lunar squadron can hold out. Earth itself is scarcely secure and their bombings are becoming more serious — Oh, Ullen, don't you understand?'

The Martian's look of confusion deepened, 'Eard is losing?'

'God, yes!'

'Den give up. Dat is de logical ding to do. Why did you start at all – you stupid Eardmen.'

Johnnie ground his teeth, 'But if we have the disintegrator, we won't lose.'

Ullen shrugged, 'Oh, Johnnie, it gets wearisome to listen to de same old story. You Eardmen have one-track minds. Look, wouldn't it make you feel better to have me read you some of my manuscript? It would do your intellect good.'

'All right, Ullen, you've asked for it, and here's everything

113

right out. If you don't tell Thorning what he wants to know, you're going to be arrested and tried for treason.'

There was a short silence, and then a confused stutter, 'T-treason. You mean dat I betray —' The historian removed his glasses and wiped them with shaking hand, 'It's not true. You're trying to frighten me.'

'Oh, no, I'm not. Korsakoff thinks you know more than you're telling. He's sure that you're either holding out for a price or, more likely, that you've sold out to the Veenies.'

'But Dorning —'

'Thorning isn't any too secure himself. He has his own skin to think of. Earth governments in moments of stress are not famous for being reasonable.' There were sudden tears in his eyes, 'Ullen, there must be something you can do. It's not only you – it's for Earth.'

Ullen's breathing whistled harshly, 'Dey tink I would *sell* my scientific knowledge. Is dat de kind of insult dey pay my sense of eddics; my scientific integrity?' His voice was thick with fury and for the first time since Johnnie knew him, he lapsed into guttural Martian. 'For dat, I say not a word,' he finished. 'Let dem put me in prison or shoot me, but dis insult I cannot forget.'

There was no mistaking the firmness in his eyes, and Johnnie's shoulders sagged. The Earthman didn't move at the glare of the signal light.

'Answer de light, Johnnie,' said the Martian, softly, 'dey are coming for me.'

In a moment, the room was crowded with green uniforms. Dr. Thorning and the two with him were the only ones present in civilian clothes.

Ullen struggled to his feet, 'Gentlemen, say nodding. I have heard dat it is dought dat I am selling what I know – *selling for money*.' He spat the words. 'It is a ding never before said of me – a ding I have not deserved. If you wish you can imprison me immediately, but I shall say nodding more – nor have anyding furder to do wid de Eard government.'

A green-garbed official stepped forward immediately, but Dr. Thorning waved him back.

'Whoa, there, Dr. Ullen,' he said jovially, 'don't jump too soon. I've just come to ask if there isn't a single additional fact

114

that you remember. Anything, no matter how insignificant —'

There was stony silence. Ullen leant heavily on his crutches but remained stolidly erect.

Dr. Thorning seated himself imperturbably upon the historian's desk, picked up the high stack of type-written pages, 'Ah, is this the manuscript young Brewster was telling me about.' He gazed at it curiously, 'Well, of course, you realize that your attitude will force the government to confiscate all this.'

'Eh?' Ullen's stern expression melted into dismay. His crutch slipped and he dropped heavily into his seat.

The physicist warded off the other's feeble clutch, 'Keep your hands off, Dr. Ullen, I'm taking care of this.' He leafed through the pages with a rustling noise. 'You see, if you are arrested for treason, your writings become subversive.'

'Subversive!' Ullen's voice was hoarse, 'Dr. Dorning, you don't know what you are saying. It is my – my great labor.' His voice caught huskily, 'Please, Dr. Dorning, give me my manuscript.'

The other held it just beyond the Martian's shaking fingers. '*If* —' he said.

'But I don't know!'

The sweat stood out on the historian's pale face. His voice came thickly. 'Time! Give me time! But let me dink – and don't, please don't harm dis manuscript.'

The other's fingers sank painfully into Ullen's shoulder, 'So help me, I burn your manuscript in five minutes, if —'

'Wait, I'll tell you. Somewhere – I don't know where – it was said dat in de weapon dey used a special metal for some of de wiring. I don't know what metal, but water spoiled it and had to be kept away – also air. It —'

'Holy jumping *Jupiter*,' came the sudden shout from one of Thorning's companions. 'Chief, don't you remember Aspartier's work on sodium wiring in argon atmosphere five years ago —'

Dr. Thorning's eyes were deep with thought, 'Wait – wait – wait – *Damn!* It was staring us in the face —'

'I know,' shrieked Ullen suddenly. 'It was in Karisto. He was discussing de fall of Gallonie and dat was one of de minor causes – de lack of dat metal – and den he mentioned —'

He was talking to an empty room, and for a while he was

115

silent in puzzled astonishment.

And then, 'My manuscript!' He salvaged it from where it lay scattered over the floor, hobbling painfully about, smoothing each wrinkled sheet with care.

'De barbarians – to treat a great scientific work so!'

Ullen opened still another drawer and scrabbled through its contents. He closed it and looked about peevishly, 'Johnnie, where did I put dat bibliography? Did you see it?'

He looked toward the window, 'Johnnie!'

Johnnie Brewster said, 'Wait a while, Ullen. Here they come now.'

The streets below were a burst of color. In a long, stiffly-moving line the Green of the Navy paraded down the avenue, the air above them snow-thick with confetti, hail-thick with ticker-tape. The roar of the crowd was dull, muted.

'Ah, de foolish people,' mused Ullen. 'Dey were happy just like dis when de war started and dere was a parade just like dis – and now anodder one. Silly!' He stumped back to his chair.

Johnnie followed, 'The government is naming a new museum after you, isn't it?'

'Yes,' was the dry reply. He peered helplessly about under the desk, 'De Ullen War Museum – and it will be filled wid ancient weapons, from stone knife to anti-aircraft gun. Dat is your queer Eard sense of de fitness of dings. *Where* in dunderation is dat bibliography?'

'Here,' said Johnnie, withdrawing the document from Ullen's vest pocket. 'Our victory was due to your weapon, ancient to you, so it *is* fit in a way.'

'Victory! Sure! Until Venus rearms and reprepares and refights for revenge. All history shows – but never mind. It is useless, dis talk.' He settled himself deeply in his chair, 'Here, let me show you a real victory. Let me read you some of de first volume of my work. It's already in print, you know.'

Johnnie laughed, 'Go ahead, Ullen. Right now I'm even willing to listen to you read your entire twelve volumes – word for word.'

And Ullen smiled gently. 'It would be good for your intellect,' he said.

THE END

'History,' you will notice, mentions Hitler's end. It was written in the first days of September 1940, when Hitler seemed at the very peak of his success. France was defeated and occupied and Britain was at bay and seemed unlikely to survive. – Still, I had no doubt as to his ultimate defeat. I did not visualize his ending in suicide, however. I thought that like Napoleon and the Kaiser, he would end his life in exile. Madagascar was the place I picked.

Also mentioned in the story are 'the tiny "Drops of Death," the highly-publicized radioactive bombs that noiselessly and inexorably ate out a fifteen-foot crater wherever they fell.'

By the time I wrote the story, uranium fission had been discovered and announced. I had not yet yeard of it, however, and I was unaware that reality was about to outstrip my prized science fictional imagination.

On October 23, 1940, I visited Campbell and outlined to him another robot story I wanted to write, a story I planned to call 'Reason.' Campbell was completely enthusiastic. I had trouble writing it and had to start over several times, but eventually it was done, and on November 18 I submitted it to John. He accepted it on the twenty-second, and it appeared in the April 1941 issue of *Astounding*.

It was the third story of mine that he had accepted and the first in which he did not ask for a revision. (He told me, in fact, that he had liked it so well, he had almost decided to pay me a bonus.)

With 'Reason,' the 'positronic robot' series was fairly launched, and my two most successful characters yet, Gregory Powell and Mike Donovan (improvements on Turner and Snead of 'Ring Around the Sun') made their appearance. Eventually, 'Reason' and others of the series that were to follow, together with 'Robbie,' which Campbell had rejected, were to appear in *I, Robot*.

The success of 'Reason' didn't mean that I was to have no further rejections from Campbell.

On December 6, 1940, influenced by the season and never stopping to think that a Christmas story must sell no later than July in order to make the Christmas issue, I began 'Christmas on Ganymede.' I submitted it to him on the twenty-third, but the holiday season did not affect his critical judgment. He rejected it.

I tried Pohl next, and, as was happening so often that year, he took it. In this case, for reasons I will describe later, the acceptance fell through. I eventually sold it the next summer (June 27, 1941, the *proper* time of year) to *Startling Stories,* the younger, sister magazine of *Thrilling Wonder Stories.*

14: Christmas on Ganymede

Olaf Johnson hummed nasally to himself and his china-blue eyes were dreamy as he surveyed the stately fir tree in the corner of the library. Though the library was the largest single room in the Dome, Olaf felt it none too spacious for the occasion. Enthusiastically he dipped into the huge crate at his side and took out the first roll of red-and-green crêpe paper.

What sudden burst of sentiment had inspired the Ganymedan Products Corporation, Inc. to ship a complete collection of Christmas decorations to the Dome, he did not pause to inquire. Olaf's was a placid disposition, and in his self-imposed job as chief Christmas decorator, he was content with his lot.

He frowned suddenly and muttered a curse. The General Assembly signal light was flashing on and off hysterically. With a hurt air Olaf laid down the tack-hammer he had just lifted, then the roll of crêpe paper, picked some tinsel out of his hair and left for officers quarters.

Commander Scott Pelham was in his deep armchair at the head of the table when Olaf entered. His stubby fingers were drumming unrhythmically upon the glass-topped table. Olaf met the commander's hotly furious eyes without fear, for nothing had gone wrong in his department in twenty Ganymedan revolutions.

The room filled rapidly with men, and Pelham's eyes hardened as he counted noses in one sweeping glance.

'We're all here. Men, we face a crisis!'

There was a vague stir. Olaf's eyes sought the ceiling and he relaxed. Crises hit the Dome once a revolution, on the average. Usually they turned out to be a sudden rise in the quota of oxite to be gathered, or the inferior quality of the last batch of karen leaves. He stiffened, however, at the next words.

'In connection with the crisis, I have one question to ask.' Pelham's voice was a deep baritone, and it rasped unpleasantly when he was angry. 'What dirty imbecilic troublemaker has

Startling Stories, January 1942
Copyright © 1941 by Better Publications, Inc.
Copyright renewed © 1968 by Isaac Asimov

been telling those blasted Ossies fairy tales?'

Olaf cleared his throat nervously and thus immediately became the center of attention. His Adam's apple wobbled in sudden alarm and his forehead wrinkled into a washboard. He shivered.

'I – I —' he stuttered, quickly fell silent. His long fingers made a bewildered gesture of appeal. 'I mean I was out there yesterday, after the last – uh – supplies of karen leaves, on account the Ossies were slow and —'

A deceptive sweetness entered Pelham's voice. He smiled. 'Did you tell those natives about Santa Claus, Olaf?'

The smile looked uncommonly like a wolfish leer and Olaf broke down. He nodded convulsively.

'Oh, you did? Well, well, you told them about Santa Claus! He comes down in a sleigh that flies through the air with eight reindeer pulling it, huh?'

'Well – er – doesn't he?' Olaf asked unhappily.

'And you drew pictures of the reindeer, just to make sure there was no mistake. Also, he has a long white beard and red clothes with white trimmings.'

'Yeah, that's right,' said Olaf, his face puzzled.

'And he has a big bag, chock full of presents for good little boys and girls, and he brings it down the chimney and puts presents inside stockings.'

'Sure.'

'You also told them he's about due, didn't you? One more revolution and he's going to visit us.'

Olaf smiled weakly. 'Yeah, Commander, I meant to tell you. I'm fixing up the tree and —'

'Shut up!' The commander was breathing hard in a whistling sort of way. 'Do you know what those Ossies have thought of?'

'No, Commander.'

Pelham leaned across the table toward Olaf and shouted:

'They want Santa Claus to visit *them*!'

Someone laughed and changed it quickly into a strangling cough at the commander's raging stare.

'And if Santa Claus doesn't visit them, the Ossies are going to quit work!' He repeated, 'Quit cold – strike!'

There was no laughter, strangled or otherwise, after that. If there were more than one thought among the entire group, it didn't show itself. Olaf expressed that thought:

'But what about the quota?'

'Well, what about it?' snarled Pelham. 'Do I have to draw pictures for you? Ganymedan Products has to get one hundred tons of wolframite, eighty tons of karen leaves and fifty tons of oxite every year, or it loses its franchise. I suppose there isn't anyone here who doesn't know that. It so happens that the current year ends in two Ganymedan revolutions, and we're five per cent behind schedule as it is.'

There was pure, horrified silence.

'And now the Ossies won't work unless they get Santa Claus. No work, no quota, no franchise – no jobs! Get that, you low-grade morons. When the company loses its franchise, we lose the best-paying jobs in the System. Kiss them good-bye, men, unless —'

He paused, glared steadily at Olaf, and added:

'Unless, by next revolution, we have a flying sleigh, eight reindeer and a Santa Claus. And by every cosmic speck in the rings of Saturn, we're going to have just that, especially a Santa!'

The faces turned ghastly pale.

'Got someone in mind, Commander?' asked someone in a voice that was three-quarters croak.

'Yes, as a matter of fact, I have.'

He sprawled back in his chair. Olaf Johnson broke into a sudden sweat as he found himself staring at the end of a pointing forefinger.

'Aw, Commander!' he quavered.

The pointing finger never moved.

Pelham tramped into the foreroom, removed his oxygen nosepiece and the cold cylinders attached to it. One by one he cast off thick woolen outer garments and, with a final, weary sigh, jerked off a pair of heavy knee-high space boots.

Sim Pierce paused in his careful inspection of the latest batch of karen leaves and cast a hopeful glance over his spectacles.

'Well?' he asked.

Pelham shrugged. 'I promised them Santa. What else could I do? I also doubled sugar rations, so they're back on the job –

121

for the moment.'

'You mean till the Santa we promised doesn't show up.' Pierce straightened and waved a long karen leaf at the commander's face for emphasis. 'This is the silliest thing I ever heard of. It can't be done. There ain't no Santa Claus!'

'Try telling that to the Ossies.' Pelham slumped into a chair and his expression became stonily bleak. 'What's Benson doing?'

'You mean that flying sleigh he says he can rig up?' Pierce held a leaf up to the light and peered at it critically. 'He's a crackpot, if you ask me. The old buzzard went down to the sub-level this morning and he's been there ever since. All I know is that he's taken the spare lectro-dissociator apart. If anything happens to the regular, it just means that we're without oxygen.'

'Well,' Pelham rose heavily, 'for my part I hope we *do* choke. It would be an easy way out of this whole mess. I'm going down below.'

He stumped out and slammed the door behind him.

In the sub-level he gazed about in bewilderment, for the room was littered with gleaming chrome-steel machine parts. It took him some time to recognize the mess as the remains of what had been a compact, snugly built lectro-dissociator the day before. In the center, in anachronistic contrast, stood a dusty wooden sleigh atop rust-red runners. From beneath it came the sound of hammering.

'Hey, Benson!' called Pelham.

A grimy, sweat-streaked face pushed out from underneath the sleigh, and a stream of tobacco juice shot toward Benson's ever-present cuspidor.

'What are you shouting like that for?' he complained. 'This is delicate work.'

'What the devil is that weird contraption?' demanded Pelham.

'Flying sleigh. My own idea, too.' The light of enthusiasm shone in Benson's watery eyes, and the quid in his mouth shifted from cheek to cheek as he spoke. 'The sleigh was brought here in the old days, when they thought Ganymede was covered with snow like the other Jovian moons. All I have to do is fix a few gravo-repulsors from the dissociator to the bottom and that'll make it weightless when the current's on.

Compressed air-jets will do the rest.'

The commander chewed his lower lip dubiously.

'Will it work?'

'Sure it will. Lots of people have thought of using repulsors in air travel, but they're inefficient, especially in heavy gravity fields. Here on Ganymede, with a field of one-third gravity and a thin atmosphere, a child could run it. Even Johnson could run it, though I wouldn't mourn if he fell off and broke his blasted neck.'

'All right, then, look here. We've got lots of this native purple-wood. Get Charlie Finn and tell him to put that sleigh on a platform of it. He's to have it extend about twenty feet or more frontward, with a railing around the part that projects.'

Benson spat and scowled through the stringy hair over his eyes.

'What's the idea, Commander?'

Pelham's laughter came in short, harsh barks.

'Those Ossies are expecting reindeer, and reindeer they're going to have. Those animals will have to stand on something, won't they?'

'Sure ... But wait, hold on! There aren't any reindeer on Ganymede.'

Commander Pelham paused on his way out. His eyes narrowed unpleasantly as they always did when he thought of Olaf Johnson.

'Olaf is out rounding up eight spiny backs for us. They've got four feet, a head on one end and a tail on the other. That's close enough for the Ossies.'

The old engineer chewed this information and chuckled nastily.

'Good! I wish the fool joy of his job.'

'So do I,' gritted Pelham.

He stalked out as Benson, still leering, slid underneath the sleigh.

The commander's description of a spinyback was concise and accurate, but it left out several interesting details. For one thing, a spinyback has a long, mobile snout, two large ears that wave back and forth gently and two emotional purple eyes. The males have pliable spines of a deep crimson color along the backbone that seem to delight the female of the species.

123

Combine these with a scaly, muscular tail and a brain by no means mediocre, and you have a spinyback – or at least you have one if you can catch one.

It was just such a thought that occurred to Olaf Johnson as he sneaked down from the rocky eminence toward the herd of twenty-five spinybacks grazing on the sparse, gritty undergrowth. The nearest spinies looked up as Olaf, bundled in fur and grotesque with attached oxygen nosepiece, approached. However, spinies have no natural enemies, so they merely gazed at the figure with languidly disapproving eyes and returned to their crunchy but nourishing fare.

Olaf's notions on bagging big game were sketchy. He fumbled in his pocket for a lump of sugar, held it out and said:

'Here, pussy, pussy, pussy, pussy, pussy!'

The ears of the nearest spinie twitched in annoyance. Olaf came closer and held out the sugar again.

'Come, bossy! Come, bossy!'

The spinie caught sight of the sugar and rolled his eyes at it. His snout twitched as he spat out his last mouthful of vegetation and ambled over. With neck stretched out, he sniffed. Then, using a rapid, expert motion, he struck at the outheld palm and flipped the lump into his mouth. Olaf's other hand whistled down upon nothingness.

With a hurt expression, Olaf held out another piece.

'Here, Prince! Here, Fido!'

The spinie made a low, tremulous sound deep in his throat. It was a sound of pleasure. Evidently this strange monstrosity before him, having gone insane, intended to feed him these bits of concentrated succulence forever. He snatched and was back as quickly as the first time. But, since Olaf had held on firmly this time, the spinie almost bagged half a finger as well.

Olaf's yell lacked a bit of the nonchalance necessary at such times. Nevertheless, a bite that can be felt through thick gloves is a *bite*!

He advanced boldly upon the spinie. There are some things that stir the Johnson blood and bring up the ancient spirit of the Vikings. Having one's finger bitten, especially by an unearthly animal, is one of these.

There was an uncertain look in the spinie's eyes as he backed slowly away. There weren't any white cubes being offered any more and he wasn't quite sure what was going to happen now. The uncertainty vanished with a suddenness he did not expect, when two glove-muffled hands came down upon his ears and jerked. He let out a high-pitched yelp and charged forward.

A spinie has a certain sense of dignity. He doesn't like to have his ears pulled, particularly when other spinies, including several unattached females, have formed a ring and are looking on.

The Earthman went over backward and remained in that position for awhile. Meantime, the spinie backed away a few feet in a gentlemanly manner and allowed Johnson to get to his feet.

The old Viking blood frothed still higher in Olaf. After rubbing the hurt spot where he had landed on his oxygen cylinder, he jumped, forgetting to allow for Ganymedan gravity. He sailed five feet over the spinie's back.

There was awe in the animal's eye as he watched Olaf, for it was a stately jump. But there was a certain amount of bewilderment as well. There seemed to be no purpose to the maneuver.

Olaf landed on his back again and got the cylinder in the same place. He was beginning to feel a little embarrassed. The sounds that came from the circle of onlookers were remarkably like snickers.

'Laugh!' he muttered bitterly. 'I haven't even begun to fight yet.'

He approached the spinie slowly, cautiously. He circled, watching for his opening. So did the spinie. Olaf feinted and the spinie ducked. Then the spinie reared and Olaf ducked.

Olaf kept remembering new profanity all the time. The husky 'Ur-r-r-r' that came out the spinie's throat seemed to lack the brotherly spirit that is usually associated with Christmas.

There was a sudden, swishing sound. Olaf felt something collide with his skull, just behind his left ear. This time he turned a back somersault and landed on the nape of his neck. There was a chorused whinny from the onlookers, and the spinie waved his tail triumphantly.

Olaf got rid of the impression that he was floating through a

125

star-studden unlimited space and wavered to his feet.

'Listen,' he objected, 'using your tail is a foul!'

He leaped back as the tail shot forward again, then flung himself forward in a diving tackle. He grabbed at the spinie's feet and felt the animal come down on his back with an indignant yelp.

Now it was a case of Earth muscles against Ganymedan muscles, and Olaf became a man of brute strength. He struggled up, and the spinie found himself slung over the stranger's shoulders.

The spinie objected vociferously and tried to prove his objections by a judicious whip of the tail. But he was in an inconvenient position and the stroke whistled harmlessly over Olaf's head.

The other spinies made way for the Earthman with saddened expressions. Evidently they were all good friends of the captured animal and hated to see him lose a fight. They returned to their meal in philosophic resignation, plainly convinced that it was kismet.

On the other side of the rocky ledge, Olaf reached his prepared cave. There was the briefest of scrambling struggles before he managed to sit down hard on the spinie's head and put enough knots into rope to hold him there.

A few hours later, when he had coralled his eighth spiny-back, he possessed the technique that comes of long practice. He could have given a Terrestrial cowboy valuable pointers on throwing a maverick. Also, he could have given a Terrestrial stevedore lessons in simple and compound swearing.

'Twas the night before Christmas – and all through the Ganymedan Dome there was deafening noise and bewildering excitement, like an exploding nova equipped for sound. Around the rusty sleigh, mounted on its huge platform of purplewood, five Earthmen were staging a battle royal with a spinie.

The spinie had definite views about most things, and one of his stubbornest and most definite views was that he would never go where he didn't want to go. He made that clear by flailing one head, one tail, three spines and four legs in every possible direction, with all possible force.

But the Earthmen insisted, and not gently. Despite loud, agonized squeaks, the spinie was lifted onto the platform,

126

hauled into place and harnessed into hopeless helplessness.

'Okay!' Peter Benson yelled. 'Pass the bottle.'

Holding the spinie's snout with one hand, Benson waved the bottle under it with the other. The spinie quivered eagerly and whined tremulously. Benson poured some of the liquid down the animal's throat. There was a gurgling swallow and an appreciative whinny. The spinie's neck stretched out for more.

Benson sighed. 'Our best brandy, too.'

He up-ended the bottle and withdrew it half empty. The spinie, eyes whirling in their sockets rapidly, did what seemed an attempt at a gay jig. It didn't last long, however, for Ganymedan metabolism is almost immediately affected by alcohol. His muscles locked in a drunken rigor and, with a loud hiccup, he went out on his feet.

'Drag out the next!' yelled Benson.

In an hour the eight spinybacks were so many cataleptic statues. Forked sticks were tied around their heads as antlers. The effect was crude and sketchy, but it would do.

As Benson opened his mouth to ask where Olaf Johnson was, that worthy showed up in the arms of three comrades, and he was putting up as stiff a fight as any spinie. His objections, however, were highly articulate.

'I'm not going anywhere in this costume!' he roared, gouging at the nearest eye. 'You hear me?'

There certainly was cause for objection. Even at his best, Olaf had never been a heart-throb. But in his present condition, he resembled a hybrid between a spinie's nightmare and a Picassian conception of a patriarch.

He wore the conventional costume of Santa. His clothes were as red as red tissue paper sewed onto his space coat could make it. The 'ermine' was as white as cotton wool, which it was. His beard, more cotton wool glued into a linen foundation, hung loosely from his ears. With that below and his oxygen nosepiece above, even the strongest were forced to avert their eyes.

Olaf had not been shown a mirror. But, between what he could see of himself and what his instinct told him, he would have greeted a good, bright lightning bolt like a brother.

By fits and starts, he was hauled to the sleigh. Others pitched in to help, until Olaf was nothing but a smothered squirm and muffled voice.

127

'Leggo,' he mumbled. 'Leggo and come at me one by one. Come on!'

He tried to spar a bit, to point his dare. But the multiple grips upon him left him unable to wriggle a finger.

'Get in!' ordered Benson.

'You go to hell!' gasped Olaf. 'I'm not getting into any patented short-cut to suicide, and you can take your bloody flying sleigh and —'

'Listen,' interrupted Benson, 'Commander Pelham is waiting for you at the other end. He'll skin you alive if you don't show up in half an hour.'

'Commander Pelham can take the sleigh sideways and —'

'Then think of your job! Think of a hundred and fifty a week. Think of every other year off with pay. Think of Hilda, back on Earth, who isn't going to marry you without a job. Think of all that!'

Johnson thought, snarled. He thought some more, got into the sleigh, strapped down his bag and turned on the gravo-repulsors. With a horrible curse, he opened the rear jet.

The sleigh dashed forward and he caught himself from going backward, over and out of the sleigh, by two-thirds of a whisker. He held onto the sides thereafter, watching the surrounding hills as they rose and fell with each lurch of the unsteady sleigh.

As the wind rose, the undulations grew more marked. And when Jupiter came up, its yellow light brought out every jag and crag of the rocky ground, toward every one of which, in turn, the sleigh seemed headed. And by the time the giant planet had shoved completely over the horizon, the curse of drink – which departs from the Ganymedan organism just as quickly as it descends – began removing itself from the spinies.

The hindmost spinie came out of it first, tasted the inside of his mouth, winced and swore off drink. Having made that resolution, he took in his immediate surroundings languidly. They made no immediate impression on him. Only gradually was the fact forced upon him that his footing, whatever it was, was not the usual stable one of solid Ganymede. It swayed and shifted, which seemed very unusual.

Yet he might have attributed this unsteadiness to his recent orgy, had he not been so careless as to drop his glance over the railing to which he was anchored. No spinie ever died of heart-failure, as far as is recorded, but, looking downward, this one almost did.

His agonized screech of horror and despair brought the other spinies into full, if headachy, consciousness. For a while there was a confused blur of squawking conversation as the animals tried to get the pain out of their heads and the facts in. Both aims were achieved and a stampede was organized. It wasn't much of a stampede, because the spinies were anchored tightly. But, except for the fact that they got nowhere, they went through all the motions of a full gallop. And the sleigh went crazy.

Olaf grabbed his beard a second before it let go of his ears. 'Hey!' he shouted.

It was something like saying 'Tut, tut' to a hurricane.

The sleigh kicked, bucked and did a hysterical tango. It made sudden spurts, as if inspired to dash its wooden brains out against Ganymede's crust. Meanwhile Olaf prayed, swore, wept and jiggled all the compressed air jets at once.

Ganymede whirled and Jupiter was a wild blur. Perhaps it was the spectacle of Jupiter doing the shimmy that steadied the spinies. More likely it was the fact that they just didn't give a hang any more. Whatever it was, they halted, made lofty farewell speeches to one another, confessed their sins and waited for death.

The sleigh steadied and Olaf resumed his breathing once more. Only to stop again as he viewed the curious spectacle of the hills and solid ground up above, and black sky and swollen Jupiter down below.

It was at this point that he, too, made his peace with the eternal and awaited the end.

'Ossie' is short for ostrich, and that's what native Ganymedans look like, except that their necks are shorter, their heads are larger and their feathers look as if they were about to fall out by the roots. To this, add a pair of scrawny, feathered arms with three stubby fingers apiece. They can speak English, but when you hear them, you wish they couldn't.

There were fifty of them in the low purplewood structure that was their 'meeting hall.' On the mound of raised dirt in the front of the room – dark with the smoky dimness of burning purplewood torches fetid to boot – sat Commander Scott Pelham and five of his men. Before them strutted the frowziest Ossie of them all, inflating his huge chest with rhythmic, booming sounds.

He stopped for a moment and pointed to a ragged hole in the ceiling.

'Look!' he squawked. 'Chimney. We make. Sannycaws come in.'

Pelham grunted approval. The Ossie clucked happily. He pointed to the little sacks of woven grass that hung from the walls.

'Look! Stockies. Sannycaws put presets!'

'Yeah,' said Pelham unenthusiastically. 'Chimney and stockings. Very nice.' He spoke out of the corner of his mouth to Sim Pierce, who sat next to him: 'Another half-hour in this dump will kill me. When is that fool coming?'

Pierce stirred uneasily.

'Listen,' he said, 'I've been doing some figuring. We're safe on everything but the karen leaves, and we're still four tons short on that. If we can get this fool business over with in the next hour, so we can start the next shift and work the Ossies at double, we can make it.' He leaned back. 'Yes, I think we can make it.'

'Just about,' replied Pelham gloomily. 'That's if Johnson gets here without pulling another bloomer.'

The Ossie was talking again, for Ossies like to talk. He said:

'Every year Kissmess comes. Kissmess nice, evvybody friendly. Ossie like Kissmess. You like Kissmess?'

'Yean, fine,' Pelham snarled politely. 'Peace on Ganymede, good will toward men – especially Johnson. Where the devil is that idiot, anyhow?'

He fell into an annoyed fidget, while the Ossie jumped up and down a few times in a thoughtful sort of manner, evidently for the exercise of it. He continued the jumping, varying it with little hopping dance steps, till Pelham's fists began making strangling gestures. Only an excited squawk from the hole in the wall dignified by the term 'window' kept Pelham from committing Ossie-slaughter.

Ossies swarmed about and the Earthmen fought for a view.

Against Jupiter's great yellowness was outlined a flying

130

sleigh, complete with reindeers. It was only a tiny thing, but there was no doubt about it. Santa Claus was coming.

There was only one thing wrong with the picture. The sleigh, 'reindeer' and all, while plunging ahead at a terrific speed, was flying upside down.

The Ossies dissolved into squawking cacophony.

'Sannycaws! Sannycaws! Sannycaws!'

The scrambled out the window like so many animated dust-mops gone mad. Pelham and his men used the low door.

The sleigh was approaching, growing larger, lurching from side to side and vibrating like an off-center flywheel. Olaf Johnson was a tiny figure holding on desperately to the side of the sleigh with both hands.

Pelham was shouting wildly, incoherently, choking on the thin atmosphere every time he forgot to breathe through his nose. Then he stopped and stared in horror. The sleigh, almost life-size now, was dipping down. If it had been an arrow shot by William Tell, it could not have aimed between Pelham's eyes more accurately.

'Everybody down!' he shrieked, and dropped.

The wind of the sleigh's passage whistled keenly and brushed his face. Olaf's voice could be heard for an instant, high-pitched and indistinct. Compressed air spurted, leaving tracks of condensing water vapor.

Pelham lay quivering, hugging Ganymede's frozen crust. Then, knees shaking like a Hawaiian hula-girl, he rose slowly. The Ossies who had scattered before the plunging vehicle had assembled again. Off in the distance, the sleigh was veering back.

Pelham watched as it swayed and hovered, still rotating. It lurched toward the dome, curved off to one side, turned back, and gathered speed.

Inside that sleigh, Olaf worked like a demon. Straddling his legs wide, he shifted his weight desperately. Sweating and cursing, trying hard not to look 'downward' at Jupiter, he urged the sleigh into wilder and wilder swings. It was wobbling through an angle of 180 degrees now, and Olaf felt his stomach raise strenuous objections.

Holding his breath, he leaned hard with his right foot and felt the sleigh swing far over. At the extremity of that swing, he released the gravo-repulsor and, in Ganymede's weak gravity, the sleigh jerked downward. Naturally, since the vehicle was bottom-heavy due to the metal gravo-repulsor beneath, it righted itself as it fell.

But this was little comfort to Commander Pelham, who found himself once more in the direct path of the sleigh.

'Down!' he yelled, and dropped again.

The sleigh *whi-i-ished* overhead, came up against a huge boulder with a *crack*, bounced twenty-five feet into the air, came down with a *rush* and a *bang* and Olaf fell over the railing and out.

Santa Claus had arrived.

With a deep, shuddering breath, Olaf swung his bag over his shoulders, adjusted his beard and patted one of the silently suffering spinies on the head. Death might be coming – in fact, Olaf could hardly wait – but he was going to die on his feet nobly, like a Johnson.

Inside the shack, into which the Ossies had once more swarmed, a *thump* announced the arrival of Santa's bag on the roof, and a second *thud* the arrival of Santa himself. A ghastly face appeared through the makeshift hole in the ceiling.

'Merry Christmas!' it croaked, and tumbled through.

Olaf landed on his oxygen cylinders, as usual, and got them in the usual place.

The Ossies jumped up and down like rubber balls with the itch.

Olaf limped heavily toward the first stocking and deposited the garishly colored sphere he withdrew from his bag, one of the many that had originally been intended as a Christmas tree ornament. One by one he deposited the rest in every available stocking.

Having completed his job, he dropped into an exhausted squat, from which position he watched subsequent proceedings with a glazed and fishy eye. The jolliness and belly-shaking good humor, traditionally characteristic of Santa Claus, were absent from this one with remarkable thoroughness.

The Ossies made up for it by their wild ecstasy. Until Olaf had deposited the last globe, they had kept their silence and their seats. But when he had finished, the air heaved and writhed under the stresses of the discordant screeches that arose. In half a second the hand of each Ossie contained a globe.

They chattered among themselves furiously, handling the globes carefully and hugging them close to their chests. Then they compared one with another, flocking about to gaze at particularly good ones.

The frowziest Ossie approached Pelham and plucked at the commander's sleeve. 'Sannycaws good,' he cackled. 'Look, he leave eggs!' He stared reverently at his sphere and said: 'Pittier'n Ossie eggs. Must be Sannycaws eggs, huh?'

His skinny finger punched Pelham in the stomach.

'No!' yowled Pelham vehemently. 'Hell, no!'

But the Ossie wasn't listening. He plunged the globe deep into the warmth of his feathers and said:

'Pitty colors. How long take for little Sannycaws come out? And what little Sannycaws eat?' He looked up. 'We take good care. We teach little Scannycaws, make him smart and full of brain like Ossie.'

Pierce grabbed Commander Pelham's arm.

'Don't argue with them,' he whispered frantically. 'What do you care if they think those are Santa Claus eggs? Come on! If we work like maniacs, we can still make the quota. Let's get started.'

'That's right,' Pelham admitted. He turned to the Ossie. 'Tell everyone to get going.' He spoke clearly and loudly. 'Work now. Do you understand? Hurry, hurry, hurry! Come on!'

He motioned with his arms. But the frowzy Ossie had come to a sudden halt. He said slowly:

'We work, but Johnson says Kissmess come evvy year.'

'Isn't one Christmas enough for you?' Pelham rasped.

'No!' squawked the Ossie. 'We want Sannycaws next year. Get more eggs. And next year more eggs. And next year. And next year. And next year. More eggs. More little Sannycaws eggs. If Sannycaws not come, we not work.'

'That's a long time off,' said Pelham. 'We'll talk about it then. By that time I'll either have gone completely crazy, or you'll have forgotten all about it.'

Pierce opened his mouth, closed it, open his mouth, closed it, opened it and finally managed to speak.

'Commander, they want him to come every year.'

'I know. They won't remember by next year, though.'

'But you don't get it. A year to them is one Ganymedan

133

revolution around Jupiter. In Earth time, that's seven days and three hours. They want Santa Claus to come every *week*.'

'Every week!' Pelham gulped. 'Johnson told them —'

For a moment everything turned sparkling somersaults before his eyes. He choked, and automatically his eye sought Olaf.

Olaf turned cold to the marrow of his bones and rose to his feet apprehensively, sidling toward the door. There he stopped as a sudden recollection of tradition hit him. Beard a-dangle, he croaked:

'Merry Christmas to all, and to all a good night!'

He made for the sleigh as if all the imps of Hades were after him. The imps weren't, but Commander Scott Pelham was.

THE END

In January of 1941 (the month in which I attained my majority), I undertook something new – a collaboration.

Fred Pohl, after all, was not merely an editor. He was also a budding writer. He has since come to be a giant in the field, but in those early days he was struggling along with only the sort of meager success I was having. Alone, and in collaboration with other Futurians, he turned out stories under a variety of pseudonyms. The one he used most frequently was 'James MacCreigh.'

As it happened, he had written, under that pseudonym, a small fantasy called 'The Little Man on the Subway,' which he apparently had hopes for but couldn't get right. He asked me if I would rewrite it, and the request flattered me. Besides, I was still trying to get into *Unknown*, and if I couldn't do it on my own, maybe I could do it by way of a collaboration. I wasn't proud – at least as far as fantasy was concerned.

I took on the task and did it virtually at a sitting. Doing it easily didn't help, however. I submitted it to Campbell for *Unknown* on January 27, 1941, and he rejected it. I had to hand it back to Pohl.

Pohl, however, with the true agent's soul, never gave up, and in 1950, long after I had utterly forgotten it, he managed to place it with a small magazine called *Fantasy Book*.

15: The Little Man on the Subway (with James MacCreigh)

Subway stations are places where people usually get out, so when no one left the first car at Atlantic Avenue station, Conductor Cullen of the I.R.T. began to get worried. In fact, no one had left the first car from the time the run to Flatbush had begun – though dozens were getting on all the time.

Odd! Very odd! It was the kind of proposition that made well-bred conductors remove their caps and scratch their heads. Conductor Cullen did so. It didn't help, but he repeated the process at Bergen Street, the next station, where again the first car lost not one of its population. And at Grand Army Plaza, he added to the headscratching process a few rare old Gaelic words that had passed down from father to son for hundreds of years. They ionized the surrounding atmosphere, but otherwise did not affect the situation.

At Eastern Parkway, Cullen tried an experiment. He carefully refrained from opening the first car's doors at all. He leaned forward eagerly, twisted his head and watched – and was treated to nothing short of a miracle. The New York subway rider is neither shy, meek nor modest, and doors that do not open immediately or sooner are helped on their way by sundry kicks. But this time there was not a kick, not a shriek, not even a modified yell. Cullen's eyes popped.

He was getting angry. At Franklin Avenue, where he again contacted the Express, he flung open the doors and swore at the crowd. Every door spouted commuters of both sexes and all ages, except that terrible first car. At those doors, three men and a very young girl got on, though Cullen could plainly see the slight bulging of the walls that the already super-crowded condition of the car had caused.

For the rest of the trip to Flatbush Avenue, Cullen ignored the first car completely, concentrating on that last stop where everyone would *have* to get off. Everyone! President, Church and Beverly Road were visited and passed, and Cullen found himself counting the stations to the Flatbush terminus.

They seemed like such a nice bunch of passengers, too. They

Fantasy Book, Volume 1, Number 6
Copyright © 1950 by Fantasy Publishing Company, Inc.

read their newspapers, stared into the whirling blackness out the window, or at the girl's legs across the way, or at nothing at all, quite like ordinary people. Only, they didn't want to get out. They didn't even want to get into the next car, where empty seats filled the place. Imagine New Yorkers resisting the impulse to pass from one car to the other, and missing the chance to leave the doors open for the benefit of the draft.

But it was Flatbush Avenue! Cullen rubbed his hands, slammed the doors open and yelled in his best unintelligible manner, 'Lasstop!' He repeated it two or three times hoarsely and several in that damned first car looked up at him. There was reproach in their eyes. Have you never heard of the Mayor's anti-noise campaign, they seemed to say.

The last other passenger had come out of the train, and the scattered new ones were coming in. There were a few curious looks at the jammed car, but not too many. The New Yorker considers everything he cannot understand a publicity stunt.

Cullen fell back on his Gaelic once more and dashed up the platform toward the motorman's booth. He needed moral assistance. The motorman should have been out of his cab, preparing for his next trip, but he wasn't. Cullen could see him through the glass of the door, leaning on the controls and staring vacantly at the bumper-stop ahead.

'Gus!' cried Cullen. 'Come out! There's a hell of —'

At that point, his tongue skidded to a halt, because it wasn't Gus. It was a little old man, who smiled politely and twiddled his fingers in greeting.

Patrick Cullen's Irish soul rebelled. With a yelp, he grabbed the edge of the door and tried to shove it open. He should have known that wouldn't work. So, taking a deep breath and commending said Irish soul to God, he made for the open door and ploughed into the mass of haunted humans in that first car. Momentum carried him six feet, and then there he stuck. Behind him, those he had knocked down picked themselves up from the laps of their fellow-travelers, apologized with true New York courtesy (consisting of a growl, a grunt, and a grimace) and returned to their papers.

Then, caught helplessly, he heard the Dispatcher's bell. It was time for his own train to be on its way. Duty called! With a superhuman effort, he inched toward the door, but it closed before he could get there, and the train commenced to move.

It occurred to Cullen that he had missed a report for the first time, and he said, 'Damn!' After the train had travelled some fifty feet, it came to him that they were going the wrong way, and this time he said nothing.

After all, what was there to say – even in the purest of Gaelic.

How *could* a train go the wrong way at Flatbush Ave. There were no further tracks. There was no further tunnel. There was a bumper-stop to prevent eccentric motormen from trying to bore one. It was absurd. Even the Big Deal couldn't do it.

But there they were!

There were stations in this new tunnel, too – cute little small ones just large enough for one car. But that was all right, because only one car was travelling. The rest had somehow become detached, presumably to make the routine trip to Bronx Park.

There were maybe a dozen stations on the line – with curious names. Cullen noticed only a few, because he found it difficult to keep his eyes from going out of focus. One was Archangel Boulevard; another Seraph Road; still another Cherub Plaza.

And then, the train slid into a monster station, that looked uncommonly like a cave, and stopped. It was huge, about three hundred feet deep and almost spherical. The tracks ran to the exact center without trusses, and the platform at its side like-wise rested comfortably upon air.

The conductor was the only person left in the car, the rest having mostly gotten off at Hosannah Square. He hung limply from the porcelain hand-grip, staring fixedly at a lip-stick advertisement. The door of the motorman's cabin opened and the little man came out. He glanced at Cullen, turned away, then whirled back.

'Hey,' he said, 'who are you?'

Cullen rotated slowly, still clutching the hand-grip. 'Only the conductor. Don't mind me. I'm quitting anyway. I don't like the work.'

'Oh dear, dear, this is unexpected.' The little man waggled his head and tch-tched. 'I'm Mr. Crumley,' he explained. 'I steal things. People mostly. Sometimes subway cars, – but they're such big, clumsy things, don't you think?'

'Mister,' groaned Cullen. 'I quit thinking two hours ago. It didn't get me anywhere. Who are you, anyway?'

137

'I told you – I'm Mr. Crumley. I'm practicing to be a god.'

'A gob?' said Cullen. 'You mean a sailor?'

'Dear, no,' frowned Mr. Crumley. 'I said, "god," as in Jehovah. Look!' He pointed out the window to the wall of the cave. Where his finger pointed, the rock billowed and rose. He moved his finger and there was a near ridge of rock describing a reversed, lower case 'h.'

'That's my symbol,' said Crumley modestly. 'Mystic, isn't it? But that's nothing. Wait till I really get things organized. Dear, dear, will I give them miracles!'

Cullen's head swivelled between the raised-rock symbol and the simpering Mr. Crumley, until he began to get dizzy, and then he stopped.

'Listen,' he demanded hoarsely. 'How did you get that car out of Flatbush Avenue? Where did that tunnel come from? Are some of them foreigners —'

'Oh, my, no!' answered Mr. Crumley. 'I made that myself and willed it so that no one would notice. It was quite difficult. It just wears the ectoplasm right out of me. Miracles with people mixed up in it are much harder than the other kind, because you have to fight their wills. Unless you have lots of Believers, you can't do it. Now that I've got over a hundred thousand, I can do it, but there was a time,' he shook his head reminiscently, 'when I couldn't even have levitated a baby – or healed a leper. Oh, well, we're wasting time. We ought to be at the nearest factory.'

Cullen brightened. 'Factory' was more prosaic. 'I once had a brother,' he said, 'who worked in a sweater factory, but —'

'Oh, goodness, Mr. Cullen. I'm referring to my Believers' Factories. I have to educate people to believe in me, don't I, and preaching is such slow work. I believe in mass production. Some day I intend to be called the Henry Ford of Utopia. Why, I've got twelve Factories in Brooklyn alone and when I manufacture enough Believers, I'll just cover the world with them.'

He sighed, 'Gracious me, if I only had enough Believers. I've got to have a million before I can let things progress by themselves and until then I have to attend to every detail myself. It is so boring! I even have to keep reminding my Believers who I am – even the Disciples. Incidentally, Cullen, – I read your mind, by the way, so that's how I know your name –

138

you want to be a Believer, of course.'

'Well, now,' said Cullen nervously.

'Oh, come now. *Some* gods would have been angry at your intrusion and done away with you,' he snapped his fingers, 'like that. Not I, though, because I think killing people is messy and inconsiderate. Just the same, you'll have to be a Believer.'

Now Patrick Cullen was an intelligent Irishman. That is to say, he admitted the existence of banshees, leprechauns and the Little Folk, and kept an open mind on poltergeists, were-wolves, vampires and such-like foreign trash. At mere super-naturalities, he was too well-educated to sneer. Still, Cullen did not intend to compromise his religion. His theology was weak, but for a mortal to claim godship smacked of heresy, not to say sacrilege and blasphemy, even to him.

'You're a faker,' he cried boldly, 'and you're headed straight for Hell the way you're going.'

Mr. Crumley clicked his tongue, 'What terrible language you use. And so unnecessary! Of course you Believe in me.'

'Oh, yeah?'

'Well, then, if you are stubborn, I'll pass a minor miracle. It's inconvenient, but now,' he made vague motions with his left hand, 'you Believe in me.'

'Certainly,' said Cullen, hurt. 'I always did. How do I go about worshipping you? I want to do this properly.'

'Just Believe in me, and that's enough. Now you must go to the factories and then we'll send you back home – they'll never know you were gone – and you can live your life like a Believer.'

The conductor smiled ecstatically, 'Oh, happy life! I *want* to go to the factories.'

'Of course you would,' replied Mr. Crumley. 'You'd be a fine Crumleyite otherwise, wouldn't you? Come!' He pointed at the door of the car, and the door slid open. They walked out and Crumley kept on pointing. Rock faded away in front, and bit down again behind. Through the wall Cullen walked, following that little figure who was his god.

That *was* a god, thought Cullen. Any god that could do that was one hell of a damn good god to believe in.

And then he was at the factory – in another cave, only smaller. Mr. Crumley seemed to like caves.

Cullen didn't pay much attention to his surroundings. He

couldn't see much anyway on account of the faint violet mist that blurred his vision. He got the impression of a slowly-moving conveyor belt, with men stationed at intervals along it. Disciples, he thought. And the parts being machined on that belt were probably non-Believers, or such low trash.

There was a man watching him, smiling. A Disciple, Cullen thought, and quite naturally made the sign to him. He had never made it before, but it was easy. The Disciple replied in kind.

'He told me you were coming,' said the Disciple. 'He made a special miracle for you, he said. That's quite a distinction. Do you want me to show you around the belt?'

'You bet.'

'Well, this is Factory One. It's the nerve center of all the factories of the country. The others give preliminary treatment only; and make only Believers. *We* make Disciples.'

Oh, boy, Disciples! 'Am I going to be a Disciple?' asked Cullen eagerly.

'After being miraculated by *him*. Of course! You're a *some-body*, you know. There are only five other people he ever took personal charge of.'

This was a glorious way to do things. Everything Mr. Crumley did was glorious. What a god! What a god!

'You started that way, too.'

'Certainly,' said the Disciple, placidly, 'I'm an important fellow, too. Only I wish I were more important, even.'

'What for?' said Cullen, in a shocked tone of voice. 'Are you murmuring against the dictates of Mr. Crumley? (may he prosper). This is sacrilege.'

The Disciple shifted uncomfortably, 'Well, I've got ideas, and I'd like to try them out.'

'You've got ideas, huh?' muttered Cullen balefully. 'Does Mr. Crumley (may he live forever) know?'

'Well – frankly, no! But just the same,' the Disciple looked over each shoulder carefully and drew closer, 'I'm not the only one. There are lots of us that think Mr. Crumley (on whom be blessings) is just a trifle old-fashioned. For instance, take the lights in this place.'

Cullen stared upwards. The lights were the same type as those in the terminal-cave. They might have been stolen from any line of the IRT subway. Perfect copies of the stop-and-go

140

signals and the exit markers.

'What's wrong?' he asked.

The Disciple sneered, 'They lack originality. You'd think a grade A god would do something new. When he takes people, he does it through the subway, and he obeys subway rules. He waits for the Dispatcher to tell him to go; he stops at every station; he uses crude electricity and so on. What we need,' the Disciple was waving his hands wildly and shouting, 'is more enterprise, more git-and-go. We've got to speed up things and run them with efficiency and vim.'

Cullen stared hotly, 'You are a heretic,' he accused. 'You are doomed to damnation.' He looked angrily about for a bell, whistle, gong or drum wherewith to summon the great Crumley, but found nothing.

The other blinked in quick thought. 'Say,' he said, bluffly, 'look at what time it is. I'm behind schedule. You better get on the belt for your first treatment.'

Cullen was hot about the slovenly assistance. Mr. Crumley was getting from this inferior Disciple, but a treatment is a treatment, so making the sign devoutly, he got on. He found it fairly comfortable despite its jerky motion. The Disciple motioned to Cullen's first preceptor – another Disciple – standing beside a sort of blackboard. Cullen had watched others while discussing Crumley and he had noticed the question and answer procedure that had taken place. He had noticed it particularly.

Consequently, he was surprised, when the second Disciple, instead of using his heavy pointer to indicate a question on the board, reversed it and brought it down upon his head.

The lights went out!

When he came to, he was under the belt, at the very bottom of the cave. He was tied up, and the Rebellious Disciple and three others were talking about him.

'He couldn't be persuaded,' the Disciple was saying. 'Crumley must have given him a double treatment or something.'

'It's the last double treatment Crumley'll ever give,' said the fat little man.

'Let's hope so. How's it coming?'

'Very well. Very well, indeed. We teleported ourselves to Section Four about two hours ago. It was a perfect miracle.'

The Disciple was pleased. 'Fine! How're they doing at Four?'

The fat little man clucked his lips. 'Well, now, not so hot. For some reason, they're getting odd effects over there. Miracles are just happening. Even ordinary Crumleyites can pass them, and sometimes they – just happen. It's extremely annoying.'

'Hmm, that's bad. If there are too many hitches, Crumley'll get suspicious. If he investigates there first, he can reconvert all of them in a jiffy, before he comes here and then without their support we might not be strong enough to stand up against him.'

'Say, now,' said the fat man apprehensively, 'we're not strong enough *now*, you know. None of this going off half-cocked.'

'We're strong enough,' pointed out the Disciple stiffly, 'to weaken him long enough to get us a new god started, and after that —'

'A new god, eh?' said another. He nodded wisely.

'Sure,' said the Disciple. 'A new god, created by us, can be destroyed by us. He'd be completely under our thumb and then instead of this one-man tyranny, we can have a sort of – er – council.'

There were general grins and everyone looked pleased.

'But we'll discuss that further some other time,' continued the Disciple briskly. 'Let's Believe just a bit. Crumley isn't stupid, you know, and we don't want him to observe any slackening. Come on, now. All together.'

They closed their eyes, concentrated a bit, and then opened them with a sigh.

'Well,' said the little, fat man, *'that's* over. I'd better be getting back now.'

From under the belt, Cullen watched him. He looked singularly like a chicken about to take off for a tree as he flexed his knees and stared upwards. Then he added to the resemblance not a little when he spread his arms, gave a little hop and fluttered away.

Cullen could follow his flight only by watching the eyes of the three remaining. Those eyes turned up and up, following the fat man to the very top of the cave, it seemed. There was an air of self-satisfaction about those eyes. They were very

142

happy over their miracles.

Then they all went away and left Cullen to his holy indignation. He was shocked to the very core of his being at this sinful rebellion, this apostasy – this – this — There weren't any words for it, even when he tried Gaelic.

Imagine trying to create a god that would be under the thumbs of the creators. It was anthropomorphic heresy (where had he heard that word, now?) and struck at the roots of all religion. Was he going to lie there and watch anything strike at the roots of all religion? Was he going to submit to having Mr. Crumley (may he swim through seas of ecstasy) deposed?

Never!

But the ropes thought otherwise, so there he stayed.

And then there was an interruption in his thoughts. There came a low, booming sound – a sound which would have been a voice if it had not been pitched so incredibly low. There was a menace to it that got immediate attention. It got attention from Cullen, who quivered in his bonds; from the others in the cave, who quivered even harder, not being restrained by ropes; from the belt itself, which stopped dead with a jerk, and quivered mightily.

The Rebellious Disciple dropped to his knees and quivered more than any of them.

The voice came again, this time in a recognizable language, 'WHERE IS THAT BUM, CRUMLEY?' it roared.

There was no wait for an answer. A cloud of shadow gathered in the center of the hall and spat a black bolt at the belt. A spot of fire leaped out from where the bolt had touched and spread slowly outward. Where it passed, the belt ceased to exit. It was far from Cullen, but there were humans nearer, and among those scurrying pandemonium existed.

Cullen wanted very much to join the flight, but unfortunately the Disciple who had trussed him up had evidently been a Boy Scout. Jerking, twisting and writhing had no effect upon the stubborn ropes, so he fell back upon Gaelic and wishing. He wished he were free. He wished he weren't tied. He wished he were far away from that devouring flame. He wished lots of things, some unprintable, but mainly those.

And with that he felt a gentle slipping pressure and down at his feet was an untidy pile of hempen fibre. Evidently the forces liberated by the rebellion were getting out of control here as well as in Section Four. What had the little fat man said? 'Miracles are just happening. Even ordinary Crumleyites can pass them, and sometimes they – just happen.'

But why waste time? He ran to the rock wall and howled a wish at it to dissolve into nothing. He howled several times, with Gaelic modifications, but the wall didn't even slightly soften. He stared wildly and then saw the hole. It was on the side of the cave, diametrically across from Cullen's position at the bottom of the hall, and about three loops of the belt up. The upward spiral passed just below it.

Somehow he made the leap that grabbed the lower lip of the spiral, wriggled his way onto it and jumped into a run. The fire of disintegration was behind him and plenty far away, but it was making time. Up the belt to the third loop he ran, not taking time to be dizzy from the circular trip. But when he got there, the hole, large, black and inviting, was just the tiniest bit higher than he could jump.

He leaned against the wall panting. The spot of fire was now two spots, crawling both ways from a twenty foot break in the belt. Everyone in the cavern, some two hundred people, was in motion, and everyone made some sort of noise.

Somehow, the sight stimulated him. It nerved him to further efforts to get into the hole. Wildly, he tried walking up the sheer wall, but this didn't work.

And then Mr. Crumley stuck his head out of the hole and said, 'Oh, mercy me, what a perfectly terrible mess. Dear, dear! Come up here, Cullen! Why do you stay down there!'

A great peace descended upon Cullen. 'Hail, Mr. Crumley.' he cried. 'May you sniff the essence of roses forever.'

Mr. Crumley looked pleased, 'Thank you, Cullen.' He waved his hand, and the conductor was beside him – a simple matter of levitation. Once again, Cullen decided in his inmost soul that here was a *god*.

'And now,' said Mr. Crumley, 'we must hurry, hurry, hurry. I've lost most of my power when the Disciples rebelled, and my subway car is stuck half-way. I'll need your help. Hurry!'

Cullen had no time to admire the tiny subway at the end of the tunnel. He jumped off the platform on Crumley's heels and dashed about a hundred feet down the tube to where the car was standing idle. He wafted into the open front door with the grace of a chorus-boy. Mr. Crumley took care of that.

'Cullen,' said Mr. Crumley, 'start this thing and take it back to the regular line. And be careful; *he* is waiting for me.'

'Who?'

'He, the new god. Imagine those fools – no, idiots – thinking they could create a controllable god, when the very essence of godship is uncontrollability. Of course, when they made a god to destroy me, they made a Destroyer, and he'll just destroy everything in sight that I created, including my Disciples.'

Cullen worked quickly. He knew how to start car 30990; any conductor would. He raced to the other end of the car for the control lever, snatched it off, and returned at top speed. That was all he needed. There was power in the rail; the lights were on; and there were no stop signals between him and God's Country.

Mr. Crumley lay himself down on a seat, 'Be very quiet. *He* may let you get past him. I'm going to blank myself out, and maybe he won't notice me. At any rate, he won't harm you – I *hope*. Dear, dear, since this all started in section four, things are *such* a mess.'

Eight stations passed before anything happened and then came Utopia Circle station and – well, nothing really *happened*. It was just an impression – an impression of people all around him for a few seconds watching him closely with a virulent hostility. It wasn't exactly people, but a person. It wasn't exactly a person either, but just a huge eye, watching – watching – watching.

But it passed, and almost immediately Cullen saw a black and white 'Flatbush Avenue' sign at the side of the tunnel. He jammed on his brakes in a hurry, for there was a train waiting there. But the controls didn't work the way they should have, and the car edged up until it was in contact with the cars before. With a soft click, it coupled and 30990 was just the last car of the train.

It was Mr. Crumley's work, of course. Mr. Crumley stood behind him, watching. 'He didn't get you, did he? No – I see he didn't.'

'Is there any more danger?' asked Cullen, anxiously.

'I don't think so,' responded Mr. Crumley sadly. 'After he has destroyed all my creation, there will be nothing left for him to destroy, and, deprived of a function, he will simply cease to exist. That's the result of this nasty, slipshod work.

I'm disgusted with human beings.'

'Don't say that,' said Cullen.

'I will,' retorted Mr. Crumley savagely, 'Human beings aren't fit to be god of. They're too much trouble and worry. It would give any self-respecting god gray hairs and I suppose you think a god looks very dignified all gray. Darn all humans! They can get along without me. From now on, I'm going to go to Africa and try the chimpanzees. I'll bet they make *much* better material.'

'But wait,' wailed Cullen. 'What about me? I *believe* in you.'

'Oh, dear, that would never do. Here! Return to normal.'

Mr. Crumley's hand caressed the air, and Cullen, once more a God-fearing Irishman, let loose a roar in the purest Gaelic and made for him.

'Why, you blaspheming spalpeen —'

But there was no Mr. Crumley. There was only the Dispatcher, asking very impolitely – in English – what the blankety-blank hell was the matter with him.

THE END

I am sorry to say that I have no clear memory, at this time, what parts of the story are mine and what parts are Pohl's. Going over it, I can say, 'This part sounds like me, this part doesn't,' but whether I'd be right or not I couldn't swear.

Fantasy Book was a very borderline publication that lasted only eight issues. 'The Little Man on the Subway' was in the sixth.

An amusing fact about this issue of a small magazine that had to make do with what it could find among the rejects of the field was that it included 'Scanners Live in Vain,' by Cordwainer Smith. This was Smith's first published story and he was not to publish another for eight years or so. In the 1960s, Smith (a pseudonym for a man whose real identity was not made clear until after his death) became a writer of considerable importance, and this first story of his became a classic.

While working on 'The Little Man on the Subway' I was also doing another 'positronic robot' story, called 'Liar!' In this one, my character Susan Calvin first appeared (she has been a character in ten of my stories up to the present time and

146

I don't eliminate the possibility that she will appear yet again).

It was while Campbell and I were discussing this story, by the way, on December 16, 1940, that the 'Three Laws of Robotics' were worked out in full. (I say it was Campbell who worked them out and he says it was I – but I know I'm right. It was he.)

'Liar!' was accepted at once by Campbell, at the end of January, without revision, and appeared in the May 1941 issue of *Astounding*. It was my fourth appearance in that magazine. The fact that it appeared the month after 'Reason' helped fix the 'positronic robot' stories in the readers' minds as a 'series.' 'Liar!' eventually appeared in *I, Robot*.

The sale of two 'positronic robot' stories, 'Reason' and 'Liar!' virtually back to back put me all on fire to do more of the same. When I suggested still another story of the sort to Campbell on February 3, 1941, he approved, but he said he didn't want me, this early in the game, tying myself down too completely into a rigid formula. He suggested I do other kinds of stories first. I was a good boy; I obeyed.

On that very day, in fact, I decided to try fantasy again. I wrote a short one (1,500 words) called 'Masks,' and heaven only knows what it was about, for I don't. I submitted it to Campbell for *Unknown* on February 10, and he rejected it. It is gone; it no longer exists.

Later that month I also wrote a short story called 'The Hazing,' intended for Pohl. I submitted it to him on February 24, and he rejected it at once. Eventually I submitted it to *Thrilling Wonder Stories*. They requested a revision, I obliged, and they accepted it on July 29, 1941.

16: The Hazing

The campus of Arcturus University, on Arcturus's second planet, Eron, is a dull place during mid-year vacations and, moreover, a hot one, so that Myron Tubal, sophomore, found life boring and uncomfortable. For the fifth time that day, he looked in at the Undergraduate Lounge in a desperate attempt at locating an acquaintance, and was at last gratified to behold Bill Sefan, a green-skinned youngster from Vega's fifth planet.

Sefan, like Tubal, had flunked Biosociology and was staying through vacation to study for a make-up exam. Things like that weave strong bonds between sophomore and sophomore.

Tubal grunted a greeting, dropped his huge hairless body – he was a native of the Arcturian System itself – into the largest chair and said:

'Have you seen the new freshmen yet?'

'Already! It's six weeks before the fall semester starts!'

Tubal yawned. 'These are a special breed of frosh. They're the very first batch from the Solarian System – ten of them.'

'Solarian System? You mean that new system that joined the Galactic Federation three–four years ago?'

'That's the one. Their world capital is called Earth, I think.'

'Well, what about them?'

'Nothing much. They're just here, that's all. Some of them have hair on the upper lip, and very silly it looks, too. Otherwise, they look like any of a dozen or so other breeds of Humanoids.'

It was at this point that the door flew open and little Wri Forase ran in. He was from Deneb's single planet, and the short, gray fuzz that covered his head and face bristled with agitation, while his large purple eyes gleamed excitedly.

'Say,' he twittered breathlessly, 'have you seen the Earthmen?'

Sefan sighed. 'Isn't anyone ever going to change the subject? Tubal was just telling me about them.'

'He was?' Forase seemed disappointed. 'But – but did he tell

Thrilling Wonder Stories, October 1942
Copyright © 1942 by Better Publications, Inc.

you these were that abnormal race they made such a fuss over when the Solarian System entered the Federation?'

'They looked all right to me,' said Tubal.

'I'm not talking about them from the physical standpoint,' said the Denebian disgustedly. 'It's the mental aspect of the case. Psychology! That's the stuff!' Forase was going to be a psychologist some day.

'Oh, that! Well, what's wrong with them?'

'Their mob psychology as a race is all wrong,' babbled Forase. 'Instead of becoming less emotional with numbers, as is the case with every other type of Humanoid known, they become *more* emotional! In groups, these Earthmen riot, panic, go crazy. The more there are, the worse it is. So help me, we even invented a new mathematical notation to handle the problem. Look!'

He had his pocket-pad and stylus out in one rapid motion; but Tubal's hand clamped down upon them before the stylus so much as made a mark.

Tubal said, 'Whoa! I've got a walloping lulu of an idea.'

'Imagine!' murmured Sefan.

Tubal ignored him. He smiled again, and his hand rubbed thoughtfully over his bald dome.

'Listen,' he said, with sudden briskness. His voice dropped to a conspiratorial whisper.

Albert Williams, late of Earth, stirred in his sleep and became conscious of a prodding finger exploring the space between his second and third ribs. He opened his eyes, swiveled his head, stared stupidly; then gasped, shot upright and reached for the light switch.

'Don't move,' said the shadowy figure beside his bed. There was a muted click, and the Earthman found himself centered in the pearly beam of a pocket flash.

He blinked and said, 'Who the blasted devil are you?'

'You are going to get out of bed,' replied the apparition stolidly. 'Dress, and come with me.'

Williams grinned savagely. 'Try and make me.'

There was no answer, but the flash beam shifted slightly and fell upon the shadow's other hand. It held a 'neuronic whip,' that pleasant little weapon that paralyzes the vocal chords and twists nerves into so many knots of agony. Williams swallowed hard, and got out of bed.

He dressed in silence, and then said:

'All right, what do I do now?'

The gleaming 'whip' gestured, and the Earthman moved toward the door.

'Just walk ahead,' said the unknown.

Williams moved out of the room, along the silent corridor, and down eight stories without daring to look back. Out upon the campus he stopped, and felt metal probe the small of his back.

'Do you know where Obel Hall is?'

Williams, nodding, began walking. He walked past Obel Hall, turned right at University Avenue, and after half a mile stepped off the roads and past the trees. A spaceship hulked dimly in the darkness, with ports closely curtained and only a dim light showing where the airlock opened a crack.

'Get in!' He was shoved up a flight of stairs and into a small room.

He blinked, looked about him and counted aloud.

'– seven, eight, nine, and I make ten. They've got us all, I guess.'

'It's no guess,' growled Eric Chamberlain sourly. 'It's a certainty.' He was rubbing his hand. 'I've been here an hour.'

'What's wrong with the mitt?' asked Williams.

'I sprained it on the jaw of the rat that brought me here. He's as tough as a spaceship's hull.'

Williams seated himself cross-legged upon the floor and rested his head against the wall.

'Has anyone any idea as to what this is all about?'

'Kidnapping!' said little Joey Sweeney. His teeth were chattering.

'What the devil for?' snorted Chamberlain. 'If any of us are milionaires, I hadn't heard of it. I know I'm not!'

Williams said, 'Look, let's not go off the deep end. Kidnaping or anything of that sort is out. These people can't be criminals. It stands to reason that a civilization that has developed psychology to the extent this Galactic Federation has, would be able to wipe out crime without raising a sweat.'

'Pirates,' grunted Lawrence Marsh. 'I don't think so, but it's just a suggestion.'

'Nuts!' said Williams. 'Piracy is a frontier phenomenon. This region of space has been civilized for tens of millennia.'

'Just the same, they had guns,' insisted Joe, 'and I don't like it.' He had left his glasses in his room and peered about in near-sighted anxiety.

'That doesn't mean much,' answered Williams. 'Now, I've been thinking. Here we are – ten newly arrived freshmen at Arcturus U. On our first night here, we're bundled mysteriously out of our rooms and into a strange spaceship. That suggests something to me. How about it?'

Sidney Morton raised his head from his arms long enough to say sleepily:

'I've thought of it, too. It looks like we're in for one hell of a hazing. Gents, I think the local sophs are just having good, clean fun.'

'Exactly,' agreed Williams. 'Anyone have any other ideas?'

Silence. 'All right, then, so there isn't anything to do but wait. Personally, I'm going to catch up on my sleep. They can wake me up if they need me.'

There was a jar at that moment and he fell off balance.

'Well, we're off – wherever we're going.'

Moments later, Bill Sefan hesitated just an instant before entering the control room. When he finally did, it was to face a highly excited Wri Forase.

'How is it working?' demanded the Denebian.

'Rotten,' responded Sefan sourly. 'If they're panicked, then I'm damned. They're going to sleep.'

'Asleep! All of them? But what were they saying?'

'How do I know? They weren't speaking Galactic, and I can't make head or tail out of their infernal foreign gibberish.'

Forase threw his hands into the air in disgust.

Tubal spoke finally. 'Listen, Forase, I'm cutting a class in Biosoc. – which I can't afford. You guaranteed the psychology of this stunt. If it turns out to be a flop, I'm not going to like it.'

'Well, for the love of Deneb,' grated Forase desperately, 'you two are a fine pair of yellow-bellies! Did you expect them to start screaming and kicking right off? Sizzling Arcturus! Wait till we get to the Spican System, will you? When we maroon them overnight —'

He tittered suddenly. 'This is going to be the fanciest trick since they tied those stink-bats to the chromatic organ on Concert Night.'

Tubal cracked a grin, but Sefan leaned back in his chair and remarked thoughtfully.

'What if someone – say, President Wynn – hears about this?'

The Arcturian at the controls shrugged. 'It's only a hazing. They'll go easy.'

'Don't play dumb, M. T. This isn't kid stuff. Planet Four, Spica – the whole Spican System, in fact – is banned to Galactic ships, and you know that. It's got a sub-Humanoid race on it. They're supposed to develop entirely free of interference until they discover interstellar travel on their own. That's the law, and they're strict about it. Space! If they find out about this, we'll be in the soup for fair.'

Tubal turned in his seat. 'How in Arcturus do you expect Prexy Wynn – damn his thick hide! – to find out about us? Now, mind you, I'm not saying the story won't spread around the campus, because half the fun will be killed if we have to keep it to ourselves. But how will names come out? No one will squeal. You know that.'

'Okay,' said Sefan, and shrugged.

And then Tubal said, 'Ready for hyper-space!'

He compressed keys and there was the queer internal wrench that marked the ship's departure from normal space.

The ten Earthmen were rather the worse for wear, and looked it. Lawrence Marsh squinted at his watch again.

'Two-thirty,' he said. 'That's thirty-six hours now. I wish they'd get this over with.'

'This isn't a hazing,' moaned Sweeney. 'It takes too long.'

Williams grew red. 'What do you all look half-dead about? They've been feeding us regularly, haven't they? They haven't tied us up, have they? I should say it was pretty evident that they were taking good care of us.'

'Or,' came Sidney Morton's discontented drawl, 'fattening us up for the slaughter.'

He paused, and everyone stiffened. There was no mistaking the queer internal wrench they had felt.

'Get *that*!' said Eric Chamberlain in sudden frenzy. 'We're back in normal space again, and that means we're only an hour or two from wherever we're going. We've got to do something!'

'Hear, hear,' Williams snorted. 'But what?'

'There are ten of us, aren't there?' shouted Chamberlain, puffing out his chest. 'Well, I've only seen one of them so far. Next time he comes in, and we've got another meal due us pretty soon, we're going to mob him.'

Sweeney looked sick. 'What about the neuronic whip he always carries?'

'It won't kill us. He can't get us all before we pin him down, anyway.'

'Eric,' said Williams bluntly, 'you're a fool.'

Chamberlain flushed and his stub-fingered fists closed slowly.

'I'm just in the mood for a little practice persuasion. Call me that again, will you?'

'Sit down!' Williams scarcely bothered to look up. 'And don't work so hard justifying my epithet. All of us are nervous and keyed-up, but that doesn't mean we ought to go altogether crazy. Not yet, anyway. First of all, even discounting the whip, mobbing our jailer won't be particularly successful.

'We've only seen one, but that one is from the Arcturian System. He's better than seven feet tall, and comfortably past the three-hundred-pound mark. He'd mop us up – all ten of us – with his bare fists. I thought you had one run-in with him already, Eric.'

There was a thickish silence.

Williams added, 'And even if we could knock him out and finish as many others as there may be in the ship, we still haven't the slightest idea where we are or how to get back or even how to run the ship.' A pause. Then, 'Well?'

'Nuts!' Chamberlain turned away, and glowered in silence.

The door kicked open and the giant Acturian entered. With one hand, he emptied the bag he carried, and with the other kept his neuronic whip carefully leveled.

'Last meal,' he grunted.

There was a general scramble for the rolling cans, still lukewarm from recent heating. Morton glared at his with disgust.

'Say,' he spoke stumblingly in Galactic, 'can't you give us a change? I'm tired of this rotten goulash of yours. This is the fourth can!'

153

'So what? It's your last meal,' the Arcturian snapped, and left.

A horrified paralysis prevailed.

'What did he mean by that?' gulped someone huskily.

'They're going to kill us!' Sweeney was round-eyed, the thin edge of panic in his voice.

Williams' mouth was dry and he felt unreasoning anger grow against Sweeney's contagious fright. He paused – the kid was only seventeen – and said huskily, 'Stow it, will you? Let's eat.'

It was two hours later that he felt the shuddering jar that meant the landing and end of the journey. In that time, no one had spoken, but Williams could feel the pall of fear choke tighter with the minutes.

Spica had dipped crimsonly below the horizon and there was a chill wind blowing. The ten Earthmen, huddled together miserably upon the rock-strewn hilltop, watched their captors sullenly. It was the huge Arcturian, Myron Tubal, that did the talking, while the green-skinned Vegan, Bill Sefan, and the fuzzy little Denebian, Wri Forase, remained placidly in the background.

'You've got your fire,' said the Arcturian gruffly, 'and there's plenty of wood about to keep it going. That will keep the beasts away. We'll leave you a pair of whips before we go, and those will do as protection, if any of the aborigines of the planet bother you. You will have to use your own wits as far as food, water and shelter are concerned.'

He turned away. Chamberlain let loose with a sudden roar, and leaped after the departing Arcturian. He was sent reeling back with an effortless heave of the other's arm.

The lock closed after the three other-world men. Almost at once, the ship lifted off the ground and shot upward. Williams finally broke the chilled silence.

'They've left the whips. I'll take one and you can have the other, Eric.'

One by one, the Earthmen dropped into a sitting position, back to the fire, frightened, half panicky.

Williams forced a grin. 'There's plenty of game about – the region is well-wooded. Come on, now, there are ten of us and they've got to come back sometime. Let's show them we Earthmen can take it. How about it, fellows?'

He was talking aimlessly now. Morton said listlessly.

'Why don't you shut up? You're not making this any easier.'

Williams gave up. The pit of his own stomach was turning cold.

The twilight blackened into night, and the circle of light about the fire contracted into a little flickering area that ended in shadows. Marsh gasped suddenly, and his eyes went wide.

'There's some – something coming!'

The stir that followed froze itself into attitudes of breathless attention.

'You're crazy,' began Williams huskily – and stopped dead at the unmistakable, slithering sound that reached his ears.

'Grab your whip!' he screamed to Chamberlain.

Joey Sweeney laughed suddenly – a strained, high-pitched laugh.

And then – there was a sudden shrieking in the air, and the shades charged down upon them.

Things were happening elsewhere, too.

Tubal's ship lazed outward from Spica's fourth planet, with Bill Sefan at the controls. Tubal himself was in his own cramped quarters, polishing off a huge flagon of Denebian liquor in two gulps.

Wri Forase watched the operation sadly.

'It cost twenty credits a bottle,' he said, 'and I only have a few left.'

'Well, don't let me hog it,' said Tubal magnanimously, 'match me bottle for bottle. It's all right with me.'

'One swig like that,' grumbled the Denebian, 'and I'd be out till the Fall exams.'

Tubal paid scant attention. 'This,' he began, 'is going to make campus history as the hazing stunt —'

And at this point, there was a sharp, singing pinging *ping-g-g-g*, scarcely muffled by intervening walls, and the lights went out.

Wri Forase felt himself pressed hard against the wall. He struggled for breath and stuttered out in gasps.

'B-by Space, we're at f-full acceleration! What's wr-rong with the equalizer?'

'Damn the equalizer!' roared Tubal, heaving to his feet. 'What's wrong with the ship?'

He stumbled out the door, into the equally dark corridor, with Forase crawling after him. When they burst into the control room, they found Sefan surrounded by the dim emergency lights, his green skin shining with perspiration.

'Meteor,' he croaked. 'It played hob with our power distributors. It's all going into acceleration. The lights, heating units and radio are all out of commission, while the ventilators are just barely limping.' He added, 'And Section Four is punctured.'

Tubal gazed about him wildly. 'Idiot! Why didn't you keep your eye on the mass indicator?'

'I did, you overgrown lump of putty,' howled Sefan, 'but it never registered! It – never – registered! Isn't that just what you'd expect from a second-hand jalopy, rented for two hundred credits? It went through the screen as if it were empty ether.'

'Shut up!' Tubal flung open the suit-compartments and groaned. 'They're all Arcturian models. I should have checked up. Can you handle one of these, Sefan?'

'Maybe.' The Vegan scratched a doubtful ear.

In five minutes, Tubal swung into the lock and Sefan, stumbling awkwardly, followed after. It was half an hour before they returned.

Tubal removed his head-piece. 'Curtains!'

Wri Forase gasped. 'You mean – we're through?'

The Arcturian shook his head. 'We can fix it, but it will take time. The radio is ruined for good, so we can't get help.'

'Get help!' Forase looked shocked. 'That's all we need. How would we explain being inside the Spican system? We might as well commit suicide as send out radio calls. As long as we can get back without help, we're safe. Missing a few more classes won't hurt us too much.'

Sefan's voice broke in dully. 'But what about those panicky Earthmen back on Spica Four?'

Forase's mouth opened, but he didn't say a word. It closed again, and if ever a Humanoid looked sick, Forase was that Humanoid.

That was only the beginning.

It took a day and a half to unscramble the space jalopy's power lines. It took two more days to decelerate to safe turning point. It took four days to return to Spica IV. Total – eight days.

When the ship hovered once more over the place where they had marooned the Earthmen, it was midmorning, and the Tubal's face as he surveyed the area through the televisor was a study in length. Shortly he broke a silence that had long since become sticky.

'I guess we've made every boner we could possibly have made. We landed them right outside a native village. There's no sign of the Earthmen.'

Sefan shook his head dolefully. 'This is a bad business.'

Tubal buried his head in his long arms clear down to the elbows.

'That's the finish. If they didn't scare themselves to death, the natives got them. Violating prohibited solar systems is bad enough – but it's just plain murder now, I guess.'

'What we've got to do,' said Sefan, 'is to get down there and find out if there are any still alive. We owe them that much. After that —'

He swallowed. Forase finished in a whisper.

'After that, it's expulsion from the U., psycho-revision – and manual labor for life.'

'Forget it!' barked Tubal. 'We'll face that when we have to.'

Slowly, very slowly, the ship circled downward and came to rest on the rocky clearing where, eight days previously, ten Earthmen had been left stranded.

'How do we handle these natives?' Tubal turned to Forase with raised eyebrow ridges (there was no hair on them, of course). 'Come on, son, give with some sub-Humanoid psychology. There are only three of us and I don't want any trouble.'

Forase shrugged and his fuzzy face wrinkled in perplexity. 'I've just been thinking about that, Tubal. I don't know any.'

'What!' exploded Sefan and Tubal in twin shouts.

'No one does,' added the Denebian hurriedly. 'It's a fact. After all, we don't let sub-Humanoids into the Federation till they're fully civilized, and we quarantine them until then. Do

157

you suppose we have much opportunity to study their psychology?'

The Arcturian seated himself heavily. 'This gets better and better. *Think*, Fuzzy-face, will you? Suggest something!'

Forase scratched his head. 'Well – uh – the best we can do is to treat them like normal Humanoids. If we approach slowly, palms spread out, make no sudden movements and keep calm, we ought to get along. Now, remember, I'm saying we *ought* to. I can't be certain about this.'

'Let's go, and damnation with certainty,' urged Sefan impatiently. 'It doesn't matter much, anyway. If I get knocked off here, I don't have to go back home.' His face took on a hunted look. 'When I think of what my family is going to say —'

They emerged from the ship and sniffed the atmosphere of Spica's fourth planet. The sun was at meridian, and loomed overhead like a large orange basketball. Off in the woods, a bird called once in a creaky caw. Utter silence descended.

'Hmph!' said Tubal, arms akimbo.

'It's enough to make you feel sleepy. No signs of life at all. Now, which way is the village?'

There was a three-way dispute about this, but it didn't last long. The Arcturian first, the other two tagging along, they strode down the slope and toward the straggling forest.

A hundred feet inside, the trees came alive, as a wave of natives dropped noiselessly from the overhanging branches. Wri Forase went under at the very first of the avalanche. Bill Sefan stumbled, stood his ground momentarily, then went over backward with a grunt.

Only huge Myron Tubal was left standing. Legs straddled wide, and whooping hoarsely, he laid about right and left. The attacking natives hit him and bounced off like drops of water from a whirling flywheel. Modeling his defense on the principle of the windmill, he backed his way against a tree.

Here he made a mistake. On the lowest branch of that tree squatted a native at once more cautious and more brainy than his fellows. Tubal had already noticed that the natives were equipped with stout, muscular tails, and had made a mental note of the fact. Of all the races in the Galaxy, only one other, Homo Gamma Cepheus, possessed tails. What he *didn't* notice, however, was that these tails were prehensile.

This he found out almost immediately, for the native in the

branch above his head looped his tail downward, flashed it about Tubal's neck and contracted it.

The Arcturian threshed wildly in agony, and the tailed attacker was jerked from his tree. Suspended head-first and whirled about in huge sweeps, the native nevertheless maintained his hold and tightened that tail-grip steadily.

The world blacked out. Tubal was unconscious before he hit the ground.

Tubal came to slowly, unpleasantly aware of the stinging stiffness of his neck. He tried vainly to rub that stiffness, and it took a few seconds to realize that he was tied tightly. The fact startled him into alertness. He became aware, first, that he was lying on his stomach; second, of the horrible din about him; third, of Sefan and Forase bundled up next to him – and last, that he could not break his bonds.

'Hey, Sefan, Forase! Can you hear me?'

It was Sefan that answered joyfully. 'You old Draconian goat! We thought you were out for good.'

'I don't die so easy,' grunted the Arcturian 'Where are we?'

There was a short pause.

'In the native village, I imagine,' Wri Forase said dully. 'Did you ever hear such a noise? The drum hasn't stopped a minute since they dumped us here.'

'Have you see anything of —'

Hands were upon Tubal, and he felt himself whirled about. He was in a sitting posture now and his neck hurt worse than ever. Ramshackle huts of thatch and green logs gleamed in the early afternoon sun. In a circle about them, watching in silence, were dark-skinned, long-tailed natives. There must have been hundreds, all wearing feathered head-dresses and carrying short, wickedly barbed spears.

Their eyes were upon the row of figures that squatted mysteriously in the foreground, and upon these Tubal turned his angry glare. It was plain that they were the leaders of the tribe. Dressed in gaudy, fringed robes of ill-tamed skins, they added further to their barbaric impressiveness by wearing tall wooden masks painted into caricatures of the human face.

With measured steps, the masked horror nearest the Humanoids approached.

'Hello,' it said, and the mask lifted up and off. 'Back so soon?'

For quite a long while, Tubal and Sefan said absolutely nothing, while Wri Forase went into a protracted fit of coughing.

Finally, Tubal drew a long breath. 'You're one of the Earthmen, aren't you?'

'That's right. I'm Al Williams. Just call me Al.'

'They haven't killed you yet?'

Williams smiled happily. 'They haven't killed any of us. Quite the contrary. Gentlemen,' he bowed extravagantly, 'meet the new tribal – er – gods.'

'The new tribal *what*?' gasped Forase. He was still coughing.

'– er – gods. Sorry, but I don't know the Galactic word for a god.'

'What do you "gods" represent?'

'We're sort of supernatural entities – objects to be worshipped. Don't you get it?'

The Humanoids stared unhappily.

'Yes, indeed,' Williams grinned, 'we're persons of great power.'

'What are you talking about?' exclaimed Tubal indignantly. 'Why should they think you were of great power? You Earth people are below average physically – well below!'

'It's the psychology of the thing,' explained Williams. 'If they see us landing in a large, gleaming vehicle that travels mysteriously through the air, and then takes off in a burst of rocket-flame – they're bound to consider us supernatural. That's elementary barbaric psychology.'

Forase's eyes seemed on the point of dropping out as Williams continued.

'Incidentally, what detained you? We figure it was all a hazing of some sort, and it was, wasn't it?'

'Say,' broke in Sefan, 'I think you're feeding us a lot of bull! If they thought you people were gods, why didn't they think we were? We had the ship, too, and —'

'That,' said Williams, 'is where *we* started to interfere. We explained – via pictures and sign language – that you people were devils. When you finally came back – and say, were we glad to see that ship coming down – they knew what to do.'

160

'What,' asked Forase, with a liberal dash of awe in his voice, 'are "devils"?'

Williams sighed. 'Don't you Galaxy people know anything?' Tubal moved his aching neck slowly. 'How about letting us up now?' he rumbled. 'I've got a crick in my neck.'

'What's your hurry? After all, you were brought here to be sacrificed in our honor.'

'*Sacrificed!*'

'Sure. You're to be carved up with knives.'

There was a horror-laden silence. 'Don't give us any of that comet-gas!' Tubal managed to grind out at last. 'We're not Earthmen who get panicky or scared, you know.'

'Oh, we know *that*! I wouldn't fool you for the world. But simple ordinary savage psychology always goes for a little human sacrifice, and —'

Sefan writhed against his bonds and tried to throw himself in a rage at Forase.

'I thought you said no one knew any sub-Humanoid psychology! Trying to alibi your ignorance, weren't you, you shriveled, fuzz-covered, pop-eyed son of a half-breed Vegan lizard! A fine mess we're in now!'

Forase shrank away. 'Now, wait! Just —'

Williams decided the joke had gone far enough.

'Take it easy,' he soothed. 'Your clever hazing blew up right in your faces – it blew up beautifully – but we're not going to carry it too far. I guess we've had enough fun out of you fellows. Sweeney is with the native chief now, explaining that we're leaving and taking you three with us. Frankly, I'll be glad to get going – Wait a while, Sweeney's calling me.'

When Williams returned two seconds later, his expression was peculiar, having turned a bit greenish. In fact, he got greener by the second.

'It looks,' he gulped throatily, 'as if our counter-haze has blow up in *our* faces. The native chief *insists* on the sacrifice!'

Silence brooded, while the three Humanoids thought over the state of affairs. For moments, none of them could say a word.

'I've told Sweeney,' Williams added, glumly, 'to go back and tell the chief that if the doesn't do as we say, something terrible

161

is going to happen to his tribe. But it's pure bluff and he may not fall for it. Uh, – I'm sorry, fellows. I guess we went too far. If it looks really bad, we'll cut you loose and join in the fight.'

'Cut us loose now,' growled Tubal, his blood running cold. 'Let's get this over with!'

'Wait!' cried Forase frantically. 'Let the Earthmen try some of his psychology. Go ahead, Earthman. Think hard!'

Williams thought until his brain began to hurt.

'You see,' he said weakly, 'we've lost some of our godlike prestige, ever since we were unable to cure the chief's wife. She died yesterday.' He nodded abstractedly to himself. 'What we need is an impressive miracle. Er – have you fellows anything in your pockets?'

He knelt beside them and began searching. Wri Forase had a stylus, a pocket-pad, a thin-toothed comb, some anti-itch powder, a sheaf of credits and a few odds and ends. Sefan had a collection of similar nondescript material.

It was from Tubal's hip pocket that Williams withdrew a small black gunlike object with a huge hand-grip and a short barrel.

'What's this?'

Tubal scowled. 'Is that what I've been sitting on all this while? It's a weld-gun that I used to fix up a meteor puncture in our ship. It's no good; power's almost gone.'

Williams' eyes kindled. His whole body galvanized with excitement.

'That's what you think! You Galaxy men never could see farther than your noses. Why don't you come down to Earth for a spell – and get a new point of view?'

Williams was running toward his fellow conspirators now.

'Sweeney,' he howled, 'you tell that damned monkey-tailed chief that in just about one second, I'm going to get sore and pull the whole sky down over his head. Get tough!'

But the chief did not wait for the message. He gestured defiance and the natives made a united rush. Tubal roared, and his muscles cracked against the bonds. The weld-gun in William's hand flared into life, its feeble power beaming outward.

The nearest native hut went up in sudden flames. Another followed – and another – and the fourth – and then the weld-gun went dead.

But it was enough. Not a native remained standing. All were groveling on their faces, wailing and shrieking for pardon. The chief wailed and shrieked loudest of all.

'Tell the chief,' said Williams to Sweeney, 'that that's just a little, insignificant sample of what we're thinking of doing to him!'

To the Humanoids, as he cut the rawhide holding them, he added complacently,

'Just some simple, ordinary savage psychology.'

It was only after they were back in their ship and off in space again that Forase locked up his pride.

'But I thought Earthmen had never developed mathematical psychology! How did you know all that sub-Humanoid stuff? No one in the Galaxy has got that far yet!'

'Well,' Williams grinned, 'we have a certain amount of rule-of-thumb knowledge about the workings of the uncivilized mind. You see – we come from a world where most people, in a manner of speaking, are still uncivilized. So we *have* to know!'

Forase nodded slowly. 'You screwball Earthmen! At least, this little episode has taught us all one thing.'

'What's that?'

'Never,' said Forase, dipping a second time into Earth slang, 'get tough with a bunch of nuts. They may be nuttier than you think!'

THE END

In going through my stories while preparing this book, I found 'The Hazing' to be the only *published* story concerning which I could remember nothing from the title alone. Even as I reread it, nothing clicked. If I had been given the story without my name on it and had been asked to read it and guess the author, I would probably have been stumped. Maybe that means something.

It does seem to me, though, that the story is set against a 'Homo Sol' background.

I had better luck with Fred Pohl with another story, 'Super-Neutron,' which I wrote at the end of the same February in which I did 'Masks' and 'The Hazing.' I submitted it to him on

March 3, 1941, and he accepted it on March 5.

By that time, less than three years after my first submission, I was clearly becoming rather impatient with rejections. At least, the news of the acceptance of 'Super-Neutron' is greeted in my diary with an 'It's about time I made a sale – five and a half weeks since the last one.'

It was at the seventeenth meeting of the Honorable Society of
Ananias that we got the greatest scare of our collective lives
and consequently elected Gilbert Hayes to the office of Perpetual President.

The Society is not a large one. Before the election of Hayes
there were only four of us: John Sebastian, Simon Murfree,
Morris Levin and myself. On the first Sunday of every month
we met at luncheon, and on these monthly occasions justified
our Society's title by gambling the dinner check on our ability
to lie.

It was quite a complicated process, with strict Parliamentary
rules. One member spun a yarn each meeting as his turn came
up, and two conditions had to be adhered to. His story had to
be an outrageous, complicated, fantastic lie; *and*, it had to
sound like the truth. Members were allowed to – and did –
attack any and every point of the story by asking questions or
demanding explanations.

Woe to the narrator who did not answer all questions immediately, or who, in answering, involved himself in a contra-
diction. The dinner-check was his! Financial loss was slight;
but the disgrace was great.

And then came that seventeenth meeting – and Gilbert Hayes.
Hayes was one of several non-members who attended occasionally to listen to the after-dinner whopper, paying his
own check, and, of course, being forbidden to participate; but
on this occasion he was the only one present aside from the
regular members.

Dinner was over, I had been voted into the chair (it was my
regular turn to preside), and the minutes had been read, when
Hayes leaned forward and said quietly, 'I'd like a chance today, gentlemen.'

I frowned, 'In the eyes of the Society you are non-existent,
Mr. Hayes. It is impossible for you to take part.'

'Then just let me make a statement,' he rejoined. 'The Solar

Astonishing Stories, September 1941
Copyright © 1941 by Fictioneers, Inc.
Copyright renewed © 1968 by Isaac Asimov

System is coming to an end at exactly seventeen and a half minutes after two this afternoon.'

There was a devil of a stir, and I looked at the electric clock over the television receiver. It was 1.14 P.M.

I said hesitantly, 'If you have anything to substantiate that extraordinary statement, it should be most interesting. It is Mr. Levin's turn today, but if he is willing to waive it, and if the rest of the Society agrees —'

Levin smiled and nodded, and the others joined in.

I banged the gavel, 'Mr. Hayes has the floor.'

Hayes lit his cigar and gazed at it pensively. 'I have little more than an hour, gentlemen, but I'll start at the beginning – which is about fifteen years ago. At that time, though I've resigned since, I was an astrophysicist at Yerkes Observatory – young, but promising. I was hot on the trail of the solution to one of the perennial puzzles of astrophysics – the source of the cosmic rays – and full of ambition.'

He paused, and continued in a different tone, 'You know, it is strange that with all our scientific advance in the last two centuries we have never found either that mysterious source or the equally mysterious reason for the explosion of a star. They are the two eternal puzzles and we know as little about them today as we did in the days of Einstein, Eddington and Millikan.

'Still, as I say, I thought I had the cosmic ray by the tail, so I set out to check my ideas by observation, as for that I had to go out in space. It wasn't, however, as easy as all that. It was in 2129, you see, just after the last war, and the Observatory was about broke – as weren't we all?

'I made the best of it. I hired an old second-hand '07 model, piled my apparatus in and set out alone. What's more, I had to sneak out of port without clearance papers, not wishing to go through the red tape the occupation army would have put me through. It was illegal, but I wanted my data – so I headed out at a right angle to the ecliptic, in the direction of the South Celestial Pole, approximately, and left Sol a billion miles behind me.

'The voyage I made, and the data I collected are unimportant. I never reported one or the other. It was the planet I found that makes the story.'

At this point, Murfree raised those bushy eyebrows of his and grunted, 'I would like to warn the gentleman, Mr. Chairman. No member has yet escaped with his skin with the phony planet.'

Hayes smiled grimly, 'I'll take my chance. – To continue; it was on the eighteenth day of my trip that I first detected the planet, and as a little orange disc the size of a pea. Naturally, a planet in that region of space is something of a sensation. I headed for it; and immediately discovered that I had not even scratched the surface of that planet's queerness. To exist there at all was phenomenal – but it likewise possessed absolutely no gravitational field.'

Levin's wine-glass crashed to the floor. 'Mr. Chairman,' he gasped, 'I demand the gentleman's immediate disqualification. No mass can exist without distorting the space in its neighborhood and thus creating a gravitational field. He has made an impossible statement, and should therefore be disqualified.' His face was an angry red.

But Hayes held his hand up, 'I demand time, Mr. Chairman. The explanation will be forthcoming in due course. To make it now would only complicate things. Please, may I continue?'

I considered, 'In view of the nature of your story, I am disposed to be lenient. Delay is granted, but please remember that an explanation will be required eventually. You will lose without it.'

'All right,' said Hayes. 'For the present, you will have to accept my statement that the planet had no gravity *at all*. That is definite, for I had complete astronomical equipment upon my ship, and though my instruments were very sensitive, they registered a dead zero.

'It worked the other way around as well, for the planet was not affected by the gravity of other masses. Again, I stress the point that it was not affected *at all*. This I was not able to determine at the time, but subsequent observation over a period of years, showed that the planet was traveling in a straight-line orbit and at a constant speed. As it was well within the sun's influence, the fact that its orbit was neither elliptical nor hyperbolic, and that, though approaching the sun, it was not accelerating, showed definitely that it was independent of solar gravity.'

'Wait a while, Hayes.' Sebastian scowled till his gold premolar gleamed. 'What held this wonderful planet together? Without gravity, why didn't it break up and drift apart?'

'Sheer inertia, for one thing!' was the immediate retort. 'There was nothing to *pull* it apart. A collision with another body of comparable size might have done it – leaving out of consideration the possibility of the existence of some other binding force peculiar to the planet.'

He sighed and continued, 'That doesn't finish the properties of the body. Its red-orange color and its low reflective power, or albedo, set me on another track, and I made the astonishing discovery that the planet was entirely transparent to the whole electro-magnetic spectrum from radio waves to cosmic rays. It was only in the region of the red and yellow portion of the visible-light octave that it was reasonably opaque. Hence, its color.'

'Why was this?' demanded Murfree.

Hayes looked at me, 'That is an unreasonable question, Mr. Chairman. I maintain that I might as well be asked to explain why glass is entirely transparent to anything above or below the ultra-violet region, so that heat, light and X-rays pass through, while it remains opaque to ultra-violet light itself. This sort of thing is a property of the substance itself and must be accepted as such without explanation.'

I whacked my gavel, 'Question declared improper!'

'I object,' declared Murfree. 'Hayes missed the point. Nothing is perfectly transparent. Glass of sufficient thickness will stop even cosmic rays. Do you mean to say that blue light would pass through an entire planet, or heat, for instance?'

'Why not?' replied Hayes. 'That perfect transparency does not exist in your experience does not mean it does not exist altogether. There is certainly no scientific law to that effect. This planet was perfectly transparent except for one small region of the spectrum. That's a definite fact of observation.'

My gavel thumped again, 'Explanation declared sufficient. Continue, Hayes.'

His cigar had gone out and he paused to relight. Then, 'In other respects, the planet was normal. It was not quite the size of Saturn – perhaps half way in diameter between it and Neptune. Subsequent experiments showed it to possess mass, though it was hard to find out how much – certainly more than twice Earth's. With mass, it possessed the usual properties of inertia and momentum – but no gravity.'

It was 1.35 now.

Hayes followed my eyes and said, 'Yes, only three-quarters of an hour is left. I'll hurry! ... Naturally, this queer planet set me to thinking, and that, together with the fact that I had already been evolving certain theories concerning cosmic rays and novae, led to an interesting solution.'

He drew a deep breath, 'Imagine – if you can – our cosmos as a cloud of – well, super-atoms which —'

'I beg your pardon,' exclaimed Sebastian, rising to his feet, 'are you intending to base any of your explanation on drawing analogies between stars and atoms, or between solar systems and electronic orbits?'

'Why do you ask?' questioned Hayes, quietly.

'Because if you do, I demand immediate disqualification. The belief that atoms are miniature solar systems is in a class with the Ptolemaic scheme of the universe. The idea has never been accepted by responsible scientists even at the very dawn of the atomic theory.'

I nodded, 'The gentleman is correct. No such analogy will be permitted as part of the explanation.'

'*I* object,' said Hayes. 'In your school course in elementary physics or chemistry, you will remember that in the study of the properties of gases, it was often pretended, for the sake of illustrating a point, that the gas molecules were tiny billiard balls. Does that mean that gas molecules *are* billiard balls?'

'No,' admitted Sebastian.

'It only means,' drove on Hayes, 'that gas molecules act similarly to billiard balls in some ways. Therefore the actions of one are better visualized by studying the actions of the other. – Well, then, I am only trying to point out a phenomenon in our universe of stars, and for the sake of ease of visualization, I compare it to a similar, and better-known, phenomenon in the world of atoms. That does not mean that stars are magnified atoms.'

I was won over. 'The point is well-taken,' I said, 'You may continue with your explanation, but if it is the judgment of the chair that the analogy becomes a false one, you will be disqualified.'

169

'Good,' agreed Hayes, 'but we'll pass on to another point for a moment. Do any of you remember the first atomic power plants of a hundred and seventy years ago and how they operated?'

'I believe,' muttered Levin, 'that they used the classical uranium fission method for power. They bombarded uranium with slow neutrons and split it up into masurium, barium, gamma rays and more neutrons, thus establishing a cyclic process.'

'That's right! Well, imagine that the stellar universe acted in ways – mind you, this is a metaphor, and not to be taken literally – like a body composed of uranium atoms, and imagine this stellar universe to be bombarded from without by objects which might act in some ways similar to the way neutrons act on an atomic scale.

'Such a super-neutron, hitting a sun, would cause that sun to explode into radiation and more super-neutrons. In other words, you would have a nova.' He looked around for disagreement.

'What justification have you for that idea?' demanded Levin.

'Two; one logical, and one observational. Logic first. Stars are essentially in matter-energy equilibrium, yet suddenly, with no observable change, either spectral or otherwise, they occasionally explode. An explosion indicates instability, but where? Not within the star, for it had been in equilibrium for millions of years. Not from a point within the universe, for novae occur in even concentration throughout the universe. Hence, by elimination, only from a point *outside* the universe.

'Secondly, observation. I came across one of these super-neutrons!'

Said Murfree indignantly: 'I suppose you mean that gravitationless planet you came across?'

'That's right.'

'Then what makes you think it's a super-neutron? You can't use your theory as proof, because you're using the super-neutron itself to bolster the theory. We're not allowed to argue in circles here.'

'I know that,' declared Hayes, stiffly. 'I'll resort to logic again. The world of atoms possesses a cohesive force in the electro-magnetic charge on electrons and protons. The world of stars possesses a cohesive force in gravity. The two forces are only alike in a very general manner. For instance, there are two kinds of electrical charges, positive and negative, but only one kind of gravity – and innumerable minor differences. Still, an analogy this far seems to me to be permissible. A neutron on an atomic scale is a mass without the atomic cohesive force – electric charge. A super-neutron on a stellar scale *ought* to be a mass without the stellar cohesive force – gravity. Therefore, if I find a body without gravity, it seems reasonable to assume it to be a super-neutron.'

'Do you consider that a rigorously scientific proof?' asked Sebastian sarcastically.

'No,' admitted Hayes, 'but it is logical, conflicts with no scientific fact I know of, and works out to form a consistent explanation of novae. That should be enough for our purpose at present.'

Murfree was gazing hard at his fingernails, 'And just where is this super-neutron of yours heading?'

'I see you anticipate,' said Hayes, sombrely. 'It was what I asked myself at the time. At 2.09½ today it hits the sun square, and eight minutes later, the radiation resulting from the explosion will sweep Earth to oblivion.'

'Why didn't you report all this?' barked Sebastian.

'Where was the use? There was nothing to be done about it. We can't handle astronomical masses. All the power available on Earth would not have sufficed to swerve that great body from its path. There was no escape within the Solar System itself, for Neptune and Pluto will turn gaseous along with the other planets, and interstellar travel is as yet impossible. Since man cannot exist independently in space, he is doomed.

'Why tell of all this? What would result after I had convinced them that the death warrant was signed? Suicides, crime waves, orgies, messiahs, evangelists and everything bad and futile you could think of. And after all, is death by nova so bad? It is instantaneous and clean. At 2.17 you're here. At 2.18 you are a mass of attenuated gas. It is so quick and easy a death, it is almost not death.'

There was a long silence after this. I felt uneasy. There are lies and lies, but this sounded like the real thing. Hayes didn't have that little quirk of the lip or that little gleam in the eye which marks the triumph of putting over a good one. He was

171

deadly, deadly serious. I could see the others felt the same. Levin was gulping at his wine, hand shaking.

Finally, Sebastian coughed loudly, 'How long ago did you discover this super-neutron and where?'

'Fifteen years ago, a billion miles or better from the sun.'

'And all that time it has been approaching the sun?'

'Yes; at a constant speed of two miles per second.'

'Good, I've got you!' Sebastian almost laughed his relief. 'Why haven't the astronomers spotted it in all this while?'

'My God,' responded Hayes, impatiently, 'it's clear you aren't an astronomer. Now, what fool would look to the Southern Celestial Pole for a planet, when they're only found in the ecliptic?'

'But,' pointed out Sebastian, 'the region is studied just the same. It is photographed.'

'Surely! For all I know, the super-neutron has been photographed a hundred times – a thousand times if you like – though the Southern Pole is the most poorly watched region of the sky. But what's to differentiate it from a star? With its low albedo, it never passed eleventh magnitude in brightness. After all, it's hard enough to detect any planets in any case. Uranus was spotted many times before Herschel realized it was a planet. Pluto took years to find even when they were *looking* for it. Remember also that without gravity, it causes no planetary perturbation, and that the absence of these removes the most obvious indication of its presence.'

'But,' insisted Sebastian, desperately, 'as it approached the sun, its apparent size would increase and it would begin to show a perceptible disc through a telescope. Even if its reflected light were very faint, it would certainly obscure the stars behind it.'

'True,' admitted Hayes. 'I will not say that a really thorough mapping of the Polar Region would not have uncovered it, but such mapping has been done long ago, and the present cursory searches for novae, special spectral types and so on are by no means thorough. Then, as the super-neutron approaches the sun, it begins to appear only in the dawn and twilight – in evening and morning star fashion – so that observation becomes much more difficult. And so, as a matter of fact, it just has not been observed – and it is what should have been expected.'

Again a silence, and I became aware that my heart was pounding. It was two o'clock even, and we hadn't been able to shake Hayes' story. We had to prove it a lie fast, or I'd die of sheer suspense. We were all of us watching the clock.

Levin took up the fight. 'It's an awfully queer coincidence that the super-neutron should be heading straight for the sun. What are the chances against it? Remember, that would be the same thing as reciting the chances against the truth of the story.'

I interposed, 'That is an illegitimate objection, Mr. Levin. To cite improbability, however great, is not sufficient. Only outright impossibility or citation of inconsistency can serve to disqualify.'

But Hayes waved his hand, 'It's all right. Let me answer. Taking an individual super-neutron and an individual star, the chances of collision, head on, are all but infinitely small. However, statistically, if you shoot enough super-neutrons into the universe, then, given enough time, every star ought to be hit sooner or later. Space must be swarming with super-neutrons – say one every thousand cubic parsecs – so that in spite of the vast distances between the stars and the relative minuteness of the targets, twenty novae occur in our single Galaxy every year – that is, there are twenty collisions between super-neutrons and stars annually.

'The situation is no different really from uranium being bombarded with ordinary neutrons. Only one neutron out of a hundred million may score a hit, but, given time, every nucleus is exploded eventually. If there is an outer-universe intelligence directing this bombardment – pure hypothesis, and *not* part of my argument, please – a year to us is probably an infinitesimal fraction of a second to them. The hits, to them, may be occurring at the rate of billions to their seconds. Energy is being developed, perhaps, to the point where the material this universe composes has become heated to the gaseous state – or whatever passes for the gaseous state there. The universe *is* expanding, you know – like a gas.'

'Still, for the very first super-neutron entering our system to head straight for the sun seems —' Levin ended in a weak stammer.

'Good Lord,' snapped Hayes, 'who told you this *was* the

first? Hundreds may have passed through the system in geologic times. One or two may have passed through in the last thousand years or so. How would we know? Even when one is headed straight for the sun, astronomers don't find it. Perhaps this is the only one that's passed through since the telescope was invented, and before then, of course.... And never forget that, having no gravity, they can go right through the middle of the system, without affecting the planets. Only a hit on the sun registers, and then it's too late.'

He looked at the clock, '2.05! We ought to see it now against the sun.' He stood up and raised the window shade. The yellow sunlight streamed in and I moved away from the dusty shaft of light. My mouth was dry as desert sand. Murfree was mopping his brow, but beads of sweat stood out all along his cheeks and neck.

Hayes took out several slips of exposed film-negative and handed them out, 'I came prepared, you see.' He held one up and squinted at the sun. 'There it is,' he remarked placidly. 'My calculations showed it would be in transit with respect to Earth at the time of collision. Rather convenient!'

I was looking at the sun, too, and felt my heart skip a beat. There, quite clear against the brightness of the sun, was a little, perfectly round, black spot.

'Why doesn't it vaporize?' stammered Murfree. 'It must be almost in the sun's atmosphere.' I don't think he was trying to disprove Hayes' story. He had gone past that. He was honestly seeking information.

'I told you,' explained Hayes, 'that it is transparent to almost all solar radiation. Only the radiation it absorbs can go into heat and that's a very small percentage of all it receives. Besides, it isn't ordinary matter. It's probably much more refactory than anything on Earth, and the Solar surface is only at 6,000 degrees Centigrade.'

He pointed a thumb over his shoulder, 'It's 2.09½, gentlemen. The super-neutron has struck and death is on its way. We have eight minutes.'

We were dumb with something that was just simply unbearable terror. I remember Hayes' voice, quite matter-of-fact, saying, 'Mercury just went!' then a few minutes later, 'Venus has gone!' and lastly, 'Thirty seconds left, gentlemen!'

The seconds crawled, but passed at last, and another thirty seconds, and still another....

And on Hayes' face, a look of astonishment grew and spread. He lifted the clock and stared at it, then peered through his film at the sun once more.

'It's gone!' He turned and faced us, 'It's unbelievable. I had thought of it, but I dared not draw the atomic analogy too far. You know that not all atomic nuclei explode on being hit by a neutron. Some, cadmium, for instance, absorb them one after the other like sponges do water. I —'

He paused again, drew a deep breath, and continued musingly, 'Even the purest block of uranium contains traces of all other elements. And in a universe of trillions of stars acting like uranium, what does a paltry million of cadmium-like stars amount to – nothing! Yet the sun is one of them! Mankind never deserved that!'

He kept on talking, but relief had finally penetrated and we listened no longer. In half-hysterical fashion, we elected Gilbert Hayes to the office of Perpetual President by enthusiastic acclamation, and voted the story the whoppingest lie ever told.

But there's one thing that bothers me. Hayes fills his post well; the Society is more successful than ever – but I think he should have been disqualified after all. His story fulfilled the second condition; it sounded like the truth. But I don't think it fulfilled the *first* condition.

I think it *was* the truth!

THE END

I had series on my mind by now. 'Super-Neutron' was certainly intended to be but the first in a long chain of very clever and very ingenious tales to be told at the meetings of the 'Honorable Society of Ananias.' It didn't work out that way. There was never a second story, not even the beginnings of one, not even the idea for one.

By the time I was writing 'Super-Neutron,' in February of 1941, I had heard of uranium fission and had even discussed it in some detail with Campbell. I managed to refer to it in the course of the story as 'the classical uranium fission method for

175

power.' I also spoke of the metal cadmium as a neutron absorber. It wasn't bad for a story that appeared in 1941, and I sometimes quote it in public to create an impression.

Notice, though, that in the same paragraph in which I mention fission, I also talk of 'masurium.' Actually, masurium was the name given to element #43 in 1926, but that discovery had proven a false alarm. The element was really discovered in 1937 and was given the now-accepted name of 'technetium.' It seems, then, that I could look years into the future and see uranium fission as a practical power source, but I couldn't look a few years into the past and see the correct name for element #43.

This brings us to March 17, 1941, and one of the key turning points of my literary career.

By that day, I had written thirty-one stories. Of these I had already sold seventeen and was yet to sell four more. Of all these stories, three perhaps, and no more, were to turn out to be of more than ephemeral value, and those were the three 'positronic robots' stories I had so far written: 'Robbie,' 'Reason' and 'Liar!'

Looking back on my first three years as a writer, then, I can judge myself to be nothing more than a steady and (perhaps) hopeful third-rater. What's more, that's all I considered myself then, too. Nor did anyone else, at that time, seriously consider me as a potential first-magnitude star in the science fiction heavens – except, maybe, Campbell.

What are the odds, then, that on March 17, 1941, I would sit down and write something that for thirty years now has been considered by a surprising number of people to be the outstanding short classic of magazine science fiction? It was one of those things that couldn't possibly happen – yet it did.

It began when I walked into Campbell's office that day and, as usual, suggested an idea. What it was I don't remember, but whatever it)was he turned it down instantly, not because it was such a bad idea but because he had something he wanted to show me that crowded everything else out of his mind. He had come across a quotation from Ralph Waldo Emerson that went: 'If the stars should appear one night in a thousand years, how would men believe and adore, and preserve for

176

many generations the remembrance of the city of God!'*

Campbell asked me what I thought would happen if the stars would appear at only very long intervals. I had nothing intelligent to suggest.

'I think men would go mad,' he said thoughtfully.

We talked about that notion for quite a while, and I went home to write a story on the subject, one that Campbell and I decided from the start was to be called 'Nightfall.'

I began it that night. I can remember the details exactly: my parents' apartment on Windsor Place in Brooklyn, across the street from the candy store; my own room, just next to the living room, is clear in my mind, with the position of my bed, my desk, my typewriter – and myself getting started.

In years to come, fans would occasionally vote in polls designed to decide the best science fiction short stories of all time. Quite frequently, 'Nightfall' would finish in first place. Just a couple of years ago, the Science Fiction Writers of America polled their membership to decide the best science fiction short stories ever published, for inclusion in a Hall of Fame anthology. ''Nightfall' finished in first place by a sizable margin. And, of course, it has been anthologized a dozen times so far.

With all this, one might argue that 'Nightfall' is the best (or at least the most popular) short science fiction story ever to appear in the magazines. Well, I often wonder, with a shudder, what might have happened on the evening of March 17, 1941, if some angelic spirit had whispered in my ear, 'Isaac, you are about to start writing the best short science fiction story of our time.'

I would undoubtedly have frozen solid. I wouldn't have been able to type a word.

But we don't know the future, and I tapped away blissfully, writing the story and completing it by April 9, 1941. That day, I submitted it to Campbell. He asked for a small revision. I took care of that, and on April 24, 1941, he bought the story.

It set several records for me. It was the longest story I had yet sold, a little over thirteen thousand words. Since Campbell

* Does anyone know in what essay, and in what connection, Emerson says this? Every once in a while I make a desultory search through quotation books or through a collection of Emerson but haven't found it yet. I hope it exists and that the quote is given correctly.

paid me a bonus (my first one), the word rate was one and a quarter cents a word, and the total check was for $166, more than twice as large as any single payment I had ever before received.*

Then, too, 'Nightfall' appeared in the September 1941 issue of *Astounding* as the lead novelette. For the first time, I made the cover of that magazine, with 'Nightfall, by Isaac Asimov' in large, bold letters.

Most important of all, the appearance of 'Nightfall' graduated me by common consent (three years after I had begun my career) into the list of first-rank science fiction writers.

Alas, the story is not included here. It appears (of course) in *Nightfall and Other Stories.*†

The excitement of writing 'Nightfall' and Campbell's hearty and unqualified praise of it ought, one might think, to have set me furiously to work at the typewriter, but it didn't. Spring 1941 was a bad time for me.

I could at any time that half year have left Columbia with a master's degree, but that would have done me no good. I had no job to go to, so I could only mark time and try to raise my value to some prospective employer by going on to the big one, the doctorate.

But that meant I had to take a series of elaborate, interminable 'qualifying examinations,' which I had to pass in order to be allowed to begin research without which I could not get the Ph.D. Passing was difficult and I didn't feel prepared at all, but I had to try it sometime, and besides, if I didn't fall short by too far, I would be allowed to continue taking courses and to repeat the qualifying examinations at some future date.

* 'Black Friar of the Flame' was three thousand words longer than 'Nightfall,' but the former was not to be sold for another half year, and since it earned merely one cent a word, it brought in only $161. Of course, first-time earnings are not the whole story, either. 'Nightfall' has earned me some thousands of dollars since 1941 and will yet earn me more; 'Black Friar of the Flame' has not yet earned me one cent over the original check – till its appearance in this book.
† In telling the story, in that collection, of how 'Nightfall' came to be written, I mentioned that I had received $150 for it, quoting from memory. Once again, I must confess fallibility. The records say $166. It is a small point, and perhaps not worth noting, but I know my readers. By explaining this now, I fend off dozens of letters that will mention the discrepancy and demand an explanation.

So in May I absented myself from the typewriter, studied earnestly for my qualifyings, took them – and didn't pass. I did well enough to earn the option of a future repeat, and I also received my M.A. as a kind of consolation prize, but I was badly disheartened all the same.

(And in the larger world outside, though Great Britain had survived air bombardment, Hitler still seemed unstoppable. He invaded the Balkans and was again winning spectacular victories, and that was disheartening, too.)

It was not till May 24, 1941, that I could bring myself to go back to my writing. I turned out 'Not Final!' which I submitted to Campbell on June 2. It was accepted on the sixth, but without a bonus.

Nicholas Orloff inserted a monocle in his left eye with all
the incorruptible Briticism of a Russian educated at Oxford
and said reproachfully, 'But, my dear Mr. Secretary! Half a
billion dollars!'

Leo Birnam shrugged his shoulders wearily and allowed his
lank body to cramp up still farther in the chair, 'The appro-
priation must go through, commissioner. The Dominion government here at Ganymede is becoming desperate. So far, I've
been holding them off, but as secretary of scientific affairs, my
powers are small.'

'I know, but —' and Orloff spread his hands helplessly.

'I suppose so,' agreed Birnam. 'The Empire government finds
it easier to look the other way. They've done it consistently up
to now. I've tried for a year now to have them understand the
nature of the danger that hangs over the entire System, but it
seems that it can't be done. But I'm appealing to you, Mr.
Commissioner. You're new in your post and can approach this
Jovian affair with an unjaundiced eye.'

Orloff coughed and eyed the tips of his boots. In the three
months since he had succeeded Gridley as colonial commissioner he had tabled unread everything relating to 'those
damned Jovian D.T.'s.' That had been according to the established cabinet policy which had labeled the Jovian affair as
'deadwood' long before he had entered office.

But now that Ganymede was becoming nasty, he found himself sent out to Jovopolis with instructions to hold the 'blasted
provincials' down. It was a nasty spot.

Birnam was speaking, 'The Dominion government has
reached the point where it needs the money so badly, in fact,
that if they don't get it, they're going to publicize everything.'

Orloff's phlegm broke completely, and he snatched at the
monocle as it dropped, 'My dear fellow!'

'I know what it would mean. I've advised against it, but
they're justified. Once the inside of the Jovian affair is out;

Astounding Science Fiction, October 1941
Copyright © 1941 by Street & Smith Publications, Inc.
Copyright renewed © 1968 by Isaac Asimov

once the people know about it; the Empire government won't stay in power a week. And when the Technocrats come in, they'll give us whatever we ask. Public opinion will see to that.'

'But you'll also create a panic and hysteria —'

'Surely! That is why we hesitate. But you might call this an ultimatum. We want secrecy, we *need* secrecy; but we need money more.'

'I see.' Orloff was thinking rapidly, and the conclusions he came to were not pleasant. 'In that case, it would be advisable to investigate the case further. If you have the papers concerning the communications with the planet Jupiter —'

'I have them,' replied Birnam, dryly, 'and so has the Empire government at Washington. That won't do, commissioner. It's the same cud that's been chewed by Earth officials for the last year, and it's gotten us nowhere. I want you to come to Ether Station with me.'

The Ganymedan had risen from his chair, and he glowered down upon Orloff from his six and a half feet of height.

Orloff flushed, 'Are you ordering me?'

'In a way, yes, I tell you there is no time. If you intend acting, you must act quickly or not at all.' Birnam paused, then added, 'You don't mind walking, I hope. Power vehicles aren't allowed to approach Ether Station, ordinarily, and I can use the walk to explain a few of the facts. It's only two miles off.'

'I'll walk,' was the brusque reply.

The trip upward to subground level was made in silence, which was broken by Orloff when they stepped into the dimly lit anteroom.

'It's chilly here.'

'I know. It's difficult to keep the temperature up to norm this near the surface. But it will be colder outside. Here!'

Birnam had kicked open a closet door and was indicating the garments suspended from the ceiling. 'Put them on. You'll need them.'

Orloff fingered them doubtfully, 'Are they heavy enough?'

Birnam was pouring into his own costume as he spoke. 'They're electrically heated. You'll find them plenty warm. That's it! Tuck the trouser legs inside the boots and lace them tight.'

He turned then and, with a grunt, brought out a double compressed-gas cylinder from its rack in one corner of the closet. He glanced at the dial reading; and then turned the stopcock. There was a thin wheeze of escaping gas, at which Birnam sniffed with satisfaction.

'Do you know how to work one of these?' he asked, as he screwed onto the jet a flexible tube of metal mesh, at the other end of which was a curiously curved object of thick, clear glass.

'What is it?'

'Oxygen nosepiece! What there is of Ganymede's atmosphere is argon and nitrogen, just about half and half. It isn't particularly breathable.' He heaved the double cylinder into position, and tightened it in its harness on Orloff's back.

Orloff staggered, 'It's heavy. I can't walk two miles with this.'

'It won't be heavy out there,' Birnam nodded carelessly upward and lowered the glass nosepiece over Orloff's head. 'Just remember to breathe in through the nose and out through the mouth, and you won't have any trouble. By the way, did you eat recently?'

'I lunched before I came to your place.'

Birnam sniffed dubiously, 'Well, that's a little awkward.' He drew a small metal container from one of his pockets and tossed it to the commissioner. 'Put one of those pills in your mouth and keep sucking on it.'

Orloff worked clumsily with gloved fingers and finally managed to get a brown spheroid out of the tin and into his mouth. He followed Birnam up a gently sloped ramp. The blind-alley ending of the corridor slid aside smoothly when they reached it and there was a faint soughing as air slipped out into the thinner atmosphere of Ganymede.

Birnam caught the other's elbow, and fairly dragged him out.

'I've turned your air tank on full,' he shouted. 'Breathe deeply and keep sucking at that pill.'

Gravity had flicked to Ganymedan normality as they crossed the threshold and Orloff after one horrible moment of apparent levitation, felt his stomach turn a somersault and explode.

He gagged, and fumbled the pill with his tongue in desperate attempt at self-control. The oxygen-rich mixture from the air

182

cylinders burned his throat, and gradually Ganymede steadied. His stomach shuddered back into place. He tried walking.

'Take it easy, now,' came Birnam's soothing voice. 'It gets you that way the first few times you change gravity fields quickly. Walk slowly and get the rhythm, or you'll take a tumble. That's right, you're getting it.'

The ground seemed resilient. Orloff could feel the pressure of the other's arm holding him down at each step to keep him from springing too high. Steps were longer now – and flatter, as he got the rhythm. Birnam continued speaking, a voice a little muffled from behind the leather flap drawn loosely across mouth and chin.

'Each to his own world,' he grinned. 'I visited Earth a few years back, with my wife, and had a hell of a time. I couldn't get myself to learn to walk on a planet's surface without a nosepiece. I kept choking – I really did. The sunlight was too bright and the sky was too blue and the grass was too green. And the buildings were right out on the surface. I'll never forget the time they tried to get me to sleep in a room twenty stories up in the air, with the window wide open and the moon shining in.

'I went back on the first spaceship going my way and don't ever intend returning. How are you feeling now?'

'Fine! Splendid!' Now that the first discomfort had gone. Orloff found the low gravity exhilarating. He looked about him. The broken, hilly ground, bathed in a drenching yellow light, was covered with ground-hugging broad-leaved shrubs that showed the orderly arrangement of careful cultivation.

Birnam answered the unspoken question, 'There's enough carbon dioxide in the air to keep the plants alive, and they all have the power to fix atmospheric nitrogen. That's what makes agriculture Ganymede's greatest industry. Those plants are worth their weight in gold as fertilizers back on Earth and worth double or triple that as sources for half a hundred alkaloids that can't be gotten anywhere else in the System. And, of course, everyone knows that Ganymedan green-leaf has Terrestrial tobacco beat bollow.'

There was the drone of a strato-rocket overhead, shrill in the thin atmosphere, and Orloff looked up.

He stopped – stopped dead – and forgot to breathe!

It was his first glimpse of Jupiter in the sky.

It is one thing to see Jupiter, coldly harsh, against the ebon backdrop of space. At six hundred thousand miles, it is majestic enough. But on Ganymede, barely topping the hills, its outlines softened and ever so faintly hazed by the thin atmosphere; shining mellowly from a purple sky in which only a few fugitive stars dare compete with the Jovian giant – it can be described by no conceivable combination of words.

At first, Orloff absorbed the gibbous disk in silence. It was gigantic, thirty-two times the apparent diameter of the Sun as seen from Earth. Its stripes stood out in faint washes of color against the yellowness beneath and the Great Red Spot was an oval splotch of orange near the western rim.

And finally Orloff murmured weakly, 'It's beautiful!'

Leo Birnam stared, too, but there was no awe in his eyes. There was the mechanical weariness of viewing a sight often seen, and besides that an expression of sick revulsion. The chin flap hid his twitching smile, but his grasp upon Orloff's arm left bruises through the tough fabric of the surface suit.

He said slowly, 'It's the most horrible sight in the System.'

Orloff turned reluctant attention to his companion, 'Eh?' Then, disagreeably, 'Oh, yes, those mysterious Jovians.'

At that, the Ganymedan turned away angrily and broke into swinging, fifteen-foot strides. Orloff followed clumsily after, keeping his balance with difficulty.

'Here, now,' he gasped.

But Birnam wasn't listening. He was speaking coldly, bitterly, 'You on Earth can afford to ignore Jupiter. You know nothing of it. It's a little pin prick in your sky, a little flyspeck. You don't live here on Ganymede, watching that damned colossus gloating over you. Up and over fifteen hours – hiding God knows what on its surface. Hiding something that's waiting and waiting and *trying to get out.* Like a giant bomb just waiting to explode!'

'Nonsense!' Orloff managed to jerk out. '*Will* you slow down. I can't keep up.'

Birnam cut his strides in half and said tensely, 'Everyone knows that Jupiter is inhabited, but practically no one ever stops to realize what that means. I tell you that those Jovians, whatever they are, are born to the purple. *They are the natural rulers of the Solar System.*'

'Pure hysteria,' muttered Orloff. 'The Empire government

has been hearing nothing else from your Dominion for a year.'

'And you've shrugged it off. Well, listen! Jupiter, discounting the thickness of its colossal atmosphere, is eighty thousand miles in diameter. That means it possesses a surface one hundred times that of Earth, and more than fifty times that of the entire Terrestrial Empire. Its population, its resources, its war potential are in proportion.'

'Mere numbers —'

'I know what you mean,' Birnam drove on, passionately. 'Wars are not fought with numbers, but with science and with organization. The Jovians have both. In the quarter of a century during which we have communicated with them, we've learned a bit. They have atomic power and they have radio. And in a world of ammonia under great pressure – a world in other words in which almost none of the metals can exist *as* metals for any length of time because of the tendency to form soluble ammonia complexes – they have managed to build up a complicated civilization. That means they have had to work through plastics, glasses, silicates and synthetic building materials of one sort or another. *That* means a chemistry developed just as far as ours is, and I'd put odds on its having developed further.'

Orloff waited long before answering. And then, 'But how certain are you people about the Jovians' last message. We on Earth are inclined to doubt that the Jovians can possibly be as unreasonably belligerent as they have been described.'

The Ganymedan laughed shortly, 'They broke off all communication after that last message, didn't they? That doesn't sound friendly on their part, does it? I assure you that we've all but stood on our ears trying to contact them.

'Here now, don't talk. Let me explain something to you. For twenty-five years here on Ganymede a little group of men have worked their hearts out trying to make sense out of the static-ridden, gravity-distorted set of variable clicks in our radio apparatus, for those clicks were our only connection with living intelligence upon Jupiter. It was a job for a world of scientists, but we never had more than two dozen at the Station at any one time. I was one of them from the very beginning and, as a philologist, did my part in helping construct and interpret the code that developed between ourselves and the Jovians, so that you can see I am speaking from the real inside.

'It was a devil of a heartbreaking job. It was five years before we got past the elementary clicks of arithmetic: three and four are seven; the square root of twenty-five is five; factorial six is seven hundred and twenty. After that, months sometimes passed before we could work out and check by further communication a single new fragment of thought.

'*But* – and this is the point – by the time the Jovians broke off relations, we understood them *thoroughly*. There was no more chance of a mistake in comprehension, than there was of Ganymede suddenly cutting loose from Jupiter. And their last message was a threat, and a promise of destruction. Oh, there's no doubt – there's no doubt!'

They were walking through a shallow pass in which the yellow Jupiter light gave way to a clammy darkness.

Orloff was disturbed. He had never had the case presented to him in this fashion before. He said, 'But the reason, man. What reason did we give them —'

'No reason! It was simply this: the Jovians had finally discovered from our messages – just where and how I don't know – that *we* were *not* Jovians.'

'Well, of course.'

'It wasn't "of course" to them. In their experiences they had never come across intelligences that were not Jovian. Why should they make an exception in favour of those from outer space?'

'You say they were scientists.' Orloff's voice had assumed a wary frigidity. 'Wouldn't they realize that alien environments would breed alien life? *We* knew it. We never thought the Jovians were Earthmen though we had never met intelligences other than those of Earth.'

They were back in the drenching wash of Jupiter light again, and a spreading region of ice glimmered amberly in a depression to the right.

Birnam answered, 'I said they were chemists and physicists – but I never said they were astronomers. Jupiter, my dear commissioner, has an atmosphere three thousand miles or more thick, and those miles of gas block off everything but the Sun and the four largest of Jupiter's moons. The Jovians know nothing of alien environments.'

Orloff considered. 'And so they decided we were aliens.

186

What next?'

'If we weren't Jovians, then, in their eyes, we weren't people. It turned out that a non-Jovian was "vermin" by definition.'

Orloff's automatic protest was cut off short by Birnam, 'In their eyes, I said, vermin we were; and vermin we are. Moreover, we were vermin with the peculiar audacity of having dared to attempt to treat with Jovians – with *human beings*. Their last message was this, word for word – "Jovians are the masters. There is no room for vermin. We will destroy you immediately." I doubt if there was any animosity in that message – simply a cold statement of fact. But they meant it.'

'But why?'

'Why did man exterminate the housefly?'

'Come, sir. You're not seriously presenting an analogy of that nature.'

'Why not, since it is certain that the Jovian considers us a sort of housefly – an insufferable type of housefly that dares aspire to intelligence.'

Orloff made a last attempt, 'But truly, Mr. Secretary, it seems impossible for intelligent life to adopt such an attitude.'

'Do you possess much of an acquaintance with any other type of intelligent life than our own?' came with immediate sarcasm. 'Do you feel competent to pass on Jovian psychology? Do you know just *how* alien Jovians must be physically? Just think of their world with its gravity at two and one half Earth normal; with its ammonia oceans – oceans that you might throw all Earth into without raising a respectable splash; with its three-thousand-mile atmosphere, dragged down by the colossal gravity into densities and pressures in its surface layers that make the sea bottoms of Earth resemble a medium-thick vacuum. I tell you we've tried to figure out what sort of life could exist under those conditions and we've given up. It's thoroughly incomprehensible. Do you expect their mentality, then, to be any more understandable? Never! Accept it as it is. They intend destroying us. That's all we know and all we need to know.'

He lifted a gloved hand as he finished and one finger pointed, 'There's Ether Station just ahead.'

Orloff's head swiveled, 'Underground?'

'Certainly! All except the Observatory. That's that steel and quartz dome to the right – the small one.'

They had stopped before two large boulders that flanked an earthy embankment, and from behind either one a nosepieced, suited soldier in Ganymedan orange, with blasters ready, advanced upon the two.

Birnam lifted his face into Jupiter's light and the soldiers saluted and stepped aside. A short word was barked into the wrist mike of one of them and the camouflaged opening between the boulders fell into two and Orloff followed the secretary into the yawning air lock.

The Earthman caught one last glimpse of sprawling Jupiter before the closing door cut off the surface altogether.

It was no longer beautiful!

Orloff did not quite feel normal again until he had seated himself in the overstuffed chair in Dr. Edward Prosser's private office. With a sigh of utter relaxation, he propped his monocle under his eyebrow.

'Would Dr. Prosser mind if I smoked in here, while we're waiting?' he asked.

'Go ahead,' replied Birnam, carelessly. 'My own idea would be to drag Prosser away from whatever he's fooling with just now, but he's a queer chap. We'll get more out of him if we wait until he's ready for us.' He withdrew a gnarled stick of greenish tobacco from its case, and bit off the edge viciously.

Orloff smiled through the smoke of his own cigarette, 'I don't mind waiting. I still have something to say. You see, for the moment, Mr. Secretary, you gave me the jitters, but, after all, granted that the Jovians intend mischief once they get at us, it remains a fact,' and here he spaced his words emphatically, 'that they can't get at us.'

'A bomb without a fuse, hey?'

'Exactly! It's simplicity itself, and not really worth discussing. You will admit, I suppose, that under no circumstances can the Jovians get away from Jupiter.'

'Under *no* circumstances?' There was a quizzical tinge in Birnam's slow reply. 'Shall we analyze that?'

He stared hard at the purple flame of his cigar. 'It's an old trite saying that the Jovians can't leave Jupiter. The fact has been highly publicized by the sensation-mongers of Earth and Ganymede and a great deal of sentiment has been driveled about the unfortunate intelligences who are irrevocably surface-

188

bound, and must forever stare into the Universe without, watching, watching, wondering, and never attaining.

'But, after all, what holds the Jovians to their planet? Two factors! That's all! The first is the immense gravity field of the planet. Two and a half Earth normal.'

Orloff nodded. 'Pretty bad!' he agreed.

'And Jupiter's gravitational potential is even worse, for because of its greater diameter the intensity of its gravitational field decreases with distance only one tenth as rapidly as Earth's field does. It's a terrible problem – *but it's been solved.*'

'Hey?' Orloff straightened.

'They've got atomic power. Gravity – even Jupiter's – means nothing once you've put unstable atomic nuclei to work for you.'

Orloff crushed his cigarette to extinction with a nervous gesture. 'But their atmosphere —'

'Yes, that's what's stopping them. They're living at the bottom of a three-thousand-mile-deep ocean of it, where the hydrogen of which it is composed is collapsed by sheer pressure to something approaching the density of *solid* hydrogen. It stays a gas because the temperature of Jupiter is above the critical point of hydrogen, but you just try to figure out the pressure that can make hydrogen *gas* half as heavy as water. You'll be surprised at the number of zeros you'll have to put down.

'No spaceship of metal or of any kind of matter can stand that pressure. No Terrestrial spaceship can land on Jupiter without smashing like an eggshell, and no Jovian spaceship can leave Jupiter without exploding like a soap bubble. That problem has not yet been solved, but it will be some day. Maybe tomorrow, maybe not for a hundred years, or a thousand. We don't know, but when it is solved, the Jovians will be on top of us. And it can be solved in a specific way.'

'I don't see how —'

'Force fields! We've got them now, you know.'

'Force fields!' Orloff seemed genuinely astonished, and he chewed the word over and over to himself for a few moments. 'They're used as meteor shields for ships in the asteroid zone – but I don't see the application to the Jovian problem.'

'The ordinary force field,' explained Birnam, 'is a feeble

rarefied zone of energy extending over a hundred miles or more outside the ship. It'll stop meteors but it's just so much empty ether to an object like a gas molecule. *But* what if you took that same zone of energy and compressed it to a thickness of a tenth of an inch. Molecules would bounce off it like this – *ping-g-g-g*! And if you used stronger generators, and compressed the field to a hundredth of an inch, molecules would bounce off even when driven by the unthinkable pressure of Jupiter's atmosphere – and then if you build a ship inside —' He left the sentence dangling.

Orloff was pale. 'You're not saying it can be done?'

'I'll bet you anything you like that the Jovians are *trying* to do it. And *we're* trying to do it right here at Ether Station.'

The colonial commissioner jerked his chair closer to Birnam and grabbed the Ganymedan's wrist. 'Why can't we bombard Jupiter with atomic bombs. Give it a thorough going-over, I mean! With her gravity, and her surface area, we can't miss.'

Birnam smiled faintly, 'We've thought of that. But atomic bombs would merely tear holes in the atmosphere. And even if you could penetrate, just divide the surface of Jupiter by the area of damage of a single bomb and find how many years we must bombard Jupiter at the rate of a bomb a minute before we begin to do significant damage. Jupiter's *big*! Don't ever forget that!'

His cigar had gone out, but he did not pause to relight. He continued in a low, tense voice. 'No, we can't attack the Jovians as long as they're on Jupiter. We must wait for them to come out – and once they do, they're going to have the edge on us in numbers. A terrific, heart-breaking edge – so we'll just have to have the edge on them in science.'

'But,' Orloff broke in, and there was a note of fascinated horror in his voice, 'how can we tell in advance what they'll have?'

'We can't. We've got to scrape up everything we can lay our hands on and hope for the best. But there's one thing we *do* know they'll have and that's force fields. They can't get out without them. And if they have them, we must, too, and that's the problem we're trying to solve here. They will not insure us victory, but without them, we will suffer certain defeat. And now you know why we need money – and more than that. We

190

want Earth itself to get to work. It's got to start a drive for scientific armaments and subordinate everything to that. You see?'

Orloff was on his feet. 'Birnam, I'm with you – a hundred percent with you. You can count on me back in Washington.'

There was no mistaking his sincerity. Birnam gripped the hand outstretched toward him and wrung it – and at the moment, the door flew open and a little pixie of a man hurtled in.

The newcomer spoke in rapid jerks, and exclusively to Birnam. 'Where'd you come from? Been trying to get in touch with you. Secretary said you weren't in. Then five minutes later you show up on your own. Can't understand it.' He busied himself furiously at his desk.

Birnam grinned. 'If you'll take time out, doc, you might say hello to Colonial Commissioner Orloff.'

Dr. Edward Prosser turned on his toe like a ballet dancer and looked the Earthman up and down twice. 'The new un, hey? We getting any money? We ought to. Been working on a shoestring ever since. At that, we might not be needing any. It depends.' He was back at the desk.

Orloff seemed a trifle disconcerted, but Birnam winked impressively, and he contented himself with a glassy stare through the monocle.

Prosser pounced upon a black leather booklet in the recesses of a pigeonhole, threw himself into his swivel chair and wheeled about.

'Glad you came, Birnam,' he said, leafing through the booklet. 'Got something to show you. Commissioner Orloff, too.'

'What were you keeping us waiting for?' demanded Birnam. 'Where were you?'

'Busy! Busy as a pig! No sleep for three nights.' He looked up, and his small puckered face fairly flushed with delight. 'Everything fell into place of a sudden. Like a jig-saw puzzle. Never saw anything like it. Kept us hopping, I tell you.'

'You've gotten the dense force fields you're after?' asked Orloff in sudden excitement.

Prosser seemed annoyed. 'No, not that. Something else. Come on.' He glared at his watch and jumped out of his seat. 'We've got half an hour. Let's go.'

An electric-motored flivver waited outside and Prosser spoke excitedly as he sped the purring vehicle down the ramps into the depths of the Station.

'Theory!' he said. 'Theory! Damned important, that. You set a technician on a problem. He'll fool around. Waste lifetimes. Get nowhere. Just putter about at random. A true scientist works with theory. Lets math solve his problems.' He overflowed with self-satisfaction.

The flivver stopped on a dime before a huge double door and Prosser tumbled out, followed by the other two at a more leisurely pace.

'Through here! Through here!' he said. He shoved the door open and led them down the corridor and up a narrow flight of stairs onto a wall-hugging passageway that circled a huge three-level room. Orloff recognized the gleaming quartz-and-steel pipe-sprouting ellipsoid two levels below as an atomic generator.

He adjusted his monocle and watched the scurrying activity below. An earphoned man on a high stool before a control board studded with dials looked up and waved. Prosser waved back and grinned.

Orloff said, 'You create your force fields here?'

'That's right! Ever see one?'

'No.' The commissioner smiled, ruefully. 'I don't even know what one *is*, except that it can be used as a meteor shield.'

Prosser said, 'It's very simple. Elementary matter. All matter is composed of atoms. Atoms are held together by interatomic forces. Take away atoms. Leave interatomic forces behind. *That's* a force field.'

Orloff looked blank, and Birnam chuckled deep in his throat and scratched the back of his ear.

'That explanation reminds me of our Ganymedan method of suspending an egg a mile high in the air. It goes like this. You find a mountain just a mile high and put the egg on top. Then, keeping the egg where it is, you take the mountain way. That's all.'

The colonial commissioner threw his head back to laugh, and the irascible Dr. Prosser puckered his lips in a pursed symbol of disapproval.

'Come, come. No joke, you know. Force fields most important. Got to be ready for the Jovians when they come.'

192

A sudden rasping bur from below sent Prosser back from the railing.

'Get behind screen here,' he babbled. 'The twenty-millimeter field is going up. Bad radiation.'

The bur muted almost into silence, and the three walked out onto the passageway again. There was no apparent change, but Prosser shoved his hand out over the railing and said, 'Feel!'

Orloff extended a cautious finger, gasped, and slapped out with the palm of his hand. It was like pushing against very soft sponge rubber or superresilient steel springs.

Birnam tried, too. 'That's better than anything we've done yet, isn't it?' He explained to Orloff, 'A twenty-millimeter screen is one that can hold an atmosphere of a pressure of twenty millimeters of mercury against a vacuum without appreciable leakage.'

The commissioner nodded, 'I see! You'd need a seven-hundred-sixty-millimeter screen to hold Earth's atmosphere then.'

'Yes! That would be a unit atmosphere screen. Well, Prosser, is this what got you excited?'

'This twenty-millimeter screen? Of course not. I can go up to two hundred fifty millimeters using the activated vanadium pentasulphide in the praseodymium breakdown. But it's not necessary. Technician would do it and blow up the place. Scientist checks on theory and goes slow.' He winked. 'We're hardening the field now. Watch!'

'Shall we get behind the screen?'

'Not necessary now. Radiation bad only at beginning.'

The burring waxed again, but not as loudly as before. Prosser shouted to the man at the control board, and a spreading wave of the hand was the only reply.

Then the control man waved a clenched fist and Prosser cried, 'We've passed fifty millimeters! Feel the field!'

Orloff extended his hand and poked it curiously. The sponge rubber had hardened! He tried to pinch it between finger and thumb so perfect was the illusion, but here the 'rubber' faded to unresisting air.

Prosser *tch-tched* impatiently. 'No resistance at right angles to force. Elementary mechanics, that is.'

The control man was gesturing again. 'Past seventy,' ex-

plained Prosser. 'We're slowing down now. Critical point is
83·42.'

He hung over the railing and kicked out with his feet at the
other two. 'Stay away! Dangerous!'

And then he yelled, 'Careful! The generator's bucking!'

The bur had risen to a hoarse maximum and the control
man worked frantically at his switches. From within the
quartz heart of the central atomic generator, the sullen red
glow of the bursting atoms had brightened dangerously.

There was a break in the bur, a reverberant roar and a blast
of air that threw Orloff hard against the wall.

Prosser dashed up. There was a cut over his eye. 'Hurt?
No? Good, good! I was expecting something of the sort.
Should have warned you. Let's go down. Where's Birnam?'

The tall Ganymedan picked himself up off the floor and
brushed at his clothes. 'Here I am. What blew up?'

'Nothing blew up. Something buckled. Come on, down we
go.' He dabbed at his forehead with a handkerchief and led the
way downward.

The control man removed his earphones as he approached
and got off his stool. He looked tired, and his dirt-smeared face
was greasy with perspiration.

'The damn thing started going at 82·8, boss. It almost caught
me.'

'It did, did it?' growled Prosser. 'Within limits of error, isn't
it? How's the generator? Hey, Stoddard!'

The technician addressed replied from his station at the
generator, 'Tube 5 died. It'll take two days to replace.'

Prosser turned in satisfaction and said, 'It worked. Went
exactly as presumed. Problem solved, gentlemen. Trouble over.
Let's get back to my office. I want to eat. And then I want to
sleep.'

He did not refer to the subject again until once more behind
the desk in his office, and then he spoke between huge bites of
a liver-and-onion sandwich.

He addressed Birnam, 'Remember the work on space strain
last June. It flopped, but we kept at it. Finch got a lead last
week and I developed it. Everything fell into place. Slick as
goose grease. Never saw anything like it.'

'Go ahead,' said Birnam, calmly. He knew Prosser suffici-

194

ently well to avoid showing impatience.

'You saw what happened. When a field tops 83·42 millimeters, it becomes unstable. Space won't stand the strain. It buckles and the field blows. *Boom!*'

Birnam's mouth dropped open and the arms of Orloff's chair creaked under sudden pressure. Silence for a while, and then Birnam said unsteadily, 'You mean force fields stronger than that are impossible?'

'They're possible. You can create them. But the denser they are, the more unstable they are. If I had turned on the two-hundred-and-fifty-millimeter field, it would have lasted one tenth of a second. Then, blooie! Would have blown up the Station! *And* myself! Technician would have done it. Scientist is warned by theory. Works carefully, the way I did. No harm done.'

Orloff tucked his monocle into his vest pocket and said tremulously, 'But if a force field is the same thing as interatomic forces, why is it that steel has such a strong interatomic binding force without bucking space? There's a flaw there.'

Prosser eyed him in annoyance. 'No flaw. Critical strength depends on number of generators. In steel, each atom is a force-field generator. That means about three hundred billion trillion generators for every ounce of matter. If we could use that many — As it is, one hundred generators would be the practical limit. That only raises the critical point to ninety-seven or thereabout.'

He got to his feet and continued with sudden fervor, 'No. Problem's over, I tell you. Absolutely impossible to create a force field capable of holding Earth's atmosphere for more than a hundredth of a second. Jovian atmosphere entirely out of question. Cold figures say that; backed by experiment. *Space won't stand it!*

'Let the Jovians do their damnedest. They can't get out! That's final! That's final! *That's final!*'

Orloff said, 'Mr. Secretary, can I send a spacegram anywhere in the Station? I want to tell Earth that I'm returning by the next ship and that the Jovian problem is liquidated – entirely and for good.'

Birnam said nothing, but the relief on his face as he shook hands with the colonial commissioner, transfigured the gaunt homeliness of it unbelievably.

And Dr. Prosser repeated, with a birdlike jerk of his head, 'That's *final*!'

Hal Tuttle looked up as Captain Everett of the spaceship *Transparent*, newest ship of the Comet Space Lines, entered his private observation room in the nose of the ship.

The captain said, 'A spacegram has just reached me from the home offices at Tucson. We're to pick up Colonel Commissioner Orloff at Jovopolis, Ganymede, and take him back to Earth.'

'Good. We haven't sighted any ships?'

'No, no! We're way off the regular space lanes. The first the System will know of us will be the landing of the *Transparent* on Ganymede. It will be the greatest thing in space travel since the first trip to the Moon.' His voice softened suddenly, 'What's wrong, Hal? This is *your* triumph, after all.'

Hal Tuttle looked up and out into the blackness of space. 'I suppose it is. Ten years of work, Sam. I lost an arm and an eye in that first explosion, but I don't regret them. It's the reaction that's got me. The problem is solved; my lifework is finished.'

'So is every steel-hulled ship in the System.'

Tuttle smiled. 'Yes. It's hard to realize, isn't it?' He gestured outward. 'You see the stars? Part of the time, there's nothing between them and us. It gives me a queazy feeling.' His voice brooded, 'Nine years I worked for nothing. I wasn't a theoretician, and never really knew where I was headed – just tried everything. I tried a little too hard and space wouldn't stand it. I paid an arm and an eye and started fresh.'

Captain Everett balled his fist and pounded the hull – the hull through which the stars shone unobstructed. There was the muffled thud of flesh striking an unyielding surface – but no response whatever from the invisible wall.

Tuttle nodded, 'It's solid enough, now – though it flicks on and off eight hundred thousand times a second. I got the idea from the stroboscopic lamp. You know them – they flash on and off so rapidly that it gives all the impression of steady illumination.

'And so it is with the hull. It's not on long enough to buckle space. It's not off long enough to allow appreciable leakage of the atmosphere. And the net effect is a strength better than steel.'

196

He paused and added slowly, 'And there's no telling how far we can go. Speed up the intermission effect. Have the field flick off and on millions of times per second – billions of times. You can get fields strong enough to hold an atomic explosion. My lifework!'

Captain Everett pounded the other's shoulder. 'Snap out of it, man. Think of the landing on Ganymede. The devil! It will be great publicity. Think of Orloff's face, for instance, when he finds he is to be the first passenger in history ever to travel in a spaceship with a force-field hull. How do you suppose he'll feel?'

Hal Tuttle shrugged. 'I imagine he'll be rather pleased.'

THE END

With 'Not Final!' I completed my third year as a writer – three years since my initial trip to Campbell's office. In that time I had earned just a hair short of a thousand dollars (not as bad as it sounds in days when college tuition was only four hundred dollars a year) and I had about a quarter of that in my savings account.

Still, you can see that there was nothing in that financial record to lead me to think that writing was a possible way of making a living – especially since I had no dream of ever writing anything but magazine science fiction.

On June 10, 1941, in the course of a talk with Fred Pohl, I mentioned my frustration at not being able to make a sale to *Unknown*. Fred said he had a good idea for a fantasy, and from that it was a short step to an agreement to go halfies. We'd talk the idea over, I would write it, and we'd split the sale, if any, fifty-fifty.

Fred must have been willing because (as I found out three days later) his magazines were doing poorly and he was being relieved of his editorial position.

It was too bad, of course, but not an irredeemable catastrophe. Pohl had had nearly two years of valuable editorial experience, and the time would come when this would stand him in good stead in a much more important and longer-enduring role as editor of *Galaxy*, which during the 1950s and

1960s was to compete with *Astounding* for leadership in the field.

As for myself, I could scarcely complain. Pohl had accepted eight of my stories (over a quarter of those I had written and nearly half of those I had sold up to then). Of these, six had already been published and one ('Super-Neutron') was safely slated for publication in the forthcoming issue of *Astonishing*. That left the ninth, 'Christmas on Ganymede.' It was not yet paid for, nor had it actually been set in type, and, regretfully, Pohl had to return it. However, I sold it within two weeks to *Thrilling Wonder Stories* for a little more than Pohl would have been able to pay me, so no harm was done even there. – And though I regretted the loss of a market, Pohl had safely seen me through the period during which I developed to the point where Campbell and *Astounding* itself could become my major market.

At first, when 'Christmas on Ganymede' was returned, I thought it was because the Pohl magazines had been suspended altogether. If the publishers had intended that, they changed their minds. *Astonishing* continued a couple of years, until it was killed by the World War II paper shortage. *Super Science Stories* survived World War II and even a little past the 1940s, and was yet to publish one more story of mine.

But back to June 10 — Taking Fred's fantasy idea, I wrote the story entirely on my own, calling it 'Legal Rights.' Once again, though, a collaboration didn't succeed. On July 8, Campbell rejected it, the first rejection I had received from him in half a year.

By that time, though, Fred was agenting again. I gave him the story, rather shamefacedly, and forgot about it. He changed the name to 'Legal Rites' (much better) and rewrote it quite a bit. Seven years later, he actually sold it.

19: Legal Rites (with James MacCreigh)

I

Already the stars were out, though the sun had just dipped under the horizon, and the sky of the west was a blood-stuck gold behind the Sierra Nevadas.

'Hey!' squawked Russell Harley. 'Come back!'

But the one-lunged motor of the old Ford was making too much noise; the driver didn't hear him. Harley cursed as he watched the old car career along the sandy ruts on its half-flat tires. Its taillight was saying a red *no* to him. *No*, you can't get away tonight; *no*, you'll have to stay here and fight it out.

Harley grunted and climbed back up the porch stairs of the old wooden house. It was well made, anyhow. The stairs, though half a century old, neither creaked beneath him nor showed cracks.

Harley picked up the bags he'd dropped when he experienced his abrupt change of mind – fake leather and worn out, they were – and carted them into the house. He dumped them on a dust-jacketed sofa and looked around.

It was stifling hot, and the smell of the desert outside had permeated the room. Harley sneezed.

'Water,' he said out loud. 'That's what I need.'

He'd prowled through every room on the ground floor before he stopped still and smote his head. Plumbing – naturally there'd be no plumbing in this hole eight miles out on the desert! A well was the best he could hope for —

If that.

It was getting dark. No electric lights either, of course. He blundered irritatedly through the dusky rooms to the back of the house. The screen door shrieked metallically as he opened it. A bucket hung by the door. He picked it up, tipped it, shook the loose sand out of it. He looked over the 'back yard' – about thirty thousand visible acres of hilly sand, rock and patches of sage and flame-tipped ocotillo.

Weird Tales, September 1950
Copyright © 1950 by Weird Tales

No well.

The old fool got water from somewhere, he thought savagely. Obstinately he climbed down the back steps and wandered out into the desert. Overhead the stars were blinding, a million million of them, but the sunset was over already and he could see only hazily. The silence was murderous. Only a faint whisper of breeze over the sand, and the slither of his shoes.

He caught a glimmer of starlight from the nearest clump of sage and walked to it. There was a pool of water, caught in the angle of two enormous boulders. He stared at it doubtfully, then shrugged. It was water. It was better than nothing. He dipped the bucket in the little pool. Knowing nothing of the procedure, he filled it with a quart of loose sand as he scooped it along the bottom. When he lifted it, brimful, to his lips, he spat out the first mouthful and swore violently.

Then he used his head. He set the bucket down, waited a second for the sand grains to settle, cupped water in his hands, lifted it to his lips. . . .

Pat. HISS. Pat. HISS. Pat. HISS —

'What the hell!' Harley stood up, looked around in abrupt puzzlement. It sounded like water dripping from somewhere, onto a red-hot stove, flashing into sizzling steam. He saw nothing, only the sand and the sage and the pool of tepid, sickly water.

Pat. HISS —

Then he saw it, and his eyes bulged. Out of nowhere it was dripping, a drop a second, a sticky, dark drop that was thicker than water, that fell to the ground lazily, in slow defiance of gravity. And when it struck each drop sizzled and skittered about, and vanished. It was perhaps eight feet from him, just visible in the starlight.

And then, 'Get off my land!' said the voice from nowhere.

Harley got. By the time he got to Rebel Butte three hours later, he was barely managing to walk, wishing desperately that he'd delayed long enough for one more good drink of water, despite all the fiends of hell. But he'd run the first three miles. He'd had plenty of encouragement. He remembered with a shudder how the clear desert air had taken milky shape around the incredible trickle of dampness and had advanced on him theateningly.

And when he got to the first kerosene-lighted saloon of Rebel Butte, and staggered inside, the saloonkeeper's fascinated stare at the front of his shoddy coat showed him strong evidence that he hadn't been suddenly taken with insanity, or drunk on the unaccustomed sensation of fresh desert air. All down the front of him it was, and the harder he rubbed the harder it stayed, the stickier it got. Blood!

'Whiskey!' he said in a strangled voice, tottering to the bar. He pulled a threadbare dollar bill from his pocket, flapped it onto the mahogany.

The blackjack game at the back of the room had stopped. Harley was acutely conscious of the eyes of the players, the bartender and the tall, lean man leaning on the bar. All were watching him.

The bartender broke the spell. He reached for a bottle behind him without looking at it, placed it on the counter before Harley. He poured a glass of water from a jug, set it down with a shot glass beside the bottle.

'I could of told you that would happen,' he said casually. 'Only you wouldn't of believed me. You had to meet Hank for yourself before you'd believe he was there.'

Harley remembered his thirst and drained the glass of water, then poured himself a shot of the whiskey and swallowed it without waiting for the chaser to be refilled. The whiskey felt good going down, almost good enough to stop his internal shakes.

'What are you talking about?' he said finally. He twisted his body and leaned forward across the bar to partly hide the stains on his coat. The saloonkeeper laughed.

'Old Hank,' he said. 'I knowed who you was right away, even before Tom came back and told me where he'd took you. I knowed you was Zeb Harley's no-good nephew, come to take Harley Hall an' sell it before he was cold in the grave.'

The blackjack players were still watching him, Russell Harley saw. Only the lean man farther along the bar seemed to have dismissed him. He was pouring himself another drink, quite occupied with his task.

Harley flushed. 'Listen,' he said, 'I didn't come in here for advice. I wanted a drink. I'm paying for it. Keep your mouth out of this.'

The saloonkeeper shrugged. He turned his back and walked

away to the blackjack table. After a couple of seconds one of the players turned, too, and threw a card down. The others followed suit.

Harley was just getting set to swallow his pride and talk to the saloonkeeper again – he seemed to know something about what Harley'd been through, and might be helpful – when the lean man tapped his shoulder. Harley whirled and almost dropped his glass. Absorbed and jumpy, he hadn't seen him come up.

'Young man,' said the lean one, 'My name's Nicholls. Come along with me, sir, and we'll talk this thing over. I think we may be of service to each other.'

Even the twelve-cylinder car Nicholls drove jounced like a hay-wagon over the sandy ruts leading to the place old Zeb had – laughingly – named 'Harley Hall.'

Russell Harley twisted his neck and stared at the heap of paraphernalia in the open rumble seat. 'I don't like it,' he complained. 'I never had anything to do with ghosts. How do I know this stuff'll work?'

Nicholls smiled. 'You'll have to take my word for it. I've had dealings with ghosts before. You could say that I might qualify as a ghost exterminator, if I chose.'

Harley growled. 'I still don't like it.'

Nicholls turned a sharp look on him. 'You like the prospect of owning Harley Hall, don't you? And looking for all the money your late uncle is supposed to have hidden around somewhere?' Harley shrugged. 'Certainly you do,' said Nicholls, returning his eyes to the road. 'And with good reason. The local reports put the figure pretty high, young man.'

'That's where you come in, I guess,' Harley said sullenly. 'I find the money – that I own anyhow – and give some of it to you. How much?'

'We'll discuss that later,' Nicholls said. He smiled absently as he looked ahead.

'We'll discuss it right now!'

The smile faded from Nicholls' face. 'No,' he said. 'We won't. I'm doing you a favor, young Harley. Remember that. In return – you'll do as I say, all the way!'

Harley digested that carefully, and it was not a pleasant

meal. He waited a couple of seconds before he changed the subject.

'I was out here once when the old man was alive,' he said. 'He didn't say nothing about any ghost.'

'Perhaps he felt you might think him – well, peculiar,' Nicholls said. 'And perhaps you would have. When were you here?'

'Oh, a long time ago,' Harley said evasively. 'But I was here a whole day, and part of the night. The old man was crazy as a coot, but he didn't keep any ghosts in the attic.'

'This ghost was a friend of his,' Nicholls said. 'The gentleman in charge of the bar told you that, surely. Your late uncle was something of a recluse. He lived in this house a dozen miles from nowhere, came into town hardly ever, wouldn't let anyone get friendly with him. But he wasn't exactly a hermit. He had Hank for company.'

'Fine company.'

Nicholls inclined his head seriously. 'Oh, I don't know,' he said. 'From all accounts, they got on well together. They played pinochle and chess – Hank's supposed to have been a great pinochle player. He was killed that way, according to the local reports. Caught somebody dealing from the bottom and shot it out with him. He lost. A bullet pierced his throat and he died quite bloodily.' He turned the wheel, putting his weight into the effort, and succeeded in twisting the car out of the ruts of the 'road,' sent it jouncing across unmarked sand to the old frame house to which they were going.

'That,' he finished as he pulled up before the porch, 'accounts for the blood that accompanies his apparition.'

Harley opened the door slowly and got out, looking uneasily at the battered old house. Nicholls cut the motor, got out and walked at once to the back of the car.

'Come on,' he said, dragging things out of the compartment. 'Give me a hand with this. I'm not going to carry this stuff all by myself.'

Harley came around reluctantly, regarded the curious assortment of bundles of dried faggots, lengths of colored cord, chalk pencils, ugly little bunches of wilted weeds, bleached bones of small animals and a couple of less pleasant things without pleasure.

Pat. HISS. Pat. HISS —

'He's here!' Harley yelped. 'Listen! He's someplace around here watching us.'

'Ha!'

The laugh was deep, unpleasant and – bodiless. Harley looked around desperately for the tell-tale trickle of blood. And he found it; from the air it issued, just beside the car, sinking gracefully to the ground and sizzling, vanishing, there.

'I'm watching you, all right,' the voice said grimly. 'Russell, you worthless piece of corruption, I've got no more use for you than you used to have for me. Dead or alive, this is my land! I shared it with your uncle, you young scalawag, but I won't share it with you. Get out!'

Harley's knees weakened and he tottered dizzily to the rear bumper, sat on it. 'Nicholls —' he said confusedly.

'Oh, brace up,' Nicholls said with irritation. He tossed a ball of gaudy twine, red and green, with curious knots tied along it, to Harley. Then he confronted the trickle of blood and made a few brisk passes in the air before it. His lips were moving silently, Harley saw, but no words came out.

There was a gasp and a chopped-off squawk from the source of the blood drops. Nicholls clapped his hands sharply, then turned to young Harley.

'Take that cord you have in your hands and stretch it around the house,' he said. 'All the way around, and make sure it goes right across the middle of the doors and windows. It isn't much, but it'll hold him till we can get the good stuff set up.'

Harley nodded, then pointed a rigid finger at the drops of blood, now sizzling and fuming more angrily than before. 'What about *that*?' he managed to get out.

Nicholls grinned complacently. 'I'll hold him here till the cows come home,' he said, 'Get moving!'

Harley inadvertently inhaled a lungful of noxious white smoke and coughed till the tears rolled down his cheeks. When he recovered he looked at Nicholls, who was reading silently from a green leather book with dog-eared pages. He said, 'Can I stop stirring this now?'

Nicholls grimaced angrily and shook his head without looking at him. He went on reading, his lips contorting over syllables that were not in any language Harley had ever heard, then snapped the book shut and wiped his brow.

'Fine,' he said. 'So far, so good.' He stepped over to windward of the boiling pot Harley was stirring on the hob over the fireplace, peered down into it cautiously.

'That's about done,' he said. 'Take it off the fire and let it cool a bit.'

Harley lifted it down, then squeezed his aching biceps with his left hand. The stuff was the consistency of sickly green fudge.

'Now what?' he asked.

Nicholls didn't answer. He looked up in mild surprise at the sudden squawk of triumph from outside, followed by the howling of a chill wind.

'Hank must be loose,' he said casually. 'He can't do us any harm, I think, but we'd better get a move on.' He rummaged in the dwindled pile of junk he'd brought from the car, extracted a paintbrush. 'Smear this stuff around all the windows and doors. All but the front door. For that I have something else.' He pointed to what seemed to be the front axle of an old Model-T. 'Leave that on the doorsill. Cold iron. You can just step over it, but Hank won't be able to pass it. It's been properly treated already with the very best thaumaturgy.'

'Step over it,' Harley repeated. 'What would I want to step over it for? *He's* out there.'

'He won't hurt you,' said Nicholls. 'You will carry an amulet with you – that one, there – that will keep him away. Probably he couldn't really hurt you anyhow, being a low-order ghost who can't materialize to any great density. But just to take no chances, carry the amulet and don't stay out too long. It won't hold him off forever, not for more than half an hour. If you ever have to go out and stay for any length of time, tie that bundle of herbs around your neck.' Nicholls smiled. 'That's only for emergencies, though. It works on the asafoetida principle. Ghosts can't come anywhere near it – but you won't like it much yourself. It has – ah – a rather definite odor.'

He leaned gingerly over the pot again, sniffing. He sneezed.

'Well, that's cool enough,' he said. 'Before it hardens, get moving. Start spreading the stuff upstairs – and make sure you don't miss any windows.'

'What are you going to do?'

'I,' said Nicholls sharply, 'will be here. Start.'

But he wasn't. When Harley finished his disagreeable task and came down, he called Nicholls' name, but the man was gone. Harley stepped to the door and looked out; the car was gone, too.

He shrugged. 'Oh, well,' he said, and began taking the dust-cloths off the furniture.

II

Somewhere within the cold, legal mind of Lawyer Turnbull, he weighed the comparative likeness of nightmare and insanity.

He stared at the plush chair facing him, noted with distinct uneasiness how the strangely weightless, strangely sourceless trickle of redness disappeared as it hit the floor, but left long, mud-ochre streaks matted on the upholstery. The sound was unpleasant, too; *Pat. HISS. Pat. HISS* —

The voice continued impatiently, 'Damn your human stupidity! I may be a ghost, but heaven knows I'm not trying to haunt you. Friend, you're not that important to me. Get this — I'm here on business.'

Turnbull learned that you cannot wet dry lips with a de-hydrated tongue. 'Legal business?'

'Sure. The fact that I was once killed by violence, and have to continue my existence on the astral plane, doesn't mean I've lost my legal rights. Does it?'

The lawyer shook his head in bafflement. He said, 'This would be easier on me if you weren't invisible. Can't you do something about it?'

There was a short pause. 'Well, I could materialize for a minute,' the voice said. 'It's hard work – damn hard, for me. There are a lot of us astral entities that can do it easy as falling out of bed, but — Well, if I have to I shall try to do it once.'

There was a shimmering in the air above the armchair, and a milky, thin smoke condensed into an intangible seated figure. Turnbull took no delight in noting that, through the figure, the outlines of the chair were still hazily visible. The figure thickened. Just as the features took form – just as Turnbull's bulging eyes made out a prominent hooked nose and a crisp beard – it thinned and exploded with a soft pop.

The voice said weakly, 'I didn't think I was that bad. I'm way out of practice. I guess that's the first daylight materialization I've made in seventy-five years.'

The lawyer adjusted his rimless glasses and coughed. *Hell's binges,* he thought, *the worst thing about this is that I'm believing it!*

'Oh, well,' he said aloud. Then he hurried on before the visitor could take offense: 'Just what did you want? I'm just a small-town laywer, you know. My business is fairly routine —'

'I know all about your business,' the voice said. 'You can handle my case – it's a land affair. I want to sue Russell Harley.'

'Harley?' Turnbull fingered his cheeks. 'Any relation to Zeb Harley?'

'His nephew – and his heir, too.'

Turnbull nodded. 'Yes, I remember now. My wife's folks live in Rebel Butte, and I've been there. Quite a coincidence you should come to me —'

The voice laughed. 'It was no coincidence,' it said softly.

'Oh.' Turnbull was silent for a second. Then, 'I see,' he said. He cast a shrewd glance at the chair. 'Lawsuits cost money, Mr. – I don't think you mentioned your name?'

'Hank Jenkins,' the voice prompted. 'I know that. Would – let's see. Would six hundred and fifty dollars be sufficient?'

Turnbull swallowed. 'I think so,' he said in a relatively unemotional tone – relative to what he was thinking.

'Then suppose we call that your retainer. I happen to have cached a considerable sum in gold when I was – that is to say, before I became an astral entity. I'm quite certain it hasn't been disturbed. You will have to call it treasure trove, I guess, and give half of it to the state, but there's thirteen hundred dollars altogether.'

Turnbull nodded judiciously. 'Assuming we can locate your trove,' he said, 'I think that would be quite satisfactory.' He leaned back in his chair and looked legal. His aplomb had returned.

And half an hour later he said slowly, 'I'll take your case.'

Judge Lawrence Gimbel had always liked his job before. But his thirteen honorable years on the bench lost their flavor for him as he grimaced wearily and reached for his gavel. This case was far too confusing for his taste.

The clerk made his speech, and the packed courtroom sat down en masse. Gimbel held a hand briefly to his eyes before he spoke.

'Is the counsel for the plaintiff ready?'

'I am, your honor.' Turnbull, alone at his table, rose and bowed.

'The counsel for the defendant?'

'Ready, your honor!' Fred Wilson snapped. He looked with a hard flicker of interest at Turnbull and his solitary table, then leaned over and whispered in Russell Harley's ear. The youth nodded glumly, then shrugged.

Gimbel said, 'I understand the attorneys for both sides have waived jury trial in this case of Henry Jenkins versus Russell Joseph Harley.'

Both lawyers nodded. Gimbel continued, 'In view of the un-usual nature of this case, I imagine it will prove necessary to conduct it with a certain amount of informality. The sole pur-pose of this court is to arrive at the true facts at issue, and to deliver a verdict in accord with the laws pertaining to these facts. I will not stand on ceremony. Nevertheless, I will not tolerate any disturbances or unnecessary irregularities. The spectators will kindly remember that they are here on privilege. Any demonstration will result in the clearing of the court.'

He looked severely at the white faces that gleamed unintel-ligently up at him. He suppressed a sigh as he said, 'The coun-sel for the plaintiff will begin.'

Turnbull rose quickly to his feet, faced the judge.

'Your honor,' he said, 'we propose to show that my client, Henry Jenkins, has been deprived of his just rights by the de-fendant. Mr. Jenkins, by virtue of a sustained residence of more than twenty years in the house located on Route 22, eight miles north of the town of Rebel Butte, with the full know-ledge of its legal owner, has acquired certain rights. In legal terminology we define these as the rights of adverse possession. The layman would call them common-law rights – squatters' rights.'

Gimbel folded his hands and tried to relax. Squatters' rights – for a ghost! He sighed, but listened attentively as Turnbull went on.

'Upon the death of Sebulon Harley, the owner of the house

208

involved – it is better known, perhaps, as Harley Hall – the defendant inherited title to the property. We do not question his right to it. But my client has an equity in Harley Hall; the right to free and full existence. The defendant has forcefully evicted my client, by means which have caused my client great mental distress, and have even endangered his very existence.'

Gimbel nodded. If the case only had a precedent somewhere. . . . But it hadn't; he remembered grimly the hours he'd spent thumbing through all sorts of unlikely law books, looking for anything that might bear on the case. It had been his better judgment that he throw the case out of court outright – a judge couldn't afford to have himself laughed at, not if he were ambitious. And public laughter was about the only certainty there was to this case. But Wilson had put up such a fight that the judge's temper had taken over. He never did like Wilson, anyhow.

'You may proceed with your witnesses,' he said.

Turnbull nodded. To the clerk he said, 'Call Henry Jenkins to the stand.'

Wilson was on his feet before the clerk opened his mouth.

'Objection!' he bellowed. 'The so-called Henry Jenkins cannot qualify as a witness!'

'Why not?' demanded Turnbull.

'Because he's dead!'

The judge clutched his gavel with one hand, forehead with the other. He banged on the desk to quieten the courtroom.

Turnbull stood there, smiling. 'Naturally,' he said, 'you'll have proof of that statement.'

Wilson snarled. 'Certainly.' He referred to his brief. 'The so-called Henry Jenkins is the ghost, spirit or specter of one Hank Jenkins, who prospected for gold in this territory a century ago. He was killed by a bullet through the throat from the gun of one Long Tom Cooper, and was declared legally dead on September 14, 1850. Cooper was hanged for his murder. No matter what hocus-pocus you produce for evidence to the contrary now, that status of legal death remains completely valid.'

'What evidence have you of the identity of my client with this Hank Jenkins?' Turnbull asked grimly.

'Do you deny it?'

Turnbull shrugged. 'I deny nothing. I'm not being cross-examined. Furthermore, the sole prerequisite of a witness is that he understand the value of an oath. Henry Jenkins was tested by John Quincy Fitzjames, professor of psychology at the University of Southern California. The results – I have Dr. Fitzjames' sworn statement of them here, which I will introduce as an exhibit – show clearly that my client's intelligence quotient is well above normal, and that a psychiatric examination discloses no important aberrations which would injure his validity as a witness. I insist that my client be allowed to testify on his own behalf.'

'But he's dead!' squawked Wilson. 'He's invisible right now!'

'My client,' said Turnbull stiffly, 'is not present just now. Undoubtedly that accounts for what you term his invisibility.' He paused for the appreciative murmur that swept through the court. Things were breaking perfectly, he thought, smiling. 'I have here another affidavit,' he said. 'It is signed by Elihu James and Terence MacRae, who respectively head the departments of physics and biology at the same university. It startes that my client exhibits all the vital phenomena of life. I am prepared to call all three of my expert witnesses to the stand, if necessary.'

Wilson scowled but said nothing, Judge Gimbel leaned forward.

'I don't see how it is possible for me to refuse the plaintiff the right to testify,' he said. 'If the three experts who prepared these reports will testify on the stand to the facts contained in them, Henry Jenkins may then take the stand.'

Wilson sat down heavily. The three experts spoke briefly – and dryly. Wilson put them through only the most formal of cross-examinations.

The judge declared a brief recess. In the corridor outside, Wilson and his client lit cigarettes and looked unsympathetically at each other.

'I feel like a fool,' said Russell Harley. 'Bringing suit against a ghost.'

'The ghost brought the suit,' Wilson reminded him. 'If only we'd been able to hold fire for a couple more weeks, till another judge came on the bench, I could've got this thing thrown right out of court.'

'Well, why couldn't we wait?'

'Because you were in such a damn hurry!' Wilson said. 'You and that idiot Nicholls – so confident that it would never come to trial.'

Harley shrugged, and thought unhappily of their failure in completely exorcising the ghost of Hank Jenkins. That had been a mess. Jenkins had somehow escaped from the charmed circle they'd drawn around him, in which they'd hoped to keep him till the trial was forfeited by non-appearance.

'That's another thing,' said Wilson. 'Where is Nicholls?'

Harley shrugged again. 'I dunno. The last I saw of him was in your office. He came around to see me right after the deputy slapped the show-cause order on me at the house. He brought me down to you – said you'd been recommended to him. Then you and him and I talked about the case for a while. He went out, after he lent me a little money to help meet your retainer. Haven't seen him since.'

'I'd like to know who recommended me to him,' Wilson said grimly. 'I don't think he'd ever recommend anybody else. I don't like this case – and I don't much like you.'

Harley growled but said nothing. He flung his cigarette away. It tasted of the garbage that hung around his neck – everything did. Nicholls had told no lies when he said Harley wouldn't much like the bundle of herbs that would ward off the ghost of old Jenkins. They smelled.

The court clerk was in the corridor, bawling something, and people were beginning to trickle back in. Harley and his attorney went with them.

When the trial had been resumed, the clerk said, 'Henry Jenkins!'

Wilson was on his feet at once. He opened the door of the judge's chamber, said something in a low tone. Then he stepped back, as if to let someone through.

Pat. HISS. Pat. HISS —

There was a concerted gasp from the spectators as the weirdly appearing trickle of blood moved slowly across the open space to the witness chair. This was the ghost – the plaintiff in the most eminently absurd case in the history of jurisprudence.

'All right, Hank,' Turnbull whispered. 'You'll have to materialize long enough to let the clerk swear you in.'

The clerk drew back nervously at the pillar of milky fog that appeared before him, vaguely humanoid in shape. A phantom hand, half transparent, reached out to touch the Bible. The clerk's voice shook as he administered the oath, and heard the response come from the heart of the cloudpillar.

The haze drifted into the witness chair, bent curiously at about hip-height, and popped into nothingness.

The judge banged his gavel wildly. The buzz of alarm that had arisen from the spectators died out.

'I'll warn you again,' he declared, 'that unruliness will not be tolerated. The counsel for the plaintiff may proceed.'

Turnbull walked to the witness chair and addressed its emptiness.

'Your name?'

'My name is Henry Jenkins.'

'Your occupation?'

There was a slight pause. 'I have none. I guess you'd say I'm retired.'

'Mr. Jenkins, just what connections have you with the building referred to as Harley Hall?'

'I have occupied it for ninety years.'

'During this time, did you come to know the late Zebulon Harley, owner of the Hall?'

'I knew Zeb quite well.'

Turnbull nodded. 'When did you make his acquaintance?' he asked.

'In the spring of 1907. Zeb had just lost his wife. After that, you see, he made Harley Hall his year-round home. He became – well, more or less of a hermit. Before that we had never met, since he was only seldom at the Hall. But we became friendly then.'

'How long did this friendship last?'

'Until he died last fall. I was with him when he died. I still have a few keepsakes he left me then.' There was a distinct nostalgic sigh from the witness chair, which by now was liberally spattered with muddy red liquid. The falling drops seemed to hesitate for a second, and their sizzling noise was muted as with a strong emotion.

Turnbull went on, 'Your relations with him were good, then?'

'I'd call them excellent,' the emptiness replied firmly. 'Every night we sat up together. When we didn't play pinochle or

212

chess or cribbage, we just sat and talked over the news of the day. I still have the book we used to keep records of the chess and pinochle games. Zeb made the entries himself, in his own handwriting.'

Turnbull abandoned the witness for a moment. He faced the judge with a smile. 'I offer in evidence,' he said, 'the book mentioned. Also a ring given to the plaintiff by the late Mr. Harley, and a copy of the plays of Gilbert and Sullivan. On the flyleaf of this book is inscribed, "To Old Hank," in Harley's own hand.'

He turned again to the empty, blood-leaking witness chair.

He said, 'In all your years of association, did Zebulon Harley ever ask you to leave, or to pay rent?'

'Of course not. Not Zeb!'

Turnbull nodded. 'Very good,' he said. 'Now, just one or two more questions. Will you tell in your own words what occurred, after the death of Zebulon Harley, that caused you to bring this suit?'

'Well, in January young Harley —'

'You mean Russell Joseph Harley, the defendant?'

'Yes. He arrived at Harley Hall on January fifth. I asked him to leave, which he did. On the next day he returned with another man. They placed a talisman upon the threshold of the main entrance, and soon after sealed every threshold and windowsill in the Hall with a substance which is noxious to me. These activities were accompanied by several of the most deadly spells in the Ars Magicorum. He further added an Exclusion Circle with a radius of a little over a mile, entirely surrounding the Hall.'

'I see,' the lawyer said. 'Will you explain to the court the effects of these activities?'

'Well,' the voice said thoughtfully, 'it's a little hard to put in words. I can't pass the Circle without a great expenditure of energy. Even if I did I couldn't enter the building because of the talisman and the seals.'

'Could you enter by air? Through a chimney, perhaps?'

'No. The Exclusion Circle is really a sphere. I'm pretty sure the effort would destroy me.'

'In effect, then, you are entirely barred from the house you have occupied for ninety years, due to the wilful acts of Russell Joseph Harley, the defendant, and an unnamed accomplice of his.'

'That is correct.'

Turnbull beamed. 'Thank you. That's all.'

He turned to Wilson, whose face had been a study in dourness throughout the entire examination. 'Your witness,' he said.

Wilson snapped to his feet and strode to the witness chair.

He said belligerently, 'You say your name is Henry Jenkins?'

'Yes.'

'That is your name now, you mean to say. What was your name before?'

'Before?' There was surprise in the voice that emanated from above the trickling blood-drops. 'Before when?'

Wilson scowled. 'Don't pretend ignorance,' he said sharply. 'Before you *died*, of course.'

'Objection!' Turnbull was on his feet, glaring at Wilson. 'The counsel for the defense has no right to speak of some hypothetical death of my client!'

Gimbel raised a hand wearily and cut off the words that were forming on Wilson's lips. 'Objection sustained,' he said. 'No evidence has been presented to identify the plaintiff as the prospector who was killed in 1850 – or anyone else.'

Wilson's mouth twisted into a sour grimace. He continued on a lower key.

'You say, Mr. Jenkins, that you occupied Harley Hall for ninety years.'

'Ninety-two years next month. The Hall wasn't built – in its present form, anyhow – until 1876, but I occupied the house that stood on the site previously.'

'What did you do before then?'

'Before then?' The voice paused, then said doubtfully, 'I don't remember.'

'You're under oath!' Wilson flared.

The voice got firmer. 'Ninety years is a long time,' it said. 'I don't remember.'

'Let's see if I can't refresh your memory. Is it true that ninety-one years ago, in the very year in which you claim to have begun your occupancy of Harley Hall, Hank Jenkins was killed in a gun duel?'

'That may be true, if you say so. I don't remember.'

'Do you remember that the shooting occurred not fifty feet from the present site of Harley Hall?'

'It may be.'

'Well, then,' Wilson thundered, 'is it not a fact that when Hank Jenkins died by violence his ghost assumed existence? That it was then doomed to haunt the site of its slaying throughout eternity?'

The voice said evenly, 'I have no knowledge of that.'

'Do you deny that it is well known throughout that section that the ghost of Hank Jenkins haunts Harley Hall?'

'Objection!' shouted Turnbull. 'Popular opinion is not evidence.'

'Objection sustained. Strike the question from the record.'

Wilson, badgered, lost his control. In a dangerously uneven voice, he said, 'Perjury is a criminal offense. Mr. Jenkins, do you deny that you are the ghost of Hank Jenkins?'

The tone was surprised. 'Why, certainly.'

'You *are* a ghost, aren't you?'

Stiffly, 'I'm an entity on the astral plane.'

'That, I believe, is what is called a ghost?'

'I can't help what it's called. I've heard you called a lot of things. Is that proof?'

There was a surge of laughter from the audience. Gimbel slammel his gavel down on the bench.

'The witness,' he said, 'will confine himself to answering questions.'

Wilson bellowed, 'In spite of what you say, it's true, isn't it, that you are merely the spirit of a human being who had died through violence?'

The voice from above the blood drops retorted, 'I repeat that I am an entity of the astral plane. I am not aware that I was ever a human being.'

The lawyer turned an exasperated face to the bench.

'Your honor,' he said, 'I ask that you instruct the witness to cease playing verbal hide-and-seek. It is quite evident that the witness is a ghost, and that he is therefore the relict of some human being, ipso facto. Circumstantial evidence is strong that he is the ghost of the Hank Jenkins who was killed in 1850. But this is a non-essential point. What is definite is that he is the ghost of someone who is dead, and hence is unqualified to

215

act as witness! I demand his testimony be stricken from the record!'

Turnbull spoke up at once. 'Will the counsel for the defense quote his authority for branding my client a ghost – in the face of my client's repeated declaration that he is an entity of the astral plane? What is the legal definition of a ghost?'

Judge Gimbel smiled. 'Counsel for the defense will proceed with the cross-examination,' he said.

Wilson's face flushed dark purple. He mopped his brow with a large bandanna, then glared at the dropping, sizzling trickle of blood.

'Whatever you are,' he said, 'answer me this question. Can you pass through a wall?'

'Why, yes. Certainly.' There was a definite note of surprise in the voice from nowhere. 'But it isn't as easy as some people think. It definitely requires a lot of effort.'

'Never mind that. You can do it?'

'Yes.'

'Could you be bound by any physical means? Would hand-cuffs hold you? Or ropes, chains, prison walls, a hermetically sealed steel chest?'

Jenkins had no chance to answer. Turnbull, scenting danger, cut in hastily. 'I object to this line of questioning. It is entirely irrelevant.'

'On the contrary,' Wilson cried loudly, 'it bears strongly on the qualifications of the so-called Henry Jenkins as a witness! I demand that he answer the question.'

Judge Gimbel said, 'Objection overruled. Witness will answer the question.'

The voice from the chair said superciliously, 'I don't mind answering. Physical barriers mean nothing to me, by and large.'

The counsel for the defense drew himself up triumphantly.

'Very good,' he said with satisfaction. '*Very* good.' Then to the judge, the words coming sharp and fast, 'I claim, your honor, that the so-called Henry Jenkins has no legal status as a witness in court. There is clearly no value in understanding the nature of an oath if a violation of the oath can bring no punishment in its wake. The statements of a man who can perjure himself freely have no worth. I demand they be stricken from the record!'

Turnbull was at the judge's bench in two strides.

'I had anticipated that, your honor,' he said quickly. 'From the very nature of the case, however, it is clear that my client can be very definitely restricted in his movements – spells, pentagrams, talismans, amulets, Exclusion Circles and whatnot. I have here – which I am prepared to deliver to the bailiff of the court – a list of the various methods of confining an astral entity to a restricted area for periods ranging from a few moments to all eternity. Moreover, I have also signed a bond for five thousand dollars, prior to the beginning of the trial, which I stand ready to forfeit should my client be confined and make his escape, if found guilty of any misfeasance as a witness.'

Gimbel's face, which had looked startled for a second, slowly cleared. He nodded. 'The court is satisfied with the statement of the counsel for the plaintiff,' he declared. 'There seems no doubt that the plaintiff can be penalized for any misstatements, and the motion of the defense is denied.'

Wilson looked choleric, but shrugged. 'All right,' he said. 'That will be all.'

'You may step down, Mr. Jenkins,' Gimbel directed, and watched in fascination as the blood-dripping column rose and floated over the floor, along the corridor, out the door.

Turnbull approached the judge's bench again. He said, 'I would like to place in evidence these notes, the diary of the late Zebulon Harley. It was presented to my client by Harley himself last fall. I call particular attention to the entry for April sixth, nineteen seventeen, in which he mentions the entrance of the United States into the First World War, and records the results of a series of eleven pinochle games played with a personage identified as "Old Hank." With the court's permission, I will read the entry for that day, and also various other entries for the next four years. Please note the references to someone known variously as "Jenkins," "Hank Jenkins" and – in one extremely significant passage – "Old Invisible."'

Wilson stewed silently during the slow reading of Harley's diary. There was anger on his face, but he paid close attention, and when the reading was over he leaped to his feet.

'I would like to know,' he asked, 'if the counsel for the plaintiff is in possession of any diaries *after* nineteen twenty?'

217

Turnbull shook his head. 'Harley apparently never kept a diary, except during the four years represented in this.'

'Then I demand that the court refuse to admit this diary as evidence on two counts,' Wilson said. He raised two fingers to tick off the points. 'In the first place, the evidence presented is frivolous. The few vague and unsatisfactory references to Jenkins nowhere specifically describe him as what he is – ghost, astral entity or what you will. Second, the evidence, even were the first point overlooked, concerns only the years up to nineteen twenty-one. The case concerns itself only with the supposed occupation of Harley Hall by the so-called Jenkins in the last twenty years – *since* 'twenty-one. Clearly, the evidence is therefore irrelevant.'

Gimbel looked at Turnbull, who smiled calmly.

'The reference to "Old Invisible" is far from vague,' he said. 'It is a definite indication of the astral character of my client. Furthermore, evidence as to the friendship of my client with the late Mr. Zebulon Harley before nineteen twenty-one is entirely relevant, as such a friendship, once established, would naturally be presumed to have continued indefinitely. Unless of course, the defense is able to present evidence to the contrary.'

Judge Gimbel said, 'The diary is admitted as evidence.'

Turnbull said, 'I rest my case.'

There was a buzz of conversation in the courtroom while the judge looked over the diary, and then handed it to the clerk to be marked and entered.

Gimbel said, 'The defense may open its case.'

Wilson rose. To the clerk he said, 'Russell Joseph Harley.'

But young Harley was recalcitrant. 'Nix,' he said, on his feet, pointing at the witness chair. 'That thing's got blood all over it! You don't expect me to sit down in that large puddle of blood, do you?'

Judge Gimbel leaned over to look at the chair. The dripdrop trickle of blood from the apparition who'd been testifying had left its mark. Muddy brown all down the front of the chair. Gimbel found himself wondering how the ghost managed to replenish its supply of the fluid, but gave it up.

'I see your point,' he said. 'Well, it's getting a bit late anyhow. The clerk will take away the present witness chair and replace it. In the interim, I declare the court recessed till tomorrow morning at ten o'clock.'

III

Russell Harley noticed how the elevator boy's back registered repulsion and disapproval, and scowled. He was not a popular guest in the hotel, he knew well. Where he made his mistake, though, was in thinking that the noxious bundle of herbs about his neck was the cause of it. His odious personality had a lot to do with the chilly attitude of the management and his fellow guests.

He made his way to the bar, ignoring the heads that turned in surprise to follow the reeking comet-tail of his passage. He entered the red-leather-and-chromium drinking room, and stared about for Lawyer Wilson.

And blinked in surprise when he saw him. Wilson wasn't alone. In the booth with him was a tall, dark figure, with his back to Harley. The back alone was plenty for recognition. Nicholls!

Wilson had seen him. 'Hello, Harley,' he said, all smiles and affability in the presence of the man with the money. 'Come on and sit down. Mr. Nicholls dropped in on me a little while ago, so I brought him over.'

'Hello,' Harley said glumly, and Nicholls nodded. The muscles of his cheeks pulsed, and he seemed under a strain, strangely uncomfortable in Harley's presence. Still there was a twinkle in the look he gave young Harley, and his voice was friendly enough – though supercilious – as he said:

'Hello, Harley. How is the trial going?'

'Ask him,' said Harley, pointing a thumb at Wilson as he slid his knees under the booth's table and sat down. 'He's the lawyer. He's supposed to know these things.'

'Doesn't he?'

Harley shrugged and craned his neck for the waitress. 'Oh, I guess so.... Rye and water!' He watched the girl appreciatively as she nodded and went off to the bar, then turned his attention back to Nicholls. 'The trouble is,' he said, 'Wilson may think he knows, but I think he's all wet.'

Wilson frowned. 'Do you imply —' he began, but Nicholls put up a hand.

'Let's not bicker,' said Nicholls. 'Suppose you answer my question. I have a stake in this, and I want to know. How's the trial going?'

Wilson put on his most open-faced expression. 'Frankly,' he said, 'not too well. I'm afraid the judge is on the other side. If you'd listened to me and stalled till another judge came along —'

'I had no time to stall,' said Nicholls. 'I have to be elsewhere within a few days. Even now, I should be on my way. Do you think we might lose the case?'

Harley laughed sharply. As Wilson glared at him he took his drink from the waitress' tray and swallowed it. The smile remained on his face as he listened to Wilson say smoothly:

'There is a good deal of danger, yes.'

'Hum.' Nicholls looked interestedly at his fingernails. 'Perhaps I chose the wrong lawyer.'

'Sure you did.' Harley waved at the waitress, ordered another drink. You want to know what else I think? I think you picked the wrong client, spelled s-t-o-o-g-e. I'm getting sick of this. This damn thing around my neck smells bad. How do I know it's any good, anyhow? Far as I can see, it just smells bad, and that's all.'

'It works,' Nicholls said succinctly. 'I wouldn't advise you to go without it. The late Hank Jenkins is not a very strong ghost – a strong one would tear you apart and chew up your herbs for dessert – but without the protection of what you wear about your neck, you would become a very uncomfortable human as soon as Jenkins heard you'd stopped wearing it.'

He put down the glass of red wine he'd been inhaling without drinking, looked intently at Wilson. 'I've put up the money in this,' he said. 'I had hoped you'd be able to handle the legal end. I see I'll have to do more. Now listen intently, because I have no intention of repeating this. There's an angle to this case that's got right by your blunted legal acumen. Jenkins claims to be an astral entity, which he undoubtedly is. Now, instead of trying to prove him a ghost, and legally dead, and therefore unfit to testify, which you have been doing, suppose you do this. . . .'

He went on to speak rapidly and to the point.

And when he left them a bit later, and Wilson took Harley up to his room and poured him into bed, the lawyer felt happy for the first time in days.

Russell Joseph Harley, a little hung over and a lot nervous, was called to the stand as first witness in his own behalf.

Wilson said, 'Your name?'

'Russell Joseph Harley.'

'You are the nephew of the late Zebulon Harley, who bequeathed the residence known as Harley Hall to you?'

'Yes.'

Wilson turned to the bench. 'I offer this copy of the late Mr. Zebulon Harley's will in evidence. All his possessions are left to his nephew and only living kin, the defendant.'

Turnbull spoke from his desk. 'The plaintiff in no way disputes the defendant's equity in Harley Hall.'

Wilson continued, 'You passed part of your childhood in Harley Hall, did you not, and visited it as a grown man on occasion?'

'Yes.'

'At any time, has anything in the shape of a ghost, specter or astral entity manifested itself to you in Harley Hall?'

'No. I'd remember it.'

'Did your late uncle ever mention any such manifestation to you?'

'Him? No.'

'That's all.'

Turnbull came up for the cross-examination.

'When, Mr. Harley, did you last see your uncle before his death?'

'It was in nineteen thirty-eight. In September, some time – around the tenth or eleventh of the month.'

'How long a time did you spend with him?'

Harley flushed unaccountably. 'Ah – just one day,' he said.

'When before that did you see him?'

'Well, not since I was quite young. My parents moved to Pennsylvania in nineteen twenty.'

'And since then – except for that one-day visit in nineteen thirty-eight – has any communication passed between your uncle and yourself?'

'No, I guess not. He was a rather queer duck – solitary. A little bit balmy, I think.'

'Well, you're a loving nephew. But in view of what you've just said, does it sound surprising that your uncle never told you of Mr. Jenkins? He never had much chance to, did he?'

221

'He had a chance in nineteen thirty-eight, but he didn't,' Harley said defiantly.

Turnbull shrugged. 'I'm finished,' he said.

Gimbel began to look bored. He had anticipated something more in the way of fireworks. He said, 'Has the defense any further witnesses?'

Wilson smiled grimly. 'Yes, your honor,' he said. This was his big moment, and he smiled again as he said gently, 'I would like to call Mr. Henry Jenkins to the stand.'

In the amazed silence that followed, Judge Gimbel leaned forward. 'You mean you wish to call the plaintiff as a witness for the defense?'

Serenely, 'Yes, your honor.'

Gimbel grimaced. 'Call Henry Jenkins,' he said wearily to the clerk, and sank back in his chair.

Turnbull was looking alarmed. He bit his lip, trying to decide whether to object to this astonishing procedure, but finally shrugged as the clerk bawled out the ghost's name.

Turnbull sped down the corridor, out the door. His voice was heard in the anteroom, then he returned more slowly. Behind him came the trickle of blood drops: *Pat. HISS. Pat. HISS* —

'One moment,' said Gimbel, coming to life again. 'I have no objection to your testifying, Mr. Jenkins, but the State should not be subjected to the needless expense of reupholstering its witness chair every time you do. Bailiff, find some sort of a rug or something to throw over the chair before Mr. Jenkins is sworn in.'

A tarpaulin was hurriedly procured and adjusted to the chair; Jenkins materialized long enough to be sworn in, then sat.

'Tell me, Mr. Jenkins,' he said, 'just how many "astral entities" – I believe that is what you call yourself – are there?'

'I have no way of knowing. Many billions.'

'As many, in other words, as there have been human beings to die by violence?'

Turnbull rose to his feet in sudden agitation, but the ghost neatly evaded the trap. 'I don't know. I only know there are billions.'

The lawyer's cat-who-ate-canary smile remained undimmed.

222

'And all these billions are constantly about us, everywhere, only remaining invisible. Is that it?'

'Oh, no. Very few remain on Earth. Of course, still fewer have anything to do with humans. Most humans are quite boring to us.'

'Well, how many would you say are on Earth? A hundred thousand?'

'Even more, maybe. But that's a good guess.'

Turnbull interrupted suddenly. 'I would like to know the significance of these questions. I object to this whole line of questioning as being totally irrelevant.'

Wilson was a study in legal dignity. He retorted, 'I am trying to elicit some facts of major value, your honor. This may change the entire character of the case. I ask your patience for a moment or two.'

'Counsel for the defense may continue,' Gimbel said curtly.

Wilson showed his canines in a grin. He continued to the blood-dripping before him. 'Now, the contention of your counsel is that the late Mr. Harley allowed an "astral entity" to occupy his home for twenty years or more, with his full knowledge and consent. That strikes me as being entirely improbable, but shall we for the moment assume it to be the case?'

'Certainly! It's the truth.'

'Then tell me, Mr. Jenkins, have you fingers?'

'Have I – what?'

'You heard me!' Wilson snapped. 'Have you fingers, flesh-and-blood fingers, capable of making an imprint?'

'Why, no. I —'

Wilson rushed on. 'Or have you a photograph of yourself – or specimens of your handwriting – or any sort of material identification? Have you any of these?'

The voice was definitely querulous. 'What do you mean?'

Wilson's voice became harsh, menacing. 'I mean, can you prove that *you* are the astral entity alleged to have occupied Zebulon Harley's home? Was it you – or was it another of the featureless, faceless, intangible unknowns – one of the hundreds of thousands of them that, by your own admission, are all over the face of the earth, rambling where they choose, not halted by any locks or bars? Can you prove that *you* are anyone in particular?'

'Your honor!' Turnbull's voice was almost a shriek as he

223

found his feet at last. 'My client's identity was never in question!'

'It is now!' roared Wilson. 'The opposing counsel has presented a personage whom he styles "Henry Jenkins." Who is this Jenkins? What is he? Is he even an individual – or a corporate aggregation of these mysterious "astral entities" which we are to believe are everywhere, but which we never see? If he is an individual, is he *the* individual? And how can we know that, even if he says he is? Let him produce evidence – photographs, a birth certificate, fingerprints. Let him bring in identifying witnesses who have known both ghosts, and are prepared to swear that these ghosts are the same ghost. Failing this, there is no case! Your honor, I demand the court declare an immediate judgment in favor of the defendant!'

Judge Gimbel stared at Turnbull. 'Have you anything to say?' he asked. 'The argument of the defense would seem to have every merit with it. Unless you can produce some sort of evidence as to the identity of your client, I have no alternative but to find for the defense.'

For a moment there was a silent tableau. Wilson triumphant, Turnbull furiously frustrated.

How could you identify a ghost?

And then came the quietly amused voice from the witness chair.

'This thing has gone far enough,' it said above the sizzle and splatter of its own leaking blood. 'I believe I can present proof that will satisfy the court.'

Wilson's face fell with express-elevator speed. Turnbull held his breath, afraid to hope.

Judge Gimbel said, 'You are under oath. Proceed.'

There was no other sound in the courtroom as the voice said, 'Mr. Harley, here, spoke of a visit to his uncle in nineteen thirty-eight. I can vouch for that. They spent a night and a day together. They weren't alone. I was there.'

No one was watching Russell Harley, or they might have seen the sudden sick pallor that passed over his face.

The voice, relentless, went on. 'Perhaps I shouldn't have eavesdropped as I did, but old Zeb never had any secrets from me anyhow. I listened to what they talked about. Young Harley was working for a bank in Philadelphia at the time. His first big job. He needed money, and needed it bad. There was a

224

shortage in his department. A woman named Sally —'

'Hold on!' Wilson yelled. 'This has nothing to do with your identification of yourself. Keep to the point!'

But Turnbull had begun to comprehend. He was shouting, too, almost too excited to be coherent. 'Your honor, my client must be allowed to speak. If he shows knowledge of an intimate conversation between the late Mr. Harley and the defendant, it would be certain proof that he enjoyed the late Mr. Harley's confidence, and thus, Q.E.D., that he is no other than the astral entity who occupied Harley Hall for so long!'

Gimbel nodded sharply. 'Let me remind counsel for the defense that this is his own witness. Mr. Jenkins, continue.'

The voice began again, 'As I was saying, the woman's name —'

'Shut up, damn you!' Harley yelled. He sprang upright, turned beseechingly toward the judge. 'He is twisting it! Make him stop! Sure, I knew my uncle had a ghost. He's it, all right, curse his black soul! He can have the house if he wants it – I'll clear out. I'll clear out of the whole damned state!'

He broke off into babbling and turned about wildly. Only the intervention of a marshal kept him from hurtling out of the courtroom.

Banging of the gavel and hard work by the court clerk and his staff restored order in the courtroom. When the room had returned almost to normalcy, Judge Gimbel, perspiring and annoyed, said, 'As far as I am concerned, identification of the witness is complete. Has the defense any further evidence to present?'

Wilson shrugged morosely. 'No, your honor.'

'Counsel for the plaintiff?'

'Nothing, your honor. I rest my case.'

Gimbel plowed a hand through his sparse hair and blinked. 'In that case,' he said, 'I find for the plaintiff. An order is entered hereby that the defendant, Russell Joseph Harley, shall remove from the premises of Harley Hall all spells, pentagrams, talismans and other means of exorcism employed; that he shall cease and desist from making any attempts, of whatever nature, to evict the tenant in the future; and that Henry Jenkins, the plaintiff, shall be permitted the full use and occupancy of the premises designated as Harley Hall for the full term of his natural – ah – existence.'

The gavel banged. 'The case is closed.'

'Don't take it so hard,' said a mild voice behind Russell Harley. He whirled surlily. Nicholls was coming up the street after him from the courthouse, Wilson in tow.

Nicholls said, 'You lost the case, but you've still got your life. Let me buy you a drink. In here, perhaps.'

He herded them into a cocktail lounge, sat them down before they had a chance to object. He glanced at his expensive wrist watch. 'I have a few minutes,' he said. 'Then I really must be off. It's urgent.'

He hailed a barman, ordered for all. Then he looked at young Harley and smiled broadly as he dropped a bill on the counter to pay for the drinks.

'Harley,' he said, 'I have a motto that you would do well to remember at times like these. I'll make you a present of it, if you like.'

'What is it?'

' "The worst is yet to come." '

Harley snarled and swallowed his drink without replying. Wilson said, 'What gets me is, why didn't they come to us before the trial with that stuff about this charmingly illicit client you wished on me? We'd have had to settle out of court.'

Nicholls shrugged. 'They had their reasons,' he said. 'After all, one case of exorcism, more or less, doesn't matter. But lawsuits set precedents. You're a lawyer, of sorts, Wilson; do you see what I mean?'

'Precedents?' Wilson looked at him slackjawed for a moment; then his eyes widened.

'I see you understand me.' Nicholls nodded. 'From now on in this state – and by virtue of the full-faith-and-credence clause of the Constitution, in *every* state of the country – a ghost has a legal right to haunt a house!'

'Good lord!' said Wilson. He began to laugh, not loud, but from the bottom of his chest.

Harley stared at Nicholls. 'Once and for all,' he whispered, 'tell me – what's your angle on all this?'

Nicholls smiled again.

'Think about it a while,' he said lightly. 'You'll begin to

understand.' He sniffed his wine once more, then sat the glass down gently —

And vanished.

THE END

As I've mentioned before, I was never a reader of *Weird Tales*, and its type of fiction did not captivate me. In 1950, though, when 'Legal Rites' finally appeared, *Weird Tales* was nearing the end of its thirty-year road and I'm rather glad I made its pages at least once before its end, even if only as half of a collaboration. It was the longest story in the issue and it received the cover.

'Legal Rites' and 'The Little Man on the Subway' are the only pieces of fiction I ever wrote in collaboration, and I didn't really enjoy the process. Later on in my career, I had occasion to collaborate on four or five non-fiction books and never really enjoyed that either, nor were any of the collaborations successful. I'm essentially a loner and like to take full responsibility for what I write.

In the case of 'Legal Rites' it seems to me that the beginning is mostly Pohl's rewriting; the trial scene is mostly mine; the ending – I don't remember.

Fantasy was not the only type of story I kept bullheadedly trying, over and over, without much success. Another type was the broadly farcical. I never sold either type to Campbell, but I at least sold the latter elsewhere.

Even while I was writing 'Legal Rites,' I was working on another robot story, but a humorous one – or what I considered humor. I called it 'Source of Power' and at least knew better than to waste time trying it on Campbell. I sent it directly to *Thrilling Wonder*, and when it was rejected there, I tried *Amazing*.

Amazing bought it on October 8, 1941 – my first sale to that magazine since those exciting beginning days of the fall of 1938. When it appeared on the stands (two days after Pearl Harbor) in the February 1942 issue, I found that *Amazing* had retitled it 'Robot AL-76 Goes Astray.'

Although 'Robot AL-76 Goes Astray' was a 'positronic robot' story, it didn't really fit in with the other three I had

227

thus far written. When *I, Robot*, my first collection of 'positronic robot' stories, was put together, in 1950, I did not include 'Robot AL-76 Goes Astray' in that volume. When, however, in 1964, *The Rest of the Robots* was put together, I felt honor-bound by the title, if nothing else, to include *all* the remaining robot stories published till then, and therefore 'Robot AL-76 Goes Astray' was included.

August 1, 1941 ('Robot AL-76 Goes Astray' was then still working its slow way through the typewriter, because the Nazi invasion of the Soviet Union distracted me) was another important day in my writing career. I went to see John Campbell that day and, not liking to come to him without an idea, I thought hard on the subway ride there.

The fate of 'Pilgrimage' (soon to become 'Black Friar of the Flame') was still rankling, and I wanted to write another future-historical. I therefore suggested to him that I do a short story against the background of the slow fall of the Galactic Empire (something I intended to model quite frankly on the fall of the Roman Empire).

Campbell caught fire. We spent two hours together, and by the time it was over it was not going to be a short story at all, but an indefinitely long series of stories dealing with the fall of the First Galactic Empire and the rise of the Second.

I submitted the first story of the series, 'Foundation,' to Campbell on September 8, 1941, and it was accepted on the fifteenth. It appeared in the May 1942 issue of *Astounding*.

Over the next eight years I was to write seven more stories of what came to be called the 'Foundation' series, and these were finally collected into three volumes, *Foundation, Foundation and Empire*, and *Second Foundation*, which collectively were called *The Foundation Trilogy*.

Of all my science fiction, these books were most successful. First published in 1951, 1952 and 1953, respectively, they have been in print constantly as hard-covers ever since, despite the appearance of numerous soft-cover editions. And in 1966, at the 24th World Science Fiction Convention, in Cleveland, the 'Foundation' series received a Hugo (science fiction's equivalent of the Oscar) as the 'Best All-Time Series.'

After 'Foundation' I was ready to try a serious positronic

robot story for the first time in half a year. This one, 'Runaround,' was submitted to Campbell on October 20, 1941, and he accepted it on the twenty-third. It appeared in the March 1942 issue of *Astounding* and was eventually included in *I, Robot*.

I then had to get to work at once on a sequel to 'Foundation.' 'Foundation' had been brought to an inconclusive ending on the assumption that a sequel would be forthcoming, and I had to come through. On November 17, the sequel, 'Bridle and Saddle,' which was the second story of the 'Foundation' series, was submitted to Campbell, and he accepted it the same day – a record in speed. What's more, it was the longest story I had yet written – eighteen thousand words – and even though I received no bonus, the check, for $180, was the largest single check I had yet received. 'Bridle and Saddle' was eventually included in *Foundation*.

Now, at last, I had a series of *long* stories going, together with my 'positronic robot' series of short stories. I was feeling quite good.

On November 17, 1941, the day I submitted and sold 'Bridle and Saddle,' Campbell told me his plan for starting a new department in *Astounding*, one to be called 'Probability Zero.' This was to be a department of short-shorts, five hundred to one thousand words, which were to be in the nature of plausible and entertaining Munchausen-like lies. Campbell's notion was that, aside from the entertainment value of these things, they would offer a place where beginners could penetrate the market without having to compete quite so hard with established writers. It would form a stairway to professional status.

This was a good idea in theory and even worked a little. Ray Bradbury, later to be one of the best-known and successful of all science fiction writers, broke into the field with a 'Probability Zero' item in the July 1942 *Astounding*. Hal Clement and George O. Smith also published in 'Probability Zero' near the very start of their careers.

Unfortunately, it didn't work *enough*. Campbell had to start the department going with professionals, hoping to let the amateurs carry on once they saw what it was Campbell wanted. There were, however, never enough amateurs who could meet Campbell's standards even for short-shorts of an undemanding nature, and after twelve appearances of 'Probability Zero' over a space of two and a half years, Campbell gave up.

On November 17, however, he was just beginning, and he wanted me to do a 'Probability Zero' for him. I was delighted that he considered me to be at that stage of virtuosity where he could order me to do something for him according to measure. I promptly sat down and wrote a short-short called 'Big Game.' On November 24, 1941, I showed it to Campbell. He glanced over it and, rather to my astonishment, handed it back. It wasn't what he wanted.

I wish I could remember what 'Big Game' was about, for I thought enough of it to try submitting it to *Collier's* magazine (an over-awing *slick*) in 1944 – and it was, of course, rejected. The title, however, recalls nothing to my mind, and the story now no longer exists.

I tried a second time and did a humorous little positronic robot story called 'First Law.' I showed it to Campbell on December 1, and he didn't like that, either. This time, though, I kept the story. Thank goodness, I had finally learned that stories must be carefully saved for eternity, however many times they are rejected, and however firmly you imagine they are retired. 'Big Game' was the eleventh of my stories to disappear, but it was also the *last*.

In the case of 'First Law' there came a time when a magazine that did not exist in 1941 was to ask me for something. The magazine in question was *Fantastic Universe*, whose editor, Hans Stefan Santesson, asked me for a story at rates that would have been fine in 1941 but that by the mid-1950s I was reluctant to accept. I remembered 'First Law,' however, and sent it in. Santesson took it and ran it in the October 1956 issue of *Fantastic Universe*, and, eventually, I included it in *The Rest of the Robots*.

But back to 'Probability Zero' —

I tried a third time with a short-story called 'Time Pussy,' which I wrote on the morning of Sunday, December 7, 1941, finishing it just before the radio went crazy with the news of Pearl Harbor. I brought it in to Campbell the next day (life goes on!), and this time he took it, but 'not too enthusiastically,' according to my diary.

This was told me long ago by old Mac, who lived in a shack just over the hill from my old house. He had been a mining prospector out in the Asteroids during the Rush of '37, and spent most of his time now in feeding his seven cats.

'What makes you like cats so much, Mr. Mac?' I asked him.

The old miner looked at me and scratched his chin. 'Well,' he said, 'they reminds me o' my leetle pets on Pallas. *They* was something like cats – same kind of head, sort o' – and the cleverest leetle fellers y' ever saw. All dead!'

I felt sorry and said so. Mac heaved a sigh.

'Cleverest leetle fellers,' he repeated. 'They was four-dimensional pussies.'

'Four-dimensional, Mr. Mac? But the fourth dimension is time.' I had learned that the year before, in the third grade.

'So you've had a leetle schooling, hey?' He took out his pipe and filled it slowly. 'Sure, the fourth dimension is time. These pussies was about a foot long and six inches high and four inches wide and stretched somewheres into middle o' next week. That's four dimensions, ain't it? Why, if you petted their heads, they wouldn't wag their tails till next day, mebbe. Some o' the big ones wouldn't wag till day after. Fact!'

I looked dubious, but didn't say anything.

Mac went on: 'They was the best leetle watchdogs in all creation, too. They had to be. Why, if they spotted a burglar or any suspicious character, they'd shriek like a banshee. And when one saw a burglar today, he'd shriek yesterday, so we had twenty-four hours' notice every time.'

My mouth opened. 'Honest?'

'Cross my heart! Y' want to know how we used to feed them? We'd wait for them to go to sleep, see, and then we'd know they was busy digesting their meals. These leetle time pussies, they always digested their meals exactly three hours before they ate it, on account their stomachs stretched that far back in time. So when they went to sleep, we used to look at the time, get their dinner ready and feed it to them exactly three hours later.'

He had lit his pipe now and was puffing away. He shook his head sadly. 'Once, though, I made a mistake. Poor leetle time pussy. His name was Joe, and he was just about my favorite, too. He went to sleep one morning at nine and somehow I got the idea it was eight. Naturally, I brought him his feed at eleven. I looked all over for him, but I couldn't find him.'

'What had happened, Mr. Mac?'

'Well, no time pussy's insides could be expected to handle his breakfast only *two* hours after digesting it. It's too much to expect. I found him finally under the tool kit in the outer shed. He had crawled there and died of indigestion an hour before. Poor leetle feller! After that, I always set an alarm, so I never made that mistake again.'

There was a short, mournful silence after that, and I resumed in a respectful whisper: 'You said they all died, before. Were they all killed like that?'

Mac shook his head solemnly. 'No! They used to catch colds from us fellers and just die anywhere from a week to ten days before they caught them. They wasn't too many to start with, and a year after the miners hit Pallas they wasn't but about ten left and them ten sort o' weak and sickly. The trouble was, leetle feller, that when they died, they went all to pieces; just rotted away fast. Especially the little four-dimensional jigger they had in their brains which made them act the way they did. It cost us all millions o' dollars.'

'How was that, Mr. Mac?'

'Y' see, some scientists back on Earth got wind of our leetle time pussies, and they knew they'd all be dead before they could get out there next conjunction. So they offered us all a million dollars for each time pussy we preserved for them.'

'And did you?'

'Well, we tried, but they wouldn't keep. After they died, they were just no good any more, and we had to bury them. We tried packing them in ice, but that only kept the outside all right. The inside was a nasty mess, and it was the inside the scientists wanted.

'Natur'lly, with each dead time pussy costing us a million dollars, we didn't want that to happen. One of us figured out that if we put a time pussy into hot water when it was about to

232

die, the water would soak all through it. Then, after it died, we could freeze the water so it would just be one solid chunk o' ice, and *then* it would keep.'

My lower jaw was sagging. 'Did it work?'

'We tried and we tried, son, but we just couldn't freeze the water fast enough. By the time we had it all iced, the four-dimensional jigger in the time pussy's brain had just corrupted away. We froze the water faster and faster but it was no go. Finally, we had only one time pussy left, and he was just fixing to die, too. We was desperate – and then one of the fellers thought o' something. He figured out a complicated contraption that would freeze all the water just like that – in a split second.

'We picked up the last leetle feller and put him into the hot water and hooked on the machine. The leetle feller gave us a last look and made a funny leetle sound and died. We pressed the button and iced the whole thing into a solid block in about a quarter of a second.' Here Mac heaved a sigh that must have weighed a ton. 'But it was no use. The time pussy spoiled inside o' fifteen minutes and we lost the last million dollars.'

I caught my breath. 'But Mr. Mac, you just said you iced the time pussy in a quarter of a second. It didn't have *time* to spoil.'

'That's just it, leetle feller,' he said heavily. 'We did it *too* doggoned fast. The time pussy didn't keep because we froze that hot water so darned fast that *the ice was still warm*!'

THE END

The most unusual thing about this small item is that it was not published under my own name. Campbell wanted one item in that first 'Probability Zero' to appear to be by a non-professional, just to encourage the newcomers he hoped would try to break in. He had three entries in that first department and the other two were by L. Sprague de Camp and Malcolm Jameson. Both were longer-established and (despite 'Nightfall') more renowned than I. As low man, it was up to me to use a pseudonym and pretend to be a newcomer.

I saw Campbell's point and, just a little sullenly, agreed. I used the name George E. Dale. It is the only time I ever used a pseudonym in the magazines. In later years I used the pseudonym Paul French on a series of six teen-age science fiction novels for reasons that are another story altogether. That was a special case, and in 1971 and 1972 those six novels appeared as paperbacks under my own name. Now 'Time Pussy' appears here under my own name, and the record is at last absolutely clean.

APPENDIX – The Sixty Stories of the Campbell Years

STORY (WORDS)	MAGAZINE ISSUE	COLLECTION
1. Cosmic Corkscrew (9,000)	—	—
2. THE CALLISTAN MENACE (6,500)	*Astonishing Stories* April 1940	*The Early Asimov* (Vol. I)
3. Marooned off Vesta (6,400)	*Amazing Stories* March 1939	*Asimov's Mysteries*
4. This Irrational Planet (3,000)	—	—
5. RING AROUND THE SUN (5,000)	*Future Fiction* March 1940	*The Early Asimov* (Vol. I)
6. The Weapon (4,000)	—	—
7. Paths of Destiny (6,000)	—	—
8. Knossos in Its Glory (6,000)	—	—
9. THE MAGNIFICENT POSSESSION (5,000)	*Future Fiction* July 1940	*The Early Asimov* (Vol. I)
10 TRENDS (6,900)	*Astounding Science Fiction* July 1939	*The Early Asimov* (Vol. I)
11. THE WEAPON TOO DREADFUL TO USE (6,500)	*Amazing Stories* May 1939	*The Early Asimov* (Vol. I)
12. The Decline and Fall (6,000)	—	—
13. BLACK FRIAR OF THE FLAME (16,000)	*Planet Stories* Spring 1942	*The Early Asimov* (Vol. I)
14. Robbie (Strange Playfellow) (6,500)	*Super Science Stories* September 1940	*I, Robot*
15. HALF-BREED (9,000)	*Astonishing Stories* February 1940	*The Early Asimov* (Vol. I)
16. THE SECRET SENSE (5,000)	*Cosmic Stories* March 1941	*The Early Asimov* (Vol. I)
17. Life Before Birth (6,000)	—	—
18. The Brothers (6,000)	—	—
19. HOMO SOL (7,200)	*Astounding Science Fiction* September 1940	*The Early Asimov* (Vol. II)
20. HALF-BREEDS ON VENUS (10,000)	*Astonishing Stories* December 1940	*The Early Asimov* (Vol. II)
21. THE IMAGINARY (7,200)	*Super Science Stories* November 1942	*The Early Asimov* (Vol. II)
22. The Oak (6,000)	—	—
23. HEREDITY (10,500)	*Astonishing Stories* April 1941	*The Early Asimov* (Vol. II)
24. HISTORY (5,000)	*Super Science Stories* March 1941	*The Early Asimov* (Vol. II)
25. Reason (7,000)	*Astounding Science Fiction* April 1941	*I, Robot*
26. CHRISTMAS ON GANYMEDE (6,000)	*Startling Stories* January 1942	*The Early Asimov* (Vol. II)
27. THE LITTLE MAN ON THE SUBWAY (4,000)	*Fantasy Book* Vol. 1, No. 6	*The Early Asimov* (Vol. II)

STORY (WORDS)	MAGAZINE ISSUE	COLLECTION
28. Liar! (7,000)	*Astounding Science Fiction* May 1941	*I, Robot*
29. Masks (1,500)	—	—
30. THE HAZING (5,000)	*Thrilling Wonder Stories* October 1942	*The Early Asimov* (Vol. II)
31. SUPER-NEUTRON (5,000)	*Astonishing Stories* September 1941	*The Early Asimov* (Vol. II)
32. Nightfall (13,200)	*Astounding Science Fiction* September 1941	*Nightfall and Other Stories*
33. NOT FINAL! (7,000)	*Astounding Science Fiction* October 1941	*The Early Asimov* (Vol. II)
34. LEGAL RITES (7,500)	*Weird Tales* September 1950	*The Early Asimov* (Vol. II)
35. Robot AL-76 Goes Astray (5,000)	*Amazing Stories* February 1942	*The Rest of the Robots*
36. Foundation (12,500)	*Astounding Science Fiction* May 1942	*Foundation*
37. Runaround (7,000)	*Astounding Science Fiction* March 1942	*I, Robot*
38. Bridle and Saddle (18,000)	*Astounding Science Fiction* June 1942	*Foundation*
39. Big Game (1,000)	—	—
40. First Law (1,000)	*Fantastic Universe* October 1956	*The Rest of the Robots*
41. TIME PUSSY (1,000)	*Astounding Science Fiction* April 1942	*The Early Asimov* (Vol. II)
42. Victory Unintentional (7,000)	*Super Science Stories* August 1942	*The Rest of the Robots*
43. AUTHOR! AUTHOR! (12,000)	—	*The Early Asimov* (Vol. III)
44. DEATH SENTENCE (7,000)	*Astounding Science Fiction* November 1943	*The Early Asimov* (Vol. III)
45. Catch That Rabbit (7,000)	*Astounding Science Fiction* February 1944	*I, Robot*
46. The Big and the Little (22,500)	*Astounding Science Fiction* August 1944	*Foundation*
47. The Wedge (6,000)	*Astounding Science Fiction* October 1944	*Foundation*
48. Dead Hand (25,000)	*Astounding Science Fiction* April 1945	*Foundation and Empire*
49. BLIND ALLEY (8,500)	*Astounding Science Fiction* March 1945	*The Early Asimov* (Vol. III)
50. Escape (Paradoxical Escape) (7,000)	*Astounding Science Fiction* August 1945	*I, Robot*
51. The Mule (50,000)	*Astounding Science Fiction* November 1945 December 1945	*Foundation and Empire*
52. Evidence (7,000)	*Astounding Science Fiction* September 1946	*I, Robot*
53. Little Lost Robot (10,000)	*Astounding Science Fiction* March 1947	*I, Robot*
54. Now You see It — (25,000)	*Astounding Science Fiction* January 1948	*Second Foundation*
55. NO CONNECTION (7,000)	*Astounding Science Fiction* June 1948	*The Early Asimov* (Vol. III)

STORY (WORDS)	MAGAZINE ISSUE	COLLECTION
56. THE ENDOCHRONIC PROPERTIES OF RESUBLIMATED THIOTIMOLINE (3,000)	*Astounding Science Fiction* March 1948	*The Early Asimov* (Vol. III)
57. Grow Old with Me (Pebble in the Sky) (70,000)	—	*Pebble in the Sky*
58. THE RED QUEEN'S RACE (7,000)	*Astounding Science Fiction* January 1949	*The Early Asimov* (Vol. III)
59. MOTHER EARTH (15,000)	*Astounding Science Fiction* May 1949	*The Early Asimov* (Vol. III)
60. — And Now You Don't (50,000)	*Astounding Science Fiction* November 1949 December 1949 January 1950	*Second Foundation*

(*Note: Stories in capital letters appear in* The Early Asimov.)

THE WORLD'S GREATEST SCIENCE FICTION AUTHORS NOW AVAILABLE IN PANTHER BOOKS

Robert Silverberg

Tower of Glass	60p	☐
Recalled to Life	50p	☐
A Time of Changes	50p	☐

Poul Anderson

Fire Time	75p	☐
Orbit Unlimited	60p	☐
Long Way Home	50p	☐
The Corridors of Time	50p	☐
Time and Stars	50p	☐
After Doomsday	50p	☐
Star Fox	40p	☐
Trader to the Stars	35p	☐

Philip José Farmer

The Stone God Awakens	80p	☐
Time's Last Gift	50p	☐
Traitor to the Living	85p	☐
To Your Scattered Bodies Go	85p	☐
The Fabulous Riverboat	85p	☐
Strange Relations	35p	☐

A E van Vogt

The Undercover Aliens	50p	☐
Rogue Ship	75p	☐
The Mind Cage	75p	☐
Slan	75p	☐
Moonbeast	85p	☐
The Voyage of the Space Beagle	50p	☐
The Book of Ptath	75p	☐
The War Against the Rull	70p	☐
Away and Beyond	75p	☐
Destination Universe!	75p	☐

ISAAC ASIMOV, GRAND MASTER OF SCIENCE FICTION – NOW AVAILABLE IN PANTHER BOOKS

The Left Hand of the Electron (Non-Fiction)	75p	☐
The Stars in their Courses (Non-Fiction)	60p	☐
Buy Jupiter!	75p	☐
The Gods Themselves	80p	☐
The Early Asimov *Volume 1*	60p	☐
The Early Asimov *Volume 2*	50p	☐
The Early Asimov *Volume 3*	75p	☐
The Early Asimov Gift Set	£1.75	☐
Earth is Room Enough	75p	☐
The Stars Like Dust	75p	☐
The Martian Way	50p	☐
Foundation	75p	☐
Foundation and Empire	75p	☐
Second Foundation	75p	☐
The Foundation Trilogy Gift Set	£1.75	☐
The Currents of Space	75p	☐
Nightfall One	75p	☐
Nightfall Two	75p	☐
The End of Eternity	75p	☐
I, Robot	75p	☐
The Caves of Steel	75p	☐
The Rest of the Robots	75p	☐
Asimov's Mysteries	85p	☐
The Naked Sun	75p	☐
Nebula Award Stories 8 (Edited by Isaac Asimov)	60p	☐

All these book are available at your local bookshop or newsagent, or can be ordered direct from the publisher. Just tick the titles you want and fill in the form below.

Name ....

Address ....

Write to Panther Cash Sales, PO Box 11, Falmouth, Cornwall TR10 9EN.

Please enclose remittance to the value of the cover price plus:

UK: 22p for the first book plus 10p per copy for each additional book ordered to a maximum charge of 82p.

BFPO and EIRE: 22p for the first book plus 10p per copy for the next 6 books, thereafter 3p per book.

OVERSEAS: 30p for the first book and 10p for each additional book.

Granada Publishing reserve the right to show new retail prices on covers, which may differ from those previously advertised in the text or elsewhere.